A Woman's Touch

NORMA EATON

Paperback-Press
an imprint of A & S Publishing
A & S Holmes, Inc.

ISBN: 0692294449
ISBN-13: 978-0-692-29444-4

TABLE OF CONTENTS

ACKNOWLEDGMENTS

To my husband Gary for going above and beyond the call during my time of need.

My favorite saying by the late Maya Angelou sums it up: "Life is not measured by the number of breaths we take, but by the moments that take our breath away."

Babe, you take my breath away.

PROLOGUE

SOUTHERN CALIFORNIA

"NO! That's N.O."

"Come on Max. Just one hit to take the edge off. I'll get the money."

"That's what you said the last three times, Ruby."

"Please, Maxie, please. I'm hurting."

"I have a little coke left from when I was using, but I'm broke and my supplier said cash only from now on. We're in too deep with him now. I've tapped out Mother's account until her next disability check comes in."

"Just one hit, Maxie, to get me on my feet. I'll turn some tricks. I'll get the money."

"Look at you. Who'd have you? You're washed up."

She dropped to the nearest chair and sobbed. Max lit a cigarette and handed it to her. She took a long drag and let the smoke out slowly as she wiped at the streaks of three-day-old mascara on her cheeks.

"I know where to get some money. Real money. Half a mil even. Maybe more." She wiped her nose on the sleeve of her dirty jacket.

"You're delusional."

"I'm serious. I've thought about it before, but I need help in pulling it off."

"Pulling what off?"

She looked him straight in the eye. "Kidnapping."

Max snorted. "Your brain is definitely fried. Get outta here. Who would you know to kidnap that'd be worth half a mil?"

"Give me one snort and I'll tell you."

He let out a loud HA! "So that's what this is leading up to. You just want a snort."

"No, no, Max. I just need a clear head to think things out."

"You actually have someone in mind to kidnap?"

"Definitely. We'd have enough money to leave the country and live high on the hog." She rubbed her nose again. "Now give me the coke."

"If I do, this better not be one of your hair-brained ideas just to get your fix. You need to get off this stuff."

"Maxie," she whined, sidling over to him and running her fingers through his hair. "We've had some good times, haven't we? We can have even better times. You and me. You remember how good it used to be when I had money. I was a real looker then. You couldn't keep your hands off me. Remember?"

"Yeah." He looked puzzled and pushed her away. "I never did know exactly how you had that much money, but I know you sure went through it fast along with your looks---went right up your nose." He shrugged. "But who was I to gripe. I was doing the same thing. Only thing is, I knew how to pace myself. In fact, I've given it up---turned over a new leaf. I remember when I didn't use and my life was not great but better than I have now."

"It could be great, Maxie. I just need some money to get myself back on my feet. Come on, handsome." She edged up to him again, rubbing herself against his arm.

He shoved her away.

She let her breath out noisily. "We're wasting time. Gimme the coke."

As he pulled a small plastic bag from his desk drawer, she practically salivated looking at the white powder. "You won't regret this."

"I'd better not." He yanked the bag back away from her. "Where'd you get that money you had when I first met you eight

2

years ago."

"It was my sister's." She grabbed at the bag but he pulled it away again.

"You don't have a sister."

"She died. She left me her money she got from---" She hesitated. "That's all you get to know until you give me what I need."

He eyed her suspiciously as he tapped out a line of coke on the coffee table, rolled a dollar bill into a straw and handed it to her. "This better be good, Ruby, or this will be the last time you see me. You'll be on your own. I want to help you get clean and sober but you've got to want to."

Paying him no mind, she grabbed the makeshift straw and snorted the powder. She leaned back, smiling while the drug swirled through her brain.

Max cocked one eyebrow. "Let's hear this million dollar scheme."

"Heard of Mayhew Enterprises---Mayhew Department Stores---Mayhew everything?"

"Sure. Who hasn't? They're mostly back East somewhere, aren't they?"

"Yeah, home offices are in St. Louis but they have stores and other businesses all over. I've kept up with some of it."

"What's that got to do with you?"

"My sister was married to the young Patrick Mayhew, but his old man took a liking to her too. His name is Christopher and he doted on her and bought her furs, jewelry, expensive cars---you name it. She called him her cash cow sugar daddy. Oh, she said the sex was good with Patrick but he was a little tighter with his money so she made sure she kept *daddy* happy." She sniffed again. "Anyway, that doesn't matter. What *does* matter is," she turned her head toward Max and smiled, "she had a kid just before she died. He was going to be our *retirement plan* so to speak. She said he would be worth a bundle. I'm just carrying on with her wishes."

"And where's the kid now."

"Don't know exactly, but I'm sure he's with his father somewhere. That's why I need you. You're computer smart. Maybe you can find him."

"And that's the kid you're planning on kidnapping? How old is he now?"

"Around ten or eleven, I think. The Mayhews will never miss the money. They've got enough to choke a whole herd of horses."

Max thought a moment. "I don't know. I sure need the money to help out with Mama." He rubbed his hands across his face and hair. "Ain't never kidnapped no one before."

"Don't worry about it. It's not like we're going to kill someone." She smiled wryly. "Unless we have to."

CHAPTER ONE

REMOTE CABIN IN MONTANA

I realize, Mr. Mayhew, that this whole matter is distasteful to you and if there could have been any other way I certainly would not have bothered you." Janet looked impatiently around the large room, avoiding contact with Patrick Mayhew's uncompromising stare. "But, it was our only alternative."

Why was he staring at her? Why doesn't he at least say *something?* She tried to suppress her feeling of irritation with him as best she could but wondered why she was bothering. After all, she wasn't running for Miss Congeniality and his personal appraisal of her was not her prime interest at the moment.

"I'm only here to get these papers signed and back to St. Louis. Five minutes of your time is all I need." She made her voice sound as pleasant as she could manage. "I might add, this could all have been done at the airport. Driving all the way out here to your home was not necessary." She breathed out noisily, then, putting her true feelings in quick restraint, pasted a smile across her face.

One corner of his mouth turned up slightly in a wry grin. "I always thought that under these kinds of circumstances you would need a little privacy. You know...a place where you could be a little more...uh...friendly." Weighing her with a critical squint, he laughed inwardly. *His father had tried to ploy him with many things in the past, but this took the cake...sending an attractive woman to "woo" him back to St. Louis. He had to give the old man credit, though. She WAS beautiful and it wasn't going to be all that unpleasant to play along with the game for a while--just to teach them a lesson.*

Janet pressed her palm against the side of her skirt, feeling the smoothness of the fabric as she drew a deep breath. His attitude toward her and suggestive remarks had annoyed her since their first meeting at the airport.

She raised one brow. "Just what do you mean by 'these kinds of circumstances'?"

His gaze lowered as did his voice. "Oh, come now, Miss...what did you say your name was?"

"Raye. Janet Raye."

"Yes, well, Miss Raye," he continued with his taunting voice, "we both know the real reason you're here." He strolled forward, reached out and cupped her chin with one finger to tilt her face upward. "So why not get on with it."

A soft shadow of annoyance swept across her features and she suddenly felt consumed with humiliation. Her irritation increased when she realized her body was trembling, no longer able to hide her exasperation. With the help of her high heels, she proudly stretched her slight frame to its full five feet one and pulled away from him.

"I don't know what silly games you're playing, Mr. Mayhew, but I assure you I am only here for the express reason I gave you—to get your signature on these documents."

"Do you know you're eyes turn purple when you're angry?"

She paid him no mind. "It is *vital* to the company. There are certain transactions that require either your father's or your authorization. With your father incapacitated, we had no choice but to turn to you."

She watched his cocky expression turn serious for a moment, noting his clamped mouth and piercing gaze. Gold flecks mixed with the hazel in his eyes gave them a very unique look. Nice eyes, she thought, and for a brief second wished she could have met him under more pleasant circumstance.

She almost laughed at herself. Pleasant? A dog fight would have been more pleasant than this day had been. She had overslept this morning and was so rushed she had to forego breakfast in order to meet her flight. Her empty stomach had not gotten over its many flip-flops from the ascent over the mountains through the turbulent weather and then the rapid descent to land at the remote airstrip in Montana. Barely catching a breath, she suddenly found herself in Patrick Mayhew's Jeep riding over the roughest terrain she had ever seen. As if that weren't enough, she then had to climb the steep, rocky path that led to his cabin in her best high-heeled alligator open-toed shoes.

The muscle flicking in Patrick's jaw brought her back to business at hand making her aware of his gaze traveling over her face. The gold in his eyes enhanced the sun streaks in his rusty blond hair. There was a scattering of gray in his sideburns and a few crinkling worry lines across his forehead which were the only tell-tale signs to indicate that he was in his middle thirties.

His brows suddenly pulled into a frown before he dropped his gaze from hers and turned away. She waivered slightly at the impact his scrutiny had had on her.

"If you would...uh," she stammered, spreading the papers out on the table, "sign right here, I can be on my way," adding, "I'm sure you'll find everything in order."

She sighed. This whole dreary day was beginning to

take its toll on her composure. It was still unsettling to her that all flights out had been cancelled due to the pending storm and she was stuck here without even a change of clothes. She had not planned to stay overnight, thinking her business with Patrick Mayhew would only take a few minutes and she would be back in St. Louis on the return flight. She was tired and hungry and the fact that this infuriating man disliked her for some reason she was unable to ascertain only made things more intolerable.

"I'd really like to get these signed." She sounded as weary as she felt. "I need to find a motel." She glanced up speculatively. "You DO have a motel around here, don't you?" Her tone was a little testy and she knew it, but hunger always made her mean.

"I can see my father has taught you well," Patrick commented dryly. "Business first, last and always."

"There you go again! I don't know what you are talking about. Are you going to sign these?"

"As a matter of fact, no," he answered nonchalantly. "Not until my lawyer...

She cut him off. "Then why did you bring me all the way out here? We should have gone directly to your lawyer's office." Her patience had run out.

Though he didn't answer her question as to why he had brought her here, his face spoke for him. His left eyebrow rose a fraction, displaying that subtle dirty insinuation that she was growing very tired of. "I wanted you to have every opportunity to persuade me to come back to St. Louis...to Mayhew Enterprises. I don't want you to feel I didn't give you every chance to carry out your orders."

The very tone of his voice made her feel ashamed of something, and she certainly had nothing to be ashamed of. Cal Wilder, the company attorney and long-time family friend of the Mayhews, had warned her that Patrick would be difficult to deal with, but she had always taken pride in herself for being able to handle even the most cantankerous people. In this case, she was afraid Cal's description of "difficult" was a gross understatement.

"I am merely after your signature on these documents." Exasperated, she breathed in noisily. "I really don't understand your reluctance."

He let out a laugh. "I don't hear from my father for years, then he sends some beautiful elf with some papers for me to…"

"Elf?!" She stared blankly at him with her mouth open. Fingering the cross she wore around her neck, she prayed, *God give me patience and strength to deal with this man.* Her small stature and cherubic features had always been a thorn in her side. Even though she was twenty-seven years old, she was thought by most to look *too young* to be taken seriously; a fact which made it very difficult for her authority in the company to be readily accepted by some of the stockholders. Christopher's confidence in her abilities quelled most of those fears, but still a battle she was constantly fighting.

"I assure you," she stated emphatically, "that I am a grown woman." She kept her voice low, surprising herself at her ability to hold her temper in check. *Thank you, God.*

His look was one of faint skepticism, his soft hazel eyes roaming languidly from her feet to the top of her head.

Nervously pushing back a wayward wisp of hair from her temple, she felt her face flush under his seductive scrutiny. That same agitating quiver ran down her spine that she had felt earlier when he touched her face. The subtle softening in his expression left her to believe he wasn't always the tyrant he appeared to be. His gaze dropped from her eyes to her throat, to the curve of her breast beneath her suit jacket then back to her throat again.

He walked to the other side of the room thinking her skin looked like apricot cream and imagining it would taste like honey. He gave himself a mental shake. *Snap out of it. I'm only going to play this cat and mouse game for a lark...I'm not going to actually fall for her.*

His plan was to just wait for her to make her move, pretend to respond until he tired of the game, and then send her packing...right back to dear old dad with a clear-cut message that he wanted no part of the family business or his father.

"Yes," he finally said, nodding his head approvingly. "I'll have to agree with you. You have all the curves in the right places to qualify for a grown woman."

She blushed like a school girl. It wasn't just what he said, but also the way he said it that made her skin prickle. The sensation was not all that unpleasant...just hard to rationalize. She cleared her throat. "Is there nothing I can do to persuade you to sign these papers?"

"You answer that," he returned cockily.

Ignoring the insinuation, she picked up the pen and held it out to him, tapping her foot lightly as she waited for him to take the hint and sign the papers.

On the third tap of her foot, she felt the familiar zing of a runner scampering up her leg. She glanced down dejectedly and stared at her bare toe sticking through the nylons she had spent too much for. She had wanted to look just right for her meeting with Patrick Mayhew. Now that she had met him, she wished she had worn a gunny sack and saved the money she spent on her outfit. Ruining her hose was just another sharp reminder that she was stranded here without as much as a toothbrush.

"Darn!"

"What's the matter?"

Walking to a nearby chair and seating herself, she began rearranging the foot of her stocking to the underneath side of her foot to hide the gaping hole. In a tone less than cheerful, she answered, "Had I known I was coming to the land where the deer and the antelope play, I would have worn my mountain-climbing boots."

Her remark amused him and he let out an unexpected

laugh.

She glanced up in surprise. For some reason she couldn't picture him ever laughing...except when he was making a sarcastic remark. She thought he was probably born without a sense of humor at all. She liked hearing him laugh. He seemed much younger when he laughed. His lips parted in a dazzling display of straight white teeth. They were a gorgeous contrast to his ruddy complexion. She studied him openly for a moment, enjoying the view. He was not exactly head-turning handsome, but when he smiled there was something very, very appealing about him.

Seeing the amusement in his eyes, she laughed too, and for a few brief moments they were just two ordinary people enjoying each other's company. "I should have been prepared," she apologized, "and dressed more appropriately."

"St. Louis, this *ain't*," he jested.

"Well, one thing's the same," she told him, rising and returning to the papers on the table.

"What's that?"

"The weather...the same unpredictable spring weather."

"Yeah," he answered, glancing out the window. "Only here it can get very treacherous this time of year." He glanced up to the skylight in the loft. "Sounds like the rain has turned to sleet."

"We had really better get on with our business, Mr. Mayhew. I really see no reason why your lawyer needs to be involved. I'm sure if you would just take a few seconds to read these over, you'll agree..." She could tell by the smug look on his face, he was not going to sign. She twiddled with her cross again and hoped God was still with her on that *patience* wish. "I'd like to get to a motel before the storm gets any worse. I'm booked on the early morning flight, weather permitting, and there's no reason we can't get this wrapped up today." She was rambling, making conversation, trying to calm her quickening pulse as Patrick walked near her, stopping so close she could smell his musk-scented aftershave.

"Just like that?" he asked, his voice low and husky.

"Just like what?" The tensing of her body betrayed her usually cool composure.

"You're not going to *entice* me?"

"What in the world are you talking about?"

"Don't be coy, Miss Raye." His face was a mask of smugness.

"I'm getting a little weary of your snide accusations, Mr. Mayhew."

"I like a girl who plays hard to get, but aren't you carrying this a bit far?" His large hand snaked around her neck and pulled her toward him.

She pulled back sharply, gripping his wrist and literally flinging his hand away. "I'm asking you once more," she said with stilted calmness. "Will you sign these papers?"

He turned and walked away, suddenly very interested in starting a fire in the fireplace. "I'm not about to just up and sign something one of my father's... uh... *messengers* brings me without knowing what it's all about."

She didn't like the way he stressed messengers, sensing he was reading another meaning into her association with Christopher Mayhew.

"Your father did not send me here. It's just something that has to be done in light of his sudden heart attack. In fact, he knows nothing about this."

"I'll bet," he cut in abruptly.

Dear God this man is exasperating. Give me strength. She raised her voice a pitch higher. "He's much too ill to even be approached about business. If he wasn't, I wouldn't be standing here right now." She took a deep breath. "I thought my secretary explained all this to you when she called to tell you I was coming."

He turned sideways, giving her a wary glance. "She said it was urgent business."

"That's right. It is urgent. There are business transactions that were in the works that must be settled—"

"Ohhhhh, heck yes," he cut in, "anything for the good of the company. We mustn't forget Christopher Mayhew's empire."

Her eyes narrowed as she noted the look of distrust that veiled Patrick's face when he spoke of his father. "I don't know what's between you and your father, but why can't you trust me?"

"You represent him, don't you?"

She nodded.

"Then as far as I'm concerned you *are* Christopher Mayhew and let's just say I've learned to be extremely cautious when it comes to dealings with my father."

His tone startled her. The only thing she knew about Patrick Mayhew was what Cal Wilder had told her and the newspaper clippings she had accidentally run across in Christopher's personal file cabinet when she was looking for his insurance policy. It was an article about Patrick's marriage and subsequent divorce from a girl nearly twelve years ago.

When she thought of Christopher Mayhew, she thought of the kindly old gentleman she knew who had treated her like a daughter the ten years she had known him. He was a man whom she trusted with her life and held a deep moral obligation to for all the things he had done for her. She had seen him reading the bible nearly every morning before business hours. The only personal thing he had ever said to her was that he had done some things in his life he was not proud of and could never forgive himself but was seeking God's forgiveness. He very seldom spoke of his son but when he did it was with a quiet reverence that made her know there was a deep love for Patrick. There was dissention between the two men, Cal had told her that much but she never knew exactly what. She never asked...never pried...but now her curiosity was piqued.

The fire had begun to blaze and she walked closer to the hearth. Her light-weight suit felt like sheer gauze against the chill. The warmth felt good as she rubbed her hands up and down her arms.

She hesitated a second, then came right out and asked, "Just what do you have against your father?"

Patrick straightened to his full, towering six feet and looked down at her with hard, hazel eyes. Their coldness sent another chill through her body much more severe than the temperature in the room.

"I'm sorry. I shouldn't have asked."

He turned back to the fire, giving her an opportunity to study his profile freely. It was the profile of a man who had been hurt badly...who had harbored a great pain for a number of years.

A swath of sandy wavy hair tumbled carelessly across his forehead, giving him an even more casual look than his western clothes. There was a tug at her heart for this man, giving her a strong desire to reach up and brush his hair back. Suddenly his jaw thrust forward. He straightened his shoulders at the same time running his fingers through his hair, putting it back in place.

His troubled gaze softened against the innocence of her own gaze. "He's a bit too ambitious for my taste." His voice was soft, his eyes never leaving hers. *So lovely,* he mused. *It was becoming more and more difficult not to really be attracted to her.*

"And ambition is a bad thing?"

He turned his attention back to the fire. "No, except when you sacrifice your family for it."

Somehow she couldn't imagine the old Mr. Mayhew neglecting his family. He had always talked so kindly about them. No, the Christopher Mayhew she knew and the one Patrick was talking about was not the same person. She owed a great deal to Christopher...not that he expected anything from her...but because he had given her a sense of belonging she had never felt in the foster homes she was reared in. Her loyalty to the old man was unshakable and she was ready and willing to do anything to keep his company intact during his illness.

There was no point belaboring the issue of Patrick signing the papers any longer so, with a sigh, she walked casually over to the table and put the documents back into the manila folder. She glanced at the tall rusty-haired man she had met only hours ago. Somehow it seemed she had known him longer. In other ways she wondered if she would *ever* really know him. Did she even want to?

"If you insist on having your lawyer look these over, then very well." She conceded as she pulled her cell phone out of her purse and noted there was no reception. "May I use your phone to call my office to let them know I'm being detained? My cell doesn't seem to be working."

"Cell reception is dicey here and especially during a storm."

"We can see your lawyer this afternoon and I can still catch the early morning flight."

"We can't do that.

"What?" Disappointment clearly showed in her voice.

"He's out of town until Monday."

CHAPTER TWO

*T*his being Friday meant she would be stuck here three more days. She nearly wilted at the thought. Giving him a pleading look, she said, "It's *very* important that I get back as soon as possible. I can't impress upon you enough how ill Christopher is. I'll be needed at the office in his absence.

"Christopher, huh?" He chuckled ironically and shook his head. "I'm Mr. Mayhew, but he's Christopher." His raking gaze left her feeling dirty as he continued. "I see he hasn't changed much...still has a way with the young girls." His smug smile was unnerving.

Her eyes snapped. "I'm hardly classified as a *young girl* and besides, I've known your father considerably longer than I've know you. Ten years longer, in fact," she emphasized. "That's how long I've been with Mayhew Enterprises. I'm Administrative Assistant to your father."

He eyed her with amusement. "What did the old man do? Rob the cradle?"

His teasing tone grated on her nerves. "You're indicating something smutty between your father and me and that just is not—"

"Christopher Mayhew smutty?" He threw his head

back and let out a loud laugh. "Heavens no, Miss Raye. My father would *never* do anything smutty to a woman...especially one as young and beautiful as you."

Her face heated.

"You *are* beautiful you know. I can see his attraction." He seemed to be dwelling on her face a little too long.

"Just what kind of relationship do you think I have with your father?"

He studied her intently for a second. "That's very good, Miss Raye...that indignant look on your face. Wow, if looks could kill, I'd be toast." He chuckled snidely. "I could almost believe you if I didn't know my father quite so well. I can smell a Christopher Mayhew plot a mile away. Your flawless beauty, your impeccable taste in clothing, not to mention your jewelry...just simple, tasteful, *expensive* diamond cross around that delectable neck."

She fumed and clutched the cross. "This belonged to my mother. It's the only thing I have left to remember her by."

"Sorry." His tone was one of honesty. "But tell me, just where did your clothes come from?"

"Of course, they came from Mayhew Department Store. I buy all my clothes there...note I said buy. I would be a little remiss if I didn't patronize Mayhew's wouldn't you think? I happen to be very loyal to the company businesses. Not like some people I know." She knew she sounded childish but just couldn't help the dig.

"And I'll bet you get a real good discount, too, don't you?" he taunted.

She dropped her shoulders. "Our conversation is becoming asinine. I'd greatly appreciate it if you would take me to the nearest motel. I'll make my call from there."

She gathered up her purse and laid the folder containing the documents back on the table. "I'll just leave these with you. After you have your lawyer go over them and determine that you aren't being cut out of the Will, you can mail them to me. My only request is that you do it as promptly–" She was interrupted by his sarcastic laugh.

"Cut out of the Will? Oh, that's rich. Do you think that's what I'm concerned about?"

"Well, why else the distrust? It's just a simple case of giving me Power of Attorney to act on your behalf during your father's absence. It's a necessary formality since you are still the co-owner."

"Maybe I'm particular who acts on my behalf, or maybe I don't want to take the chance on signing something that would necessitate my getting involved in the business again. It was never my desire to be co-owner and I made myself very clear on that part."

A flicker of a smile hovered the corners of his mouth. "And besides, what makes you think if you left them with me that I wouldn't burn them up or something. Don't you think you should stay around and look after dear old dad's interest?" *Now why'd I say that! She could be gone and forgotten and I wouldn't have to let her try to entice me. My mind knows the right thing to do, but tell that to my stupid body.*

If she didn't know better, she would swear he wanted her to stay. But why? Well, whatever the reason, he was right. It would be better if she saw to it that those papers were signed before she left Montana. She would actually only be out of the office one more business day...Monday. If they saw his lawyer early enough Monday, she could be back in St. Louis that night.

"I don't distrust you as much as you do me. I know you wouldn't destroy the documents, but I do think it best I stay until our business is finished. You never did answer me, but I presume you do have a motel in this..." She couldn't think of an appropriate word to describe where she was. "...community."

He smiled. "We have a very nice motel just a few miles from here. This is part of the United States, Ms.

Raye," he goaded.

Her sense of humor took over and she glanced around at the rustic interior of the cabin. The stone fireplace in the far corner, the massive leather and wood furniture all showed blatant signs of roughing it. "You couldn't prove it by me," she returned in the same teasing manner.

He chuckled at her feistiness. "Probably not a place you'd expect the son of Christopher Mayhew to be comfortable in. Is that what you're thinking?"

"No, that is *not* what I was thinking." She lifted a jacket from the coat rack and handed it to him. "Could we please go? I really don't care to get involved in a family squabble. We obviously do not share the same opinion of your father and there is no point in belaboring the point."

His expression grew serious as he reached out to take the jacket from her. His steady gaze bore into hers as their hands brushed together. Her skin pickled with the softness of his touch, sending tingles up her arm. His rugged appeal was so bracing, it caused her cheeks to flush, and she could well see how some women would be attracted to him. Cal Wilder had told her he was difficult but he failed to tell her just how good Patrick would look in a western shirt and tight jeans that made her light-headed every time he moved. Maybe it was the altitude, she told herself, trying to prove that she was immune to his good-looks. Or maybe it was hunger, her growling stomach suggested.

"I wish for your sake, this could have been avoided," she said calmly, "but your father's heart attack was quite sudden. We wouldn't have involved you if we had had time to make other arrangements."

"You use *we* quite easily, Miss Raye."

"If you don't like the way things are being run, then I suggest that you come back to St. Louis and run them yourself."

"Ah, the plot thickens. The real reason you're here comes shining through at last...to get me to come back."

"Oooooo!" She whirled around and walked heatedly to the door, then turned back remembering she had no way to leave.

"Why don't you just stay here," he said huskily. "After all, we're almost family."

He was the most infuriating man she had ever known. How could she have been so foolish as to see anything good about him? "We are not almost, nor will we ever be *family*. I'm sickened to death of your insinuations."

His own temper piqued. "Insinuations? It's obvious you're running things in my father's company during his illness, and from what little I know of legal matters, those papers you have give you full control. You're a true-blue Mayhew all right. Maybe not in name, but in every other respect. You're ambitious, career-minded...no true feelings whatsoever between your knees and your neck unless it would be for the *good of the company.*"

"And you *certainly* make it obvious that that is the area on a woman that captures *your* prime interest!"

Their gazes locked, each assessing the other with resentment.

"Why am I wasting my breath on you?" She tried to regain some semblance of rationality. "I'm only concerned with helping your father, but you think I'm trying to run off with the family jewels or something."

"No, you wouldn't need to resort to that. I'm sure there are other ways to get them."

"At the risk of repeating myself," she said very deliberately, "someone has to run the company in the interim and you are obviously not interested."

"I never wanted any part of my father's business."

"It doesn't make any difference what you want, you've got it and I'm not going to let you destroy it. Not as long as I have a breath left in my body!" Her eyes were blazing, uncompromising.

Patrick took a step backward and sucked in his breath.

A pang of envy shot through him over the fact that his father could elicit such love and devotion...something he himself had never known from a woman. He let his gaze wander over her body from head to toe. She was small, yet every bit a woman with a very womanly body. His eyes took in her long dark hair shining like wet mahogany, her violet eyes framed by long black lashes giving them wide innocent beauty.

She drew a long calming breath. "I had been told you were impossible to deal with, but I didn't realize just how much."

He laughed out loud. "And who told you that, Miss Raye...my father?"

"No, it wasn't your father."

"Who then?"

"Let's just say you live up to your reputation."

"If what they mean by my being impossible to deal with is that you can't buy me, they're right...with money, that is," he added with a smile. He was toying with her and enjoying every minute of it.

When their eyes met for a brief moment, it caused that annoying prickling sensation to wash over her. She had never in her life felt such a mixture of emotions. As much as she adored the old Mr. Mayhew, she loathed the son at this very moment. Or at least she thought she did. Then why were these strange feelings running rampant through her veins every time he looked at her with his deep, piercing hazel eyes?

"I'm not here to ply you with money, Mr. Mayhew."

"I guessed that." His tone was suggestive. "That's been tried many times before."

"I am fully aware that you have returned every profit-sharing check issued to you by the company. Even if you are co-owner, and deserve part of the profits, I do not question your motives by refusing the money."

"Since they know money doesn't work, they would

probably try...hmmmm...let me think. What haven't they lured me with?" His eyes gave her the once-over. "Maybe they thought a beautiful woman might convince me to come back. What do you think, Miss Raye?"

Janet's brow furrowed. "I give up." She threw her hands in the air. For the life of her, she couldn't imagine anyone not wanting to be part of the Mayhew conglomerate. It had been her life these past few years and she was proud to have worked her way up to Administrative Assistant. She eagerly learned the business and welcomed the opportunity to work while attending college. She returned Christopher Mayhew's kindness with her trust and devotion to the business.

Since she had been orphaned, she looked forward to the day she would have a family of her own, but for right now her career came first. That and the fact that she had not found anyone she wanted to settle down with since Mark. Mark Wilson...she hadn't thought of him for ages. Funny. Thinking of him didn't hurt anymore. *When did the hurt stop?* She felt relieved...but her marital status was the last thing she needed to be hashing over in her mind right now. She was not quite twenty-eight years old...plenty of time for children.

Suddenly she realized that Patrick was still staring at her. His eyes had softened and his voice was deep and raspy. "I will say, they sent a very tempting offer this time. I might just have to make an exception."

Her body jerked at his insinuating remark. "I am *not* an offering!"

"Too bad," he taunted, "it might have been interesting."

"I really don't like your attitude. In fact, there's not much I like about you at all."

A deep chuckle greeted her. "You're not the first woman who has said that..."

"Not surprising."

He cocked one eyebrow as he continued suggestively, "...and changed her mind."

She felt her cheeks heat again. Even though she repeatedly told herself she didn't care what he thought of her, she did. Maybe it was because he was the son of a man she admired, she didn't know exactly. She did know she just couldn't let him think badly of her.

"Not that I owe you any explanation..." Her voice seemed to be coming from someone far calmer than she actually felt. "But I want you to know that I really do love Christopher Mayhew." She saw the blood drain from Patrick's face. "Oh, not in the way you're suggesting. I love him like a daughter. He's been the only real father I've known."

He quirked an eyebrow. "My, my, what a break. And you said we would never be family. Sharing the same father should give us a mountain of conversational chit-chat."

"I see it's no use trying to convince you. Your mind is obviously closed to the truth."

She fidgeted nervously with the clasp on her purse. "I don't suppose there's taxi service."

He chuckled. "Motel we have...cabs, no. I'm afraid you're at my mercy."

"Then could we please go now? I'd like to get a room and something to eat." There was really no point in letting him rile her, so she tried to be as courteous as possible. "The flight over the mountains was a little too unsettling for me to eat on the plane."

He glanced at the clock on the wall then back to her. "It *is* way past lunch time." His voice was suddenly minus the previous sarcasm, but she wasn't sure she trusted him...like waiting for the other shoe to drop. "I could rustle us up something here. There's no café near the motel."

"No, thank you." She was still a little skeptical of his sudden hospitality. "Buffalo burgers are not on my diet."

He laughed. Despite his reluctance to believe her true mission here, he liked exchanging barbs with her. Her quick retorts amused him. "We're not quite that primitive, little one. I was thinking more on the lines of an omelet...or would you prefer quiche?"

His grin was contagious and she couldn't hold back her smile. "An omelet would be fine," she told him, too hungry to argue. She needed to at least try to be civil. The last thing she wanted to do was alienate him further from his father. *His father!* She flinched. Poor Christopher. When she left St. Louis this morning, he was still in intensive care.

"Would you mind if I called the hospital to check on your father?"

"Sure...although," he hesitated, "I called just before I picked you up at the airport. He's still critical but stable."

She looked toward him warily. "So you *do* have some feelings for your father. Or were you just checking out my story?"

He stared at her for a moment, then, "I don't wish him dead, if that's what you mean." He nervously raked his fingers through his hair. "When your secretary called, she was a little sketchy about him, so I thought I'd find out for myself."

Janet smiled inwardly. *He cares. He's not so tough.*

As if to excuse his show of concern, he quickly added, "But just because he's laid up, doesn't alter the fact that he could have still sent you here..."

This time she laughed out loud. "You don't believe that."

"It's possible."

"Trust me."

He jammed his hands in the back pockets of his jeans and rocked back and forth on the heels of his cowboy boots. He looked at everything in the room but her, then finally let his breath out. "I'm going to give you the benefit of the doubt," he finally said, adding, "for now."

"Good...let's eat."

He smiled, feeling a great load off his shoulders. He never was one for cat and mouse games anyway. "If I fix you lunch, would you do me a favor?" he asked, hanging the jacket he had tossed on a chair back on the coat rack.

"Anything I can," she answered cautiously.

He shook his head negatively at her obvious wariness. "All I want is for you to stop with the Mister stuff."

"I will if you'll agree to call a small truce between us until our business is settled."

He smiled down at her and nodded agreement, his hand still resting on the coat rack.

His grin caused another surge of heat to bolt through her body as she absently fingered the sleeve of the jacket he had just hung up, noting it was awfully short to fit a man of Patrick's size. She took the jacket off the rack and held it up to her shoulders. It was almost a perfect fit.

Without her having to ask, he awkwardly offered, without thinking, "That's Matt's," then caught himself, "my...er...partner."

She wrinkled her nose, doubting him.

He floundered. "He's sort of a roommate."

She gave him a teasing grin. "I think I get the picture. You hate women and you have a petite *Bunkie* named Matt."

"Whoa, there. It's not what you think...and who said I hated women?"

"Well, you haven't exactly showered me with respect since I've been here."

He hastily looked away and walked toward the kitchen.

"Well, have you?"

He turned back. "Miss Raye..."

"Janet."

"Janet," he repeated, "Just so there's no misunderstanding, I *do* like women."

"Wonderful," she said, never once doubting the fact. "And I like men. Is there any other mind-boggling facts we really need to know about each other this very moment?"

"No."

"Good. Let's eat."

They both laughed as her stomach let out another hungry growl.

CHAPTER THREE

*J*anet stared at her plate of food. It reminded her of a folded foam rubber Frisbee with something oozing from the center. Mindful it was impolite for a guest to gag at the table, she kept her composure as she pressed her fork into the glob and watched it bounce back up. "I'd like to say Grace if you don't mind."

"Sure," he said, putting his fork back down.

She reached out to take his hand in prayer. He stared for a moment, then put his hand in hers. *Mmmm, smooth skin* was all he could think about as her soft voice began its message.

"Dear God, thank you for the many blessings you have bestowed on us. We ask that you watch over Christopher and that your healing hands will guide the doctors to restore him to good health again. Bless this food that Patrick has so graciously prepared for the nourishment of our bodies. Let your light shine through us so that others may see the joy you bring to our lives. We pray in our precious Lord Jesus' name. Amen."

When she looked up, her gaze met Patrick's for a moment as he softly said, "Amen."

They quietly resumed eating. She finally managed to tear off a sliver of omelet and put it in her mouth.

"How're your eggs? Patrick asked, making conversation as he sliced his own with a knife.

So that's what this is, Janet thought. "Uh...different. Such an unusual shade of gray."

"Yeah, well, I probably got a little heavy with the pepper again," he said, examining his forkful closely. "As you've probably guessed, I'm not the best cook in the world. In fact, omelets are the only meal I know how to cook at all."

That fact was also up for debate, Janet wanted to say, but instead remarked, "I suppose your *Bunkie* does most of the cooking."

He glanced at her nervously. "Well, some. More coffee?"

Since she hadn't had an opportunity to touch her full cup, she knew he was trying to change the subject. "Why so evasive?" She flashed him a teasing smile. "Do I detect some dark secret?"

She noted he was unable to look her in the eye. "Ah, I thought so. So Matt is short for Matilda...so your roommate *is* a woman. So what? Why the big mystery? It happens all the time. It would certainly take a lot more than that to shock me." She laughed and tried to sound I-don't-care despite a pang of jealousy. How silly, she thought. She didn't even know the man, yet she was feeling envy toward the woman who shared his life. When she glanced up, his expression had turned to a smile.

"You don't have to eat that if you don't want to. It really is bad. I should have warmed up a can of soup."

"No, this is fine, I was just thinking." She hesitated, then went on. "It really isn't any of my business, and for all I know you might be married. It's just that I don't see why it should make you so uncomfortable to talk about the woman you live with unless, of course, you suspected I came here to seduce you and a wife might spoil my plans?" She looked him straight in the eye.

He stared back at her for a long time, thinking how easy it would be to just let her think that. But the honesty in her eyes made him feel more and more like a jerk for the way he had acted.

She heard him suck in a long breath and let it out again before he spoke. "I'm not married and Matt stands for Matthew." He added no further detail.

A giggle of relief almost surfaced which lasted only until she took another bite of her eggs. If anything could wipe a smile off a face, it was Patrick's cooking.

They finished lunch in relative silence. Although she wanted to learn more about him, he didn't seem to want to discuss himself. Finally, as she cleared the table, she asked, "Whatever made you settle in Montana?" It was a question she thought didn't come too close to his private life.

"I came here to get away from it all for a while, fell in love with the country and decided to stay."

Janet set the dirty dishes in the sink and looked out the window at the country he loved. It looked bleak to her, especially as the worsening storm made a miserable view. "It's so...remote...so lonely."

He stepped close behind her and she felt his breath on her neck. "You have to see past the sleet and the gray." He motioned with his hand. "Look through the obvious." His voice was full of respect. "See the mountains? I think they challenge anyone to conquer them." His hands touched the sides of her head, turning her face toward the view he was referring to.

Glad her back was to him so he couldn't see the pleasure she felt by his touch. *Why do I feel this way? I'm being ridiculous.*

"Do you see what I mean?" His husky voice lulled her into a near stupor.

"Yes, I think so." Her breathing was unsteady.

Just then a loud howl split the solitude and Janet nearly jumped out of her skin. Without realizing it, she whirled herself into Patrick's arms.

"What *was* that?!"

He tightened his hold on her. "That's just some wild animal calling to its mate. I keep them around to scare young girls into my arms," he joked. "But don't worry, they're easy to run off. All I'd have to do would be to open the door and yell real loud and they'd hightail it right out of here."

She stepped back suddenly aware she had flung herself at him. She would never convince him that she wasn't here to *woo* him if she kept this up. Still she felt warm and safe when he was holding her.

She turned away. "Somehow I just can't imagine you needing scary animals around to have girls—" She stopped, berating herself for saying her thoughts out loud.

"Why, thank you, Janet. You *can* be complimentary and nice."

There was a trace of laughter in his voice and she smiled in spite of herself. "How would you know about complimentary and nice?"

He threw back his head and let out a peal of laughter. "Touché!"

"Well, I haven't seen a lot of niceness out of you yet."

Amusement filled the eyes that met hers. "I can remedy that," he said softly, sending a quake through her body.

"I'll just bet you could. I never had any doubt as to your ability to, shall we say, *please* a woman if you *wanted* to."

"And you don't think I would want to, shall we say, *please* you?"

"There's a big difference between wanting to please and taking someone up on what you suspect is an *offer*."

His eyes were apologizing before he even spoke the

words. "I was obviously wrong about your being sent here by my father, and I'm truly sorry about the way I acted." He smiled. "How's that for nice?"

"Then you'll sign the papers?"

Exhaling slowly, his smile waned. "There's a lot you don't understand. I have my reasons for being cautious."

Her gaze turned flat with frustration as he continued.

"I *will* sign them if my lawyer finds them in order."

"I assure you they *are* in order. Cal drew them up personally. You surely trust Cal." Cal Wilder was the only link between Patrick and his father. She knew he had acted as liaison in the past. "Cal wouldn't involve you in anything unless it was absolutely necessary. If the stockholders get wind of the seriousness your father's illness, they might..."

He nodded. "Yes, Cal has always been straight with me, but he works for Mayhew Enterprises. I won't take the chance."

Her irritation turned to near pity as her eyes met his troubled ones. Wondering what was behind his stance, she examined his expression for answers but realized none would be forthcoming. With this realization, she succumbed to a new desire to respect his privacy.

As her own expression changed, she saw something darken in Patrick's eyes. She moved away, turning to the dirty dishes in the sink. "I'll just wash these, then we really must be getting to the motel. You said yourself the weather gets treacherous." She rambled nervously until she felt his hand grasp her arm and turn her toward him. His eyes dropped to her slightly parted lips and his own opened slowly as he leaned closer to her upturned face.

She could feel his breath against her lips and almost taste his kiss when she felt his body jerk. His expression turned from passion to anger and his grip tightened almost painfully. From the look on his face, she thought he was about to toss her aside but instead his lips came crushing down on hers and his tongue forced entry to hungrily probe the recess of her mouth. He crushed her body so close to his that she could barely breathe. Her heart pounded against her ribs like a million stampeding stallions.

She twisted from his hold and, without thinking, slapped him soundly across his face, and then immediately clasped her hand to her mouth with shock at her behavior.

Both were breathing heavily, their eyes locked defiantly. He looked as shocked as she felt. The contempt that had blazed in his eyes seconds ago had left them reddened and, if she didn't know better, she would swear they were beginning to mist. *Did he regret his actions?*

After a while, she found her voice. "What—what was *that* all about?" She did not wait for an answer. "I...what can I say to make you believe I did *not* come here to seduce you."

He turned away from her. "I know that...that's what makes it so darned..." He turned back to her and started to reach out to touch her, then pulled back and jammed his hands in his pockets. "You're so innocent, so...," he searched for words, "trusting."

"Then I don't understand you at all. If you felt that way about me, why did you kiss me like that?"

"I don't know. Curiosity got the best of me. You just looked like you needed to be kissed."

Heat rushed to her face. "If I had needed to be kissed it wouldn't have been like that! I don't know what kinds of women you've kissed, but I can't imagine any of them being cast under your spell by that kind of behavior."

"I'm sorry about that. I was kissing you before I even realized what I was doing. When it actually dawned on me, I didn't want it to feel good with you. I wanted to frighten you away."

Her temper surfaced. "*You* wanted to frighten me, *you* didn't want it to feel good...*you, you, you.* What about me? What about *my* feelings?" She paced back and forth in front of him. "You're right, Mr. Mayhew, I am trusting and maybe even gullible at times, but I'm happy with myself. It's certainly a lot better than...," " she waved her hands toward him, unable to hold her temper in check, "running away to play cowboy in some God-forsaken country, distrusting everyone who darkens your doorstep!"

His eyes widened. "What a little spitfire, you are. I want you to know I feel I deserve your telling me off." He pulled his hands slowly from his pockets and hesitatingly placed them on her shoulders. "I didn't mean to hurt you...only scare you away."

"Why?"

His eyes traveled the perimeter of her face before he answered. "I don't exactly know. I guess it was easier that way. Easier than dealing with my own feelings." He smiled down at her.

She smiled back. His warm expression sent a refreshing apology to her without words having to be spoken. "Don't jump to conclusions too soon. I'm not one of your wild animals. I don't scare off so easily."

They looked at each other for a long moment, their eyes dancing together like they knew some hidden secret.

"You may not scare off easily, little one, but you are certainly wild." He chuckled and rubbed his jaw. "In more ways than one."

She lowered her eyelids. "I shouldn't have slapped you. I've never done anything like that in my life. I don't know what came over me."

"You sure pack quite a wallop for an elf. Who are you anyway, Mighty Mouse?"

"Please don't joke," she said seriously. "I owe you an apology for my shoddy behavior. May God forgive me."

"I think I displayed quite a bit of shoddiness myself. Maybe God wasn't looking."

She laughed. "He's *always* looking. Still, I shouldn't have hit you. I've been kissed before when it was...uh...less than delightful," she added with a smile, "and I'm usually a little more docile under such circumstances."

"I don't suppose you'd like to try it all over again?"

"I don't suppose I would." No matter how distasteful she tried to make herself believe his kiss was, her pulse quickened at the very thought of such a strong passion in a man.

"Well then, I guess I'd better get you to a motel." His eyes were locked tenderly with hers.

"Yes," she responded half-heartedly, "I guess you'd better."

CHAPTER FOUR

After their slippery trip down the path, Janet sat shivering on the passenger side of the Jeep waiting for the vehicle to warm up while Patrick scraped the ice from the windshield.

"I'll have to admit," he said as he climbed in behind the wheel, "Mother Nature isn't setting a good example for visitors from Missouri. Can't really blame you for having a hard time seeing what I love about the Big Sky country...but believe me it gets in your blood." He put the four-wheel in gear and started over the bumpy road.

Through chattering teeth, she asked, "What does one do for a living out here? Surely you can't just live on the beauty of it all."

He smiled at her gibe. "I do a little of this and a lot of that," he joked.

"Sounds absolutely fascinating. I'm surprised everyone's not doing it."

He laughed again and she felt herself enjoying the camaraderie, her own laughter rippling through the crisp air.

"You have a nice laugh."

"I was about to say the same about you." Her voice wavered from being jostled around in her seat as he turned the Jeep from side to side to avoid potholes.

"Sorry about this. I've been meaning to work on this road to smooth it out, but I've been too busy."

"Doing a little of this or was it a lot of that?"

He gave her a quick amused glance before turning his attention back to the road. "You called me a cowboy...well, sometimes I am. I used to break horses and I still help brand during roundup."

"Break horses?"

"Tame them...make then hold a saddle. You know, so people can ride them."

"Oh, of course. I forgot for a moment what break meant. I've seen that in movies." She turned to him, her eyes widening. "Isn't that dangerous?"

"Nah...just a little hard on the old caboose sometimes when you get bucked off. And I've had my share of that."

"You don't do that anymore?"

"Very rarely." He smiled at her. "But I'm still a cowboy."

"And is Matt an Indian?"

"What?" His brow knitted. "Why do you ask that?"

"Seems all that's lacking is an Indian sidekick, a white horse and silver bullets. I watch old movies." She snickered.

Their laughter was interrupted by squawking noises from the radio. Patrick reached out and turned the squelch button to allow the message to come through.

"All Rangers report immediately to the rescue station. Repeat. All Rangers report immediately to the rescue station. Hunting party reports two men failed to return to camp. Bring warm clothing and extra food. This may be a long night."

Janet shivered once again as she looked out into the evening, picturing two lost men in the cold.

"I'll have to turn back," he said, making a sharp U-turn.

"Turn back? But—"

"I said I was a cowboy sometimes. Mostly I'm a Ranger."

"You mean you have to—"

"Yes. I work for the government. This is part of my job. Looking for missing persons in the mountains. Sometimes we help fight fires. Sometimes we—"

"That's enough." She shuddered. She couldn't imagine anyone *loving* this life. "Couldn't you just take the time to drop me off at the motel?"

"You heard them. Report immediately. This is an emergency. No, I don't have time to take you into town. You'll just have to wait at the cabin until I can get back."

"But, I don't even have a toothbrush."

"I've got a new one the dentist gave me during my last checkup. You can have it."

There were two people lost in the mountains and she was worried about brushing her teeth. "I'm being insensitive. I'm sorry." She had only been in Montana for a few hours and she had spent half that time saying she was sorry.

He didn't respond to her. His face stony, his look determined.

Despite her discomfort, she felt an overwhelming admiration for him to be so dedicated to his work. He was certainly a man any woman could be proud of. That is if she could live with the fear he might not return from one of his missions.

"Will you be safe?" she asked timidly. "I mean will there be a group of you? Will you all stay together?"

He smiled. "Don't worry. I'll be back in time to take you to the airport."

"But that's not until Monday!"

He laughed out loud. "I'm only teasing. Yes, I'll be safe. I know the mountain like the back of my hand. Besides, my partner Roger and I usually stick pretty close."

"Roger? I thought it was Matt."

"Uh...Matt is not a Ranger...Roger is."

"Oh." It was all getting a bit confusing to her so she just settled back and stared out the side window.

"Oh, nooooo!" he moaned as they pulled up to the path leading to the cabin.

"What's wrong? She saw a Bronco parked in front. "Who does that belong to?"

"Roger," he said vaguely.

"Well, he must have heard the emergency call and has come to get you."

"I don't think so," he said blandly.

After another struggle up the path, they hurriedly entered the warm cabin. Janet babbled to herself as she rubbed her hands up and down her arms. "Go directly to the fireplace, do not pass go, do not collect two hundred dollars." She stopped abruptly.

Before her stood a very pregnant young woman whom Janet guessed was in her early twenties and a boy who looked to be ten or eleven. The expressions on their faces told her they were even more surprised to see her than she was to see them. Even the large gray cat the young boy was holding was openly staring at her with huge yellow eyes.

Everyone was speechless except the cat who finally let out a loud friendly welcoming "Meow!"

*****

SOUTHERN CALIFORNIA

"Any luck yet?" Ruby hung over Max's shoulder while he slumped at his Mother's laptop computer.

"Back off, Ruby! Your breath smells like whiskey. Where'd you get it?"

"I got my ways."

"You lifted it from the liquor store again, didn't you?"

"Didn't have to. Ross was behind the counter today.

He likes what he sees." She did a hula while rubbing her hip and thigh with one hand and offering him the bottle with the other.

"Want some?"

He glanced up at her. "Want some what? Whiskey or what Ross likes." He let out a disgusted grunt. "If he's so into you, why don't you take him on your kidnapping caper?"

"Awww, Maxie, don't be jealous. Ross can't hold a candle to you. Nobody knows me like you do. Come on, take a drink. Good stuff."

"Do you want me to find this kid or party with you?"

She took a long swig from the bottle. "Find the kid. We'll have a lot of time to party when we get our hands on all that Mayhew money."

"I've discovered Patrick Mayhew is not in St. Louis or else he lives there under another name."

"Nah, he's Patrick Mayhew alright. Keep looking." She ran her finger around his ear while pressing her bosom against the back of his head. "You gonna get the money?"

"Mother's check should be in her account today."

"What about her car?"

"I don't know about that."

"Where's she going? She don't drive anymore." Ruby backed off and fell onto the couch, pouting. "We need a car. You don't think we can kidnap somebody on foot."

"Ruby, I'm doing the best I can. The home-care woman will notice if Mother's car is gone."

"So, think of something. You're her only son. Don't you think the old woman would loan her precious little boy her car for a few days."

"Okay, okay, I'll take care of it."

"We'll also need a gun."

Max turned his chair around and stared at her. "A gun!? Are you out of your mind? What do we need a gun for?"

"Insurance."

"Insurance? What are you talking about?"

She snickered and took another swallow of whiskey. "How were you going to do it, big man? Force someone into a car with a Popsicle stick?"

"I don't like it."

"Don't be such a sissy mama's boy." Smiling, she knew the right buttons to push.

"I'll get the gun." He turned back to the computer. "Remember you said we weren't going to kill anyone."

"I think I actually said, *if we don't have to.*"

CHAPTER FIVE

MONTANA

Janet watched the pregnant girl chew nervously on her bottom lip. About a million and a half explanations raced through her mind as to whom these people were and why they were here...none of which made any sense at all. The girl was obviously too young to be the boy's mother. Was he her little brother? Why were they so uneasy about being here? Why was Patrick so testy?

"I'm sorry, Buck," the young girl finally said to Patrick, a pained expression on her face.

"Buck?" Janet looked surprised. "I thought you were Pat."

"I am."

"But she called you..." She threw her hands up showing her confusion. "I'm beginning to wonder if I know *my* name." She turned to the young woman. "Are you Matilda by any chance?" She glanced suspiciously toward Patrick.

"No," the girl answered warily, looking at Patrick with an am-I-supposed-to-be-Matilda expression on her face. "I...I'm Doyne Murphy." She shrugged her shoulders. "I called before we came, Buck...er...Pat. Since there wasn't any answer, I assumed your business with...," She looked toward Janet, searching for a name.

"Janet."

"That your business with Janet was finished. Matt was worried about Carlyle being outside in the storm so we came over to let him in."

"Janet's eyes widened. "Who's Carlyle?"

The young boy stepped forward and held out the cat's paw. "This is Carlyle Cat, Ma'am, and he's very pleased to meet you."

Janet instinctively reached forward and shook the cat's paw as she smiled at the boy. "And who are you?"

"I'm Matt."

One brow raised in question. "You're...uh...Pat's partner?" she asked in astonishment.

The small brown-haired boy looked puzzled for a second, then squared his shoulders and walked cockily over to stand beside Patrick. He hoisted the cat over his shoulder and stroked it affectionately as he spoke very grownup. "Oh, yeah, Buck and I go way back. Why I remember when we used to break those wild horses together. In fact, that's where he got the nickname, Buck. He got bucked off so many times."

"That's enough, Matt," Patrick said, cutting the boy short. "There's no point in this charade any longer." He turned to Janet, a look of defeat written across his face. "You might as well know, this is my son."

Janet's mouth dropped open. "Son!?" she choked out. "I...I was never told you had a son." Then it dawned on her. No one in St. Louis knew he had a son. "You kept Matt a secret from your father?" She was dumbfounded by it all, turning to the pregnant girl. "And you?"

The girl started to say something, then closed her mouth as Patrick explained. "Doyne is Roger's wife. I asked her to pick Matt up from school and keep him at her house until after you left."

"But why?"

Patrick ran his hand around the back of his neck. "Matt and I have a good life out here. I don't want anything to jeopardize that...*and*," he emphasized, "to be blunt, I insist that you do NOT divulge Matt's existence to anyone connected with my father."

"But he's his grandson. He would be so happy to know he had..." Her eyes lit up. "This news would help him recover."

"I *said* I insist." His tone was serious, his eyes narrow slits.

"I've really got to get back," Doyne said, clearly not wanting to get caught in the middle of an argument. "I heard the emergency call on the radio on the way over here and Roger probably did too on the base unit at home. He'll be pacing the floor waiting for me to get back with the Bronco and Josh will be wanting his supper." She turned to Janet. "Josh is Roger's son by a previous marriage...my step son," she told her before Janet had to ask.

"He's my best friend," Matt offered with a big smile, making Janet smile back at him. *What a gorgeous child* she thought, looking at his bright hazel eyes the image of his father's.

"You want me to take Matt back with me, Buck?" Doyne said.

"That won't be necessary now," he answered, raking his fingers through his hair. "He can keep Miss Raye company. Kind of pointless in keeping him in hiding from her now. Besides, he can make sure she doesn't make any phone calls." He stared at Janet again, but this time he gave her a pleading look.

She knew it wasn't the phone calls he objected to, but what information she might divulge. "I'll respect your wishes," she said mildly. "I may not agree with them, but I'll respect them." She turned her attention to the young boy who was nearly her same height even with her wearing heels. "I'll be very happy to look after Matt while you're gone."

Pat let out a loud laugh. "You don't need to look *after* him, but you might need to look *out* for him. I warn you. He's eleven going on thirty."

"Well, I'm sure we'll get along fine, won't we?" She tousled his hair.

Matt smiled angelically into her eyes. He appeared to be completely captivated by her and innocently asked, "Are you really a grown-up woman?"

"See what I mean?" Patrick said out the corner of his mouth.

"The acorn doesn't fall far from the tree," she whispered, then raised her voice to the boy, "I'll soon be twenty-eight years old if that's what you're asking."

The boy's grin broadened. "Then you ARE a grown up woman!" He put the cat down and started picking up magazines and straightening pillows on the couch. "Look at this place, Dad. For crying out loud, you should have tidied up a bit. You don't even try to make a good impression." He looked pathetically at Janet. "I'm afraid it's been too much for the man," he said woefully, "all alone without a mate to help him with the grave responsibility of guiding my little footsteps in the right direction. We could sure use 'a woman's touch' around here," he added while running a finger over the table top and examining it for dust.

"Matt," Pat cautioned gravely, "can it!"

Janet could not contain her enjoyment any longer and burst forth with uncontrollable laughter. The boy's obvious display of match-making, while it clearly irritated his father, left her more than mildly amused.

"I'm under a lot of pressure here," the boy stated flatly, ignoring Janet's giggles.

"You're going to be under the tires of my Jeep," his father interjected curtly, "if you don't straighten up. What kind of impression do you think *you're* making on Miss

Raye."

"It's okay," Janet said, trying desperately to keep her chuckling under control. "I think this is going to be a memorable evening." She looked at Patrick and saw he, too, was finding it hard to keep from smiling.

"Well, I've got to get out of here," he said, taking a snowmobile suit from the coat rack. "Doyne, you go on home. I'll pick up Roger in a couple of minutes. You'd better keep the Bronco just in case." He looked at her stomach.

"Okay." She laughed. "But if it did happen, I don't think I'd be in any condition to drive myself...but if it makes you feel any better."

"It does."

Doyne hurried toward the front door, bidding her goodbyes and telling Janet she was glad to have met her even under the strange circumstances. "Oh, by the way," she called over her shoulder to Pat, "are you still planning on going to the dance tomorrow night at the Legion?" Before he could answer, she added, "Maybe Janet would like to come along and take in some of the local color."

"I don't think so," Patrick answered, pulling on a pair of insulated boots.

"Dad, you need to get out more. Enjoy yourself instead of just moping around the house every Saturday night."

Pat looked up sharply, giving his son a cautioning stare. "Moping? Since when does playing cards with you...at your insistence, I might add...constitute moping? In fact, I've seen you throw a complete fit when I've even suggested doing something else on a Saturday night."

"Tsk, tsk, tsk," Matt clucked, a grave look crossing his face. "It's unhealthy, Dad, hanging around me all the time. A boy like me doesn't need a thirty-six-year-old pal."

"Don't start it, Matt," his dad cautioned again.

"You need to be around people closer to your own age," the boy continued undauntedly. "Someone around...oh, say...twenty-eight maybe."

Janet bit her cheeks to keep from smiling as Patrick glared at his son.

"Well, think it over," Doyne said, waving goodbye to everyone.

After she left, Pat gathered up the rest of his gear and piled it by the door. Matt tossed a log on the fire and stoked it to a full blaze, then got a card table from the closet and began setting it up.

"I'm warning you, Matt," Pat said gruffly, "you are to conduct yourself like a gentleman while I'm away and do not...I repeat...do not bug Miss Raye or you'll have me to answer to."

"Yes, sir," the boy said politely, continuing to arrange two chairs opposite each other at the small table. "Be careful, Dad. I love you," he added sincerely.

I love you, too, son." The older man met the boy halfway, each hugging the other. It was such a small gesture, one which any family would do, but it brought a tear to Janet's eye.

Her feelings about Patrick Mayhew had done a complete about-face in the few short hours she had known him. The man she thought she disliked was the same man she now admired and respected. His genuine concern for Doyne and her condition, his unabashed love for his son, his protectiveness...all the tender qualities she loved in a person. If only she could convince him to make amends with his father and let Christopher know he had a grandson. She sighed. It was really none of her business. Still, she couldn't help but be curious as to the reasons he had alienated himself from his father.

"If you get hungry, there's soup."

"We'll manage," Janet assured him.

"I really am sorry you got stranded here," Patrick sympathized.

"No one can control the weather. You *can* give me that

toothbrush, though."

He grinned. "It's in the medicine cabinet still in the box. Oh, and..." he paused briefly, "you may as well sleep up in my bed in the loft."

"Oh, no, I couldn't."

"I may be gone all night. No point in wasting a perfectly comfortable bed. If I get back before morning, I'll just crash on the couch. No problem."

"Don't you think you'd better get going, Dad?" Matt impatiently tapped a deck of cards against the table.

"He hates to see me go," Pat said sarcastically, nodding a goodbye to Janet.

"God be with you." Her heart pounded lightly with apprehension.

"He's never let me down," he told her in leaving, glancing back curiously. "You really twenty-eight?"

Janet gave him a disgruntled look. "I will be next month."

He cocked his head to one side, tossing her a doubtful glance. His questioning expression unnerved her and she let her breath out in a huff. "Oh for crying out loud. What do I have to do...show you my driver's license?"

The last thing she heard was his laughter as he left...the same laugh she earlier thought sounded nice. At this particular moment, she would like to stuff a sock in his mouth.

"Hey, small fry. You gonna stand there all night?" Matt teased as he shuffled a deck of cards like a pro.

She turned slowly. "Small fry? I take it all back. We are not going to get along fine," she told him half laughing.

"Only joking, only joking," he quickly returned. "I like you just the size you are. You're just right."

"Just right?"

"Yeah. We have a lot in common. We not only can see eye to eye, but we can wear each other's jeans and T-shirts."

Janet giggled and shook her head.

"With the price of clothes now days," he continued, "that could be a great money saver."

"Matt," she warned, "I know what you're trying to do and, although I find it very amusing, I think you're getting a little carried away. I'm not going to be here long enough to share a wardrobe with you. In fact, if your father hadn't gotten that emergency call, I would have never known you even existed."

"That's just it," he said, his eyes lighting up. "It is fate don't you see?"

"That's a bit much."

"No. I believe in that stuff. I believe if you pray hard enough, someday..."

She stared intently at the boy. "You pray for a woman to come into your father's life?"

He shrugged. "I pray for a lot of things...*and*," adding emphatically, "a lot of times they come true."

"Do you do this to every woman who meets your father?"

"No." He grinned sheepishly, displaying a tiny dimple in his right cheek. "Only the ones fate sends."

She smiled tolerantly. "Well, *fate* did not send me here for what you have in mind. I need your father to sign some papers," adding rather curtly, "that could have already been signed, if he weren't so stubborn." Wishing she hadn't sounded so short, she brightened her tone. "But that's my worry, not yours."

"I knew it!" Matt threw up his hands. "Dad did it again."

"Did what?"

"Dad runs off romance faster than I can find it."

"Romance?" She let out a nervous laugh. "Aren't you a bit young to be thinking of romance?"

The boy straightened with a jolt. "Not for me. For Dad."

"Well, I know that but still…"

"I knew you and Dad had had a hassle. I could smell it."

"You certainly have quite a nose for an eleven year old kid." Janet now fully understood what Patrick had meant when he said his son was eleven going on thirty. He was a very bright boy…wise beyond his young age. She liked him. She liked him a lot and sensed they could become extremely good friends. Too bad she had to pretend he didn't exist.

"Dad's not a bad guy once you get to know him."

"I'm sure he isn't," Janet interjected. "Now, can we change the subject?"

He ignored her suggestion and continued. "He doesn't require much attention. Feed him three meals a day and he'll be your friend for life."

"Matt!" Her voice was insistent as she sat down opposite him at the card table. "Isn't there something better to do…like play cards," she said, trying desperately to get his mind on something besides pairing her up with his father. It was an idea that was about as far-fetched as you could get. They had about as much in common as oil and water. "What do you know how to play? Go fish? Rummy? War? What?"

"How about stud poker?"

"Poker? What are you, a juvenile delinquent?"

"No, just a card shark," he answered matter-of-factly, doing a tricky shuffle with the cards. "Josh and I learned how to play poker on the internet and we can beat Dad and Roger every time."

"Ahhh, the internet." She smiled. "You can learn lots of things on the internet…some good and some not so good. You and Josh are buddies, huh?"

"The best." He leaned close as if someone could hear him. "We're blood brothers."

Janet raised her brows. "Blood brothers?"

"Yeah, we cut our pinky fingers and held them together so his blood and my blood ran together." He stared at her pleadingly, "Don't tell our dads. They'd kill us."

"Oh, I think *kill* is a little strong, but no I won't tell."

He breathed a sigh of relief. "So I guess you don't play poker."

"Not so fast with your assumption." She cut the cards and slapped them back together. "I'll have you know I financed a portion of my college tuition from late night card games in the dorm. So shut up and deal!"

Matt reached in the small box he had placed on the table and handed her a bundle of wooden matches held together with a rubber band and took a bundle for himself.

"There's fifty in each bundle," he told her, dealing out two cards each, one face down, the other up. "Five match limit on the bet. Jokers, Deuces and one-eyed Jacks are wild. If you're dealt the Ace of Spades face up on the third card, you automatically forfeit the pot. The Queen of Hearts entitles you to take one match from your opponent's stack and the Four of Clubs is missing from the deck. Two Kings of the same color mean—"

"Hold it! How am I supposed to remember all those crazy rules?"

He gave the cards a couple of brushes with his fingers, snapping them loudly. His eyelids lowered cockily halfway over his hazel eyes and one side of his mouth curved in a wry grin, forming that irresistible dimple. "I didn't say it would be easy."

Exactly twenty-two minutes and seven hands later, Janet held up her one remaining match, gave it a goodbye kiss and tossed it into Matt's pile. "Here, you may as well make a clean sweep of it. One match isn't going to get me far."

"You're pretty good," he said as he bundled the matches.

"Pretty good? I lost every hand," she raged.

"Yeah, but it took seven hands. I can wipe Dad out in three. Wanna try again?"

"No. I know when I'm out-matched...pardon the pun on matches." She helped him put the rubber band around the last bundle and place it in the box. "You and your Dad have a lot of fun together, huh?"

"Sure. He's a fun guy," adding, "most of the time. It's just...." He hesitated, then went on, "He gets a little cranky whenever he has to do anything regarding Grandpa."

Janet flinched at the word, *Grandpa*. It was still new to her...thinking of Christopher having a grandson. She knew nothing would make him happier, if she could only tell him. Nothing except maybe a reconciliation with Patrick.

"You'll just have to overlook his grumpiness," the boy continued. "He's got kind of a blind spot when it comes to Mayhew Enterprises, St. Louis OR Grandpa. There's just no talking to him."

"I discovered that. Then, he's told you about your Grandpa?" She hesitated to ask.

"Oh, sure. Dad and I tell each other everything. Well, almost everything. He hedged a little on why he's so mad at Grandpa. He says I'm too young right now to understand. The only thing he told me was that Grandpa always tried to run his life and he didn't want the old man to be able to run mine."

Janet's curiosity overrode her respect for Patrick's privacy. Could she help it if the boy wanted to tell her certain things? "Then, that's why your Dad has forbidden you to ever see your Grandpa?"

"Oh, there's probably more to it than that, but anyway, he hasn't forbid me to EVER see him. He said I could do whatever I wanted after I'm twenty-one. He said by then I probably would know what I wanted out of life and nothing could change me anyway." The boy leaned back in his chair, his voice lowered thoughtfully. "It's just that while I'm a kid, he wants to keep me a secret. Oh well, I guess in ten years, I'll know what Grandpa's like. I picture him with kind of grayish hair and a round belly."

Janet chuckled softly. "He's going to simply love you, Matt." That is, she thought sadly, if he lives ten more years.

"Do you like him?"

"I adore him." She felt a bolt of guilt shoot through her for discussing Christopher with Matt. To change the subject, she asked. "What about your mother? Is she sworn to secrecy too?"

"She's dead."

"Oh, Matt, I'm so sorry," Janet apologized, feeling like a fool.

"Don't worry about it. I never knew her. She died when I was born. Dad doesn't talk much about her. They were divorced."

The pieces were beginning to fit together. Janet remembered the newspaper clippings recounting the short marriage and divorce. Matt's mother must have been pregnant at the time they were divorced but not far enough along for anyone to know except Patrick. The newspaper had said she left St. Louis without a trace and forfeited all rights to appear in court for the divorce proceedings. Patrick was granted an uncontested divorce.

Janet was still puzzled. If she left without a trace from St. Louis, how did Patrick find her? "Where were you born?"

"Dad didn't fill me in on the details, but anyway he was there when I was born...and now I'm here. I think it was fate," he added, flashing Janet a dimpled grin.

She smiled back. "I still don't quite understand keeping you a secret. I think you're right. There must be more to it."

"Beats me. I figure someday maybe he'll tell me...maybe when I'm twenty-one."

Janet marveled at the boy's mature acceptance of the situation. It was very obvious Patrick had done a fine job of *guiding his son's little footsteps in the right direction.*

"You're quite a boy." She placed her hand on top of his and gave it a squeeze.

"And you're quite a woman," he returned teasingly and placed his other hand on top of hers.

She jerked it out from under his. "I'm serious," she told him in a scolding tone of voice. "You're remarkably well-adjusted under the circumstances."

He tossed his head back, mockingly shaking his hair out of his eyes and joked, "It's a gift...just a gift."

She chuckled at his foolishness. "Gift or not, I know how hard it is to adjust to not having a mother. I barely remember my parents and I was only eight when I lost them. My little sister and I were separated and placed in foster homes."

The boy's eyes widened. "See? I told you it was fate. We have more in common than the size of our jeans. I don't have a Mom, you don't have a Mom. I tell you. You're a God-send."

She laughed. "This is crazy."

"No, it isn't. I'll bet you even carry a picture of your mother in your wallet, too." He looked her straight in the eye.

She was beginning to get caught up in this *fate* business. "You mean you...."

He shook his head yes and produced a snapshot from his billfold. She recognized a younger Patrick standing next to a pretty blond girl. She swallowed hard. Matt was a combination of his parents. His mother's smile and his father's coloring. She felt very strange. All this talk about fate. Lots of people carry pictures of their parents. Yet, it WAS eerie that this snapshot was not at all unlike the one she carried of her own parents. It had been one of the few things salvaged from the fire.

"Sometimes I think about her," Matt said, breaking the long silence. "She's always in a plaid dress and a blue apron...and when I come home from school, she's standing at the door."

"And the house smells like fresh-baked brownies," Janet interrupted, her voice sounding far off. "Only my Mom's apron is white."

Matt leaned forward excitedly. "Sometimes she drives me and my friends to school in her brown station wagon."

"My Mom drives a green car." Janet's eyes misted.

"See there...I told you. It's fate."

Janet's mind snapped back to the present. "Oh, Matt, we're being foolish. Anyone who's lost a parent pretends things like that at times."

"I think I like the part about smelling brownies best," he continued, his voice trailing to silence for a moment before he let out a chuckle. "Dad tried to make some once." He wrinkled his nose and screwed up his mouth. "Bad...real bad."

"Worse than his omelets?"

"He didn't feed you one of those?!"

Janet nodded.

"And you live to tell about it?"

She laughed. "I take it we share the same opinion of your father's cooking."

"Out of a strong will to survive, I learned to read directions on stuff out of a box. It beats omelets twenty-one times a week." They both giggled. "I make real good Kraft macaroni and cheese. Want some?"

"That sounds like ambrosia to me. I'm starved."

She set the table while Matt concocted his specialty. She caught herself humming softly as she went about her duties, privately doing a little *pretending* herself. She felt a closeness to Matt and a very at-home feeling washed over her.

"Matt?"

"Huh?"

"You don't, by any chance, have the ingredients for

brownies, do you?" Not wanting to imply she was trying to *play like* his mother, she said, "All that silly talk made me hungry for them."

Her back was toward the kitchen doorway when she heard, "Ta dah!" She turned to see Matt holding up a box.

"Betty Crocker to the rescue!" he said ceremoniously.

"Matt, I don't want you to think my making brownies has anything to do with our previous conversation about fate and all that."

"Of course not," he said brightly. "Everyone knows REAL mothers make them from scratch!"

They both broke into laughter, releasing the slight tension Janet had been experiencing.

In no time at all, Janet had the brownies mixed and baked. She took them from the oven as Matt piled their plates full of his gourmet delight.

She spread her paper napkin across her lap. "Do you want to say Grace?"

"I'll say what Josh always says." He grinned his dimpled cheeks.

"Okay, what's that?"

They took each other's hands and bowed. "Dear God. Thank you for the food on this table." He started giggling so hard he could barely finish. "Now dig in and eat all you're able."

She got caught up in the hilarity and laughed out loud. "You and Josh are certainly a pair!"

"Dad hates it when Josh does that. I think that's why Josh does it. Just to get a rise out of Dad."

"That's what best friends do. Tease each other. Sounds like you're all very close...you, Josh and your dad."

"Yeah, Dad loves Josh like a son. He's known Roger since Josh and I were around two or three. We all ran around together back then before Roger met Doyne. Dad was their best man. We're all family."

"I see that.

The meal was perfect, the company delightful and Janet could not remember enjoying an evening more.

With their stomachs full and the cabin saturated with the wonderful smell of chocolate, they both cleaned up the dirty dishes, then flopped on the couch in front of the fire. Janet moaned as she kicked off her high heels and rubbed her aching feet.

Without a word, Matt jumped up and ran to his room, returning with a pair of woolly sheepskin booties which he slipped on her feet. Janet wiggled her toes in the warm snuggies and smiled at Matt affectionately.

"Thank you. That was very thoughtful."

His face reddened slightly at her kind words and he shrugged off his embarrassment. "Been wondering who I could pawn them off on. I got them in the gift exchange at school a couple of Christmases ago. Can you imagine anyone putting booties in the boys' gift exchange? It *had* to be Weird Wilbur."

"Well, you can give Weird Wilbur a kiss from me. I love them. They feel heavenly on my feet and I will be eternally grateful."

"Kiss Weird Wilbur?" Matt fell into a fit of giggles. "If you could only see him." He stopped short. "Wait, I'll get my school pictures."

He returned with a large photo album and flipped through the pages to his class picture and pointed to a smiling boy with huge ears and a distinct overbite.

"Oh, he's not so bad," Janet kidded. "I think he's kind of cute."

Her remark only heightened Matt's hilarity. It was contagious. Janet soon joined him and suddenly something about everyone in the picture was funny.

As their laughter subsided, she turned back to the front of the album and started looking at all the pictures. The book was filled with shots of Matt from the time he was a baby to the present. There were lots of pictures of Matt with his dad on camping trips and shots of Matt and Josh as tots with their arms around each other and holding Carlyle, who had curled comfortably against Janet's thigh by now, making his presence known by his contented purring. She gave the cat a couple of strokes between pages, becoming so engrossed in the album she didn't notice Matt had leaned against her shoulder and fallen asleep. She eased her arm out and circled his shoulders, drawing the boy tight against her and brushing a stray lock of hair back from his forehead.

Janet sat that way for a long time, watching the flames leap in the fireplace, stroking Carlyle and, most of all, enjoying the feel of Matt in her arms. She knew the longer she held him, the harder it would be to forget she knew he existed, but for now she didn't care. For this one brief period of time, she wanted to allow herself the luxury of pretending she belonged to someone…that she had someone who belonged to her. It felt cozy and warm, and she laid her cheek against the boy's hair and let the evenness of his breathing and the soothing purr from Carlyle lull her into slumber.

CHAPTER SIX

Janet, wake up," Pat urged in a loud whisper. Receiving no response, he nudged her shoulder lightly. "Janet," he repeated, giving her an even heftier shake. "Hey, Squirt--you're in my bed. Wake up." By now he was speaking loudly and prodding her with both hands. "Janet!"

"Hmmm?" She lifted drowsy eyelids.

"You must suffer from acute clear-conscience to be able to sleep that soundly."

"Patrick!" She sat upright surprised to see him. "You back so soon? Did you find those people? Were they all right? Are *you* all right?" She fired one question after another although her eyes were still not fully opened.

"So soon?" He chuckled. "It's four in the morning...and, yes, they're back in their camp safe and secure. A little frigid, but safe. I'm fine and all's right with the world...so get up and go to bed."

Janet groaned and mumbled, "Four in the morn—" She slid to one side and curled back up like a baby.

"Oh, no you don't. Come on. Up you go." He lifted her upright and raised one eyelid with his thumb. "Are you in there?" He gave her a few seconds to answer, which came in the form of a half-hearted nod. "I wasn't even sure you were under all that kid and cat when I came in. I'm surprised you're not squashed to death."

She gave him a silly grin, turning her face in the direction of his voice, her eyes refusing to open by themselves. "Don't you know? Elves don't squash." She yawned and looked to each side of her. "Where ARE the kid and cat?"

"I carried the kid to bed and the cat followed. Carlyle sticks to Matt like glue. He's a one-man cat...doesn't have much to do with other human beings." He stared down at her for a moment longer. He couldn't help but notice how child-like she looked trying to force life back in her sleepy body. "You going to make it on your own, or am I going to have to carry you to bed too."

The fire had died to barely a glow, making the room dark and shadowy, but she could see well enough to be aware of his tired expression. "Why don't you just let me finish out the night here on the couch," she told him compassionately. "You need your own bed more than I do."

"Huh uh, I'm too wound up to sleep right now. I'm going to stir up the fire and just sit here for a while."

She watched him put a couple of logs in the fire box and listened to the crackling noises as tiny flickers of flame came to life. Pulling herself up off the couch and stretching out the kinks, she asked. "Do you think I would disturb anyone if I took a shower?"

"No, go ahead." He turned to look at her, eyeing her up and down. "It'll swallow you up, but you're welcome to one of my flannel shirts to sleep in."

"I'll take it," she quickly answered, already feeling how warm and comfortable flannel could be on a cold night. "I'm not picky."

He walked to the huge closet that housed his clothes and brought her back the makeshift nightgown. "Here you go. I hope Matt didn't drive you crazy. He's a pretty good kid when you get to know him."

"Funny, that's what he said about you." She laughed.

"What did you do all evening?" She noted a touch of nervousness in his voice. "Did you...did you make your call to St. Louis?"

She shook her head no. "As a matter of fact, I didn't. Frankly, I got so involved with Matt that time just got away from me. I'll call Cal at his home first thing in the morning. He'll be able to tell me how Christopher is and let my secretary know when to expect me back."

She fidgeted with the shirt she was holding, feeling a compulsion to apologize for snooping into his private life, knowing he was concerned about keeping Matt a secret. "Don't be so distrustful of me, Patrick. I told you I wouldn't say anything about your having a son and I won't."

Turning quickly, she hurried into the bathroom before he saw the guilty look on her face. Guilty for encouraging Matt to reveal intimate facts about their lives. Sometimes her over-active curiosity backed her into tight corners, and this was certainly one of those squirmy moments. She was asking him to trust her, yet at the same time doing things to make him doubt her word.

After a quick but refreshing shower, she brushed her teeth with the borrowed toothbrush and put on the over-sized shirt. She rolled the sleeves up several flaps and buttoned the front. It wasn't exactly a Dior, but it would do, she mused running her fingers through her hair.

When she re-entered the main room to climb the stairs to the loft, she heard banging of cabinet doors and mumbled cursing coming from the kitchen. She tiptoed over to the doorway and watched Patrick frantically opening and closing doors and drawers, swearing under his breath.

"Lose something?" She laughed softly at his dilemma.

"Darn that Matt!" he grumbled, shuffling through the contents of a drawer.

She took a few more steps toward him, still mildly amused. "What's the problem? What are you looking for?"

"My cigarettes! He's found them again and thrown them away. That's what he's done. I'll skin his hide!"

"I wasn't aware you smoked."

"I don't...."

She raised her brows in question.

"I mean, I did, but I quit..." He continued his relentless search, adding, "...almost. I keep a pack around for nights like this when I get uptight."

"Pretty rough up there in the mountains," she sympathized. "It must be very tense searching for lost hunters. But you said they're okay."

"Half frozen, but they'll be fine," he spat out curtly, then quickly apologized. "I didn't mean to sound testy. *They'll* be fine, but I don't know about me," he continued, opening the top cupboard doors and running his hand along the shelf. "All I could think about all night was how one word from you could ruin my whole life with Matt."

"You're wrong about your father. He would never do anything to hurt you or—"

"Ha!" he scoffed disgustedly. "How innocent you are...innocent or brainwashed!"

"I'm neither! I just know your father."

He cut her off with his penetrating stare. "I can't believe he's never told you about...nah, he wouldn't. Wouldn't want to spoil his image with you."

"What are you talking about? Told me what?"

"Nothing. Let's drop it. I don't want to argue with you. Help me find my cigarettes."

"You don't need cigarettes," she said very motherly. "They're bad for your health. If Matt threw them away, he was right in doing so."

"Now, I suppose you're a miniature Florence Nightingale coming to my rescue."

"How do you think they got the name *coffin nails*?"

She ignored his reference to her size. "Go sit on the couch. I'll get us a glass of milk and some brownies."

He dropped his shoulders in defeat. "I thought I smelled them. What's Matt been up to...playing on your sympathy with his *mother* routine?'

She looked at him quizzically for a moment, bewildered by his insensitive judgment. "It's not a *routine,* Patrick."

His expression softened. "I know," he said quietly, squeezing his fingers across his eyelids and down the bridge of his nose. "I guess being up twenty four hours straight makes me a little surly." He drew in a long calming breath. "I know he misses having a mother. I've tried to be both parents but I sure fall short."

"I think you've done a fine job." She was sincere in her praise. "He's so smart and quick and funny. Oh is he funny." She caught her voice raising in pitch as her enthusiasm for the boy rose. "He has such a healthy outlook on life. He's just a joy to be with. I can't help but—"

"But what?"

"Nothing."

"You started to say something. But what?"

She squared her shoulders boldly. "I can't help but think what a shame it is to rob him of his heritage."

"And I suppose you told him that?"

"No, I didn't." She let her breath out in a huff. "He's curious about his Grandpa, but he respects your wishes. Like me, he doesn't fully understand them, but he plans to wait until he's twenty-one before—"

"Holy cow! Did he tell you what color undershorts I wear, too?!"

"Go sit down," she ordered. "I'll get us some food and we'll discuss the color of your undershorts in a civil adult manner." She thrust her fists on her hips in an authoritative manner.

In spite of himself, he grinned, his eyes sweeping over her face and body as if seeing her for the first time tonight. Despite the baggy shirt, he liked what he saw. She was just as beautiful as the first time he saw her...maybe more so. He admired the trim taper from her calf to her ankle, smiling as his gaze dropped to her small feet, their toes wiggling against the floor.

Her cheeks flushed slightly as his eyes came back up to study her face once again. His blatant scrutiny of her caused a quickening of her pulse. His smile was a sensuous ember about to burst into flame and she was well aware of the chemistry that crackled between them.

"I...uh..." Her voice croaked and she nervously cleared her throat. "I'll get the milk."

Every curve of her body was on fire as confusion wrestled with her heart. They were no more than strangers to each other, yet she couldn't keep her body from rippling with excitement when he looked at her. Just before she turned, his grin broadened, giving way to his lighter side.

"Had I known my shirt could look that good, I would have loaned it out a long time ago."

She laughed. Among her other emotions was a sense of relief his playful remark caused, releasing some of the tension.

By the time she returned with their milk and chocolate goodies, he had stretched out full length on the couch. He raised up slightly as she handed him his glass, then she put the plate of brownies on the floor and sat down beside them, leaning back against the divan. He took a couple of big gulps of milk, then picked up a brownie and lay back down while he munched on it.

"Mmmmm, these are good," he commented tiredly. For one fleeting second a warm glow washed over him as he thought how nice it would be to come home every day to the smell of brownies and a lovely, devoted woman to share his problems with. *Good grief! I must be punch-*

drunk! I'm as bad as Matt. He crammed the rest of the chocolate morsel into his mouth and closed his eyes.

"I'm glad you like them but it's only a mix. I take no credit for their tastiness." She heard his noisy breathing and slight muffled smacking as he chewed, making her aware of just how exhausted he must be.

"I wanted to talk," she said quietly, "but I think you need to get some sleep."

"I told you, I'm too uptight to sleep right now." He reached down for another brownie. "However, I don't know if I want to talk either. I think I know what you want to talk about. You seem to have a one-track mind...Christopher Mayhew."

"Smarty." She wrinkled her nose and pouted her lips at him. I wanted to talk about Matt."

"Same thing." He yawned. "It would end up right back to the old man. You can't seem to do much that doesn't involve the welfare of Christopher Mayhew, the good of the company...."

"I'm genuinely concerned, that's all."

"Look," he interjected, "Matt and I have been able to manage quite nicely without you for a long time now, so why don't you channel your concern where it's...needed."

"You would have liked to have said, where it's *wanted*, wouldn't you?"

"You're very perceptive for a city slicker."

"You can insult me all you want, Patrick, but I won't give up being concerned. Not when I believe so strongly."

He let out a long exasperated breath. "Something told me you wouldn't." He waited a moment, then went on. "I guess I can't expect you to understand something if you've never been told." He hesitated again to collect his thoughts. "I'm not one to involve outsiders, but since you're already very much involved, maybe I *should* explain a few things to you. You're not going to like hearing it, but maybe you'll understand and leave us alone."

She felt saddened. Maybe she would understand, but it was doubtful if leaving them alone would be all that easy.

He took another bite of brownie before he continued. "These really are good. Matt's are edible, but they're usually a little scorched." He let out a low chuckle. "I tried to make some once."

"Yes. Matt said something about them."

"I guess he probably told you a lot of other things too," he added, cautiously eyeing her.

She picked at a loose thread on the sleeve of her shirt and quietly said, "That's what I wanted to talk to you about." Her tone was apologetic. "I'm afraid I didn't exactly discourage him from talking about his...his birth...his mother...his feelings about you and his Grandpa."

"Matt doesn't need much encouragement to talk about those things, or about anything for that matter so don't feel too bad. Besides, he doesn't know the full story behind all that."

"I know."

"I didn't think he had to know. Not yet. Maybe not ever. He seems to have accepted things like they are." His voice lowered tauntingly. "I just wish another certain party in this house would accept it like it is too."

Janet picked up a piece of bark from the rug and tossed it into the fire. "I told you. I'm persistent. Especially when I think it's for a good cause." She turned to him excitedly. "Your father would simply be crazy about Matt! It would give him so much to live for."

"That's *not* part of the deal!" he snapped, coming to a semi-sitting position.

She felt her nerves tense immediately at his tone of voice. "But—"

"No buts," he said sharply, dropping his body back down. "The only reason I'm even entertaining giving you an explanation is to insure that Christopher Mayhew never gets the opportunity to get his claws into my son!" His eyes caught and held hers. "You asked me not to be so distrustful of you. Well, I'm *trying* to trust you. Give me some reason to."

"You're right in feeling that way. I gave you my word to keep quiet about Matt, yet everything I've said indicates just the opposite. I'm sorry if I led you to believe I would go back on my word...I won't." She slumped back down. "That doesn't keep me from trying to change your mind, however."

The silence loomed between them like a heavy cloud until she finally turned back to look into his troubled eyes. When he spoke, his voice broke with fatigue, causing his words to falter.

"Out..side of Doyne and Roger, you're the only person I've told this to and for the life of me I don't know why I'm telling you. I guess I'm too tired tonight to think of any other way to insure your keeping Matt's existence from my father."

His stare moved from her to the ceiling. She turned away and relaxed her back against the couch and waited for him to begin.

"I don't know what you already know, but I'll just begin at the beginning." He breathed a deep breath and let it out slowly. "When I was a kid, I thought the sun rose and set with my dad. Mother was always rather sickly...a beautiful, sweet woman, but very weak and frail so Dad and I spent a lot of time together. We went to ball games, ate ice-cream cones together. He even went to PTA meetings. We did all the classic things a father and son do and more."

"Sounds nice."

"It didn't last. Mother started needing more and more care. I should say, more and more watching. She started having a problem with the bottle. The pills the doctor gave her didn't seem to work anymore for the pain and she started drinking heavily. Before anyone knew it, she was hiding bottles all over the house and spending more and more time alone in her room."

"I'm so sorry. It must have been a hard time."

"Yeah, hard. We were afraid she'd...well, anyway, Dad hired a full-time housekeeper which necessitated his making more money. Soon the more money he made, the more he had to be away from home and the worse my mother got. I always felt all she really needed was for Dad and me to spend more time with her. I tried to do what I could but I was still in school and couldn't be home all the time. Dad seemed to thrive on business ventures. Making lots of money had him totally consumed by now and nothing else mattered. He made no time at all for Mother and very little for me."

Patrick leaned back and rubbed his eyes. Remembering was painful and it clearly showed in his expression. "One day, I came home from school and she was gone. Dear old Dad had made arrangements to have her institutionalized."

"Institutionalized?" Janet gasped.

"Well, they called it a rest home...a very expensive rest home, but it was the same as institutionalized. She got so when I visited her, she just stared out the window like she didn't know me. He put her away out of his hair." He paused for a moment. "I loved her so much and he took her from me. I don't think I ever quite forgave him for that. He told me he didn't have time for her *and* his business. He couldn't *afford* the embarrassment it would cause him business-wise if the fact that his wife was a hopeless alcoholic became known."

"He told you that?"

"Not in those exact words, but he certainly implied it strongly enough. What he did say was that with Mother away, he would be able to entertain prospective clients in our home. Money! That's all he thought of."

"I'm sure he saw that your Mother was well provided for."

"His *money* saw to that!" He calmed himself. "I guess that was when I started feeling really bitter toward him. I told myself that money would never rule me...would never rob me of loved ones again, and I was determined to have nothing to do with Mayhew Enterprises. I didn't like what it had done to my father and mother...to my father and me. His goal, of course, was to get me as involved in the business as he was, but I resisted. I went away to college as far away as I could get. Mother died my senior year. Dad seemed genuinely broken by Mother's death, I'll give him that much. I wonder if he thought about her when he was with his other women."

"Other women?"

"Lots of them while Mother was incarcerated. Younger the better."

Janet leaned forward and wrapped her arms around her legs. "That explains what he told me while reading his bible one morning."

"His bible?"

"He said he had done some things he could never forgive himself for but wanted to seek God's forgiveness."

"Christopher Mayhew was reading the bible? Are we talking about the same man?"

"He reads it every morning before the work day starts. Why do you ask?"

"He's never been a very Godly man." He shook his head. "He's right. He's done some things that might be considered unforgiveable...even by God."

Janet reached up and laid her hand on his arm. "Our God is a forgiving God. All we need to do is ask. I feel Christopher is trying to repent for what he did to your Mother."

"What he did to Mother is just the tip of the iceberg."

She rested her chin on her knees while she listened and tried to keep reminding herself that the man Pat was talking about was the same, kind Christopher who lay dying in the hospital.

"Maybe it was out of moral obligation to him or that I was just trying to recapture the relationship we once had...I don't know, but I agreed to join the firm only if I could start at the bottom like any new employee. He agreed to my requests and the first day I went to work, I was made Vice President and put in charge of engineering and quality control. I was angry. He hadn't intended to comply with my wishes from the beginning. He couldn't *afford* the embarrassment of having a son who wasn't ambitious as he was."

"Patrick." She looked doubtful.

"Oh, this time you're wrong. He actually said those exact words." Patrick finished off his milk and set the empty glass on the floor. "I got my own apartment and went to work for a small plastics company in Collinsville, Illinois, a little town across the river from St. Louis...well, you know, you live there." He laughed. "I guess I'm really getting rummy from no sleep."

She smiled to herself. "All fathers want the best for their sons. I don't see making you Vice President was so wrong."

"He deliberately undermined my wishes because I was an embarrassment to him...like my Mother! I put a lot more value on my personal integrity and moral code than mere money or a top position in my father's company."

"Are you implying that all of us who are ambitious, who want to improve our standard of living are low life? We can't all be happy being cowboys!"

He breathed in noisily. "No, I didn't mean that at all. There's a difference. With my father it was push, push, push. It didn't matter to him that I wanted the self-satisfaction of making it on my own. I wanted the self-respect I felt I deserved. He tried bribing me with offers for new expensive cars, luxurious trips, a big house...anything *money* could buy, when all I really ever wanted was a father, not a business machine."

Janet shook her head in despair. The Christopher Mayhew she knew WAS a father...good and kind and loving. "People change, Patrick. I think that's what Christopher wants more than anything."

"That's *your* opinion." He hesitated for a long moment, then continued as if she hadn't spoken. "Anyway, I started working at this plastics company. Everything was going along real nice when suddenly the president of the company was mysteriously dismissed. I'll never forget the look on his face when he left that day. He was in his early fifties, had been with the company for years. He had kids in college and I think one still at home. He was a darn good man, but it is hard to find another job with that prestige at his age. I was named president."

"What's that got to do with Christopher?"

"Do you know the name of that company?"

"No."

"Diversified Plastics. Ring a bell?"

"Sure. Mayhew Enterprises owns—" She stopped.

"You hit the nail on the head. Dear old dad bought the company and promoted me to president. He didn't care whose toes he stepped on or whose lives he ruined. His son was going to be top banana or else!"

"I'm so sorry you've been hurt."

"To make a long story short, during all this hassle, I met Sylvia, my ex-wife, Matt's mother. I think the fact that my father didn't like her made me determined to marry her. I overlooked any faults she may have had. She was beautiful and a little on the wild side, which was kind of exciting at the time."

"Why didn't your father like her?"

"Same old thing. She wasn't good enough for the son of a business tycoon. He was very verbal about his disapproval of her, pointing out how flirtatious she was, how flashy she dressed, how crude her language was...just what an embarrassment she would be to the company in general. She was just too rough around the edges for his taste." He chuckled a dry humorless laugh. "The more he talked, the better she looked to me. I knew someone my father disliked so much would make me a perfect wife."

"Are you saying you only married her to spite your father? I'm beginning to feel sorry for her."

He let out a loud laugh this time. "Save your sympathy. I didn't marry out of spite, but SHE did."

"I don't understand."

"I found out later she married me to get back at my father for thinking she was gaudy and crude. I saw her as fun and exciting, so carefree, taking one day at a time. I was in love. She was acting like it. The fact that my father disapproved of her was only a bonus. I thought that would keep him from interfering in our lives."

"And I guess the next thing you're going to say is that it didn't work." She got up and put another stick of wood in the fire box. "He didn't stay out of your lives."

"You catch on fast," he said, turning to admiringly watch her go about her task. Her slender body appeared even smaller in the over-sized shirt that stopped just at her knees. He marveled again how, for a tiny person, her legs could be so curvaceous, the smooth bare skin looking like porcelain in the dim light.

As his eyes traveled back up, she turned to face him. His gaze rested momentarily on her breasts jutting against the flannel when she took in a deep breath. She watched his eyes rove appraisingly upward to her face and hair, his lazy seductive look sending a delicious shiver down her spine. Her own eyes drank in the sensuality of his physique and she wondered whatever made her think he wasn't so very handsome. He was actually lethally good-looking.

She closed her eyes to rid herself of this perfect picture, reminding herself once again how hopeless it was feeling this way about him. She couldn't deny he played havoc with her senses, but she was smart enough to know she was traveling down a dead-end street.

"You're Christopher's only child. I want to believe he was concerned for your welfare."

A look of withdrawal came over Patrick's face. Her words shocked him back to reality. *Always quick to defend his father. She definitely belonged to Christopher Mayhew lock, stock and barrel!* But hard as he tried, he could not ward off the bolt of desire that sizzled through him. His tired dreamy state left him with only one thought at the moment and that was how wonderfully soft she would feel in his arms.

His gaze riveted her eyes to his and her flesh tingled under his lustful stare. Finally finding strength to move, she grabbed an afghan off the chair and awkwardly wrapped it around her shoulders and sat back down on the floor with her back against the couch to avoid direct contact with his compelling eyes. It had been a long time since anyone looked at her that way...had touched her senses in that special way.

He began again as if nothing had transpired between them, his voice hoarse with fatigue. "After we were married, dear Dad decided since he was stuck with her, he would make her into a *suitable mate for a man in my position.*"

"Ohhhh, no. I don't know if I want to hear anymore."

"Ohhhh, yes, and you might as well hear the rest of the story. He lavished her with expensive clothes from the most prestigious designers...even had her flown to Europe for fittings. He hired a special tutor to teach her the proper social etiquette and the guy taught her how to speak with a certain aristocratic accent. Then after she had cleaned up her act, so to speak, Dad started personally taking her to various business functions and escorting her all over St. Louis. Their pictures were constantly showing up on the news and in the papers." A low ironic laugh escaped his throat. "In a few short months, I had lost the girl I married, but thanks to good old Dad, I had gained a business asset. By then, however, I didn't quite measure up to HER expectations. *Daddy*, as she called him, was more her type. He could maintain her in the style she had quickly become accustomed to."

Janet couldn't believe her ears; but, of course he was telling the truth. She had sympathy for Sylvia all right, but now it was for being so stupid! How could she jeopardize her marriage to Patrick?

"Was that when she left you?"

"Not right away. She urged me to join *Daddy's* firm. President of a small plastics firm didn't offer her much socially. Vice President of Mayhew's, on the other hand, could provide all that." He let his breath out hastily. "I was sick of the whole rat race, so while *Daddy* and my loving wife were wining and dining, I stepped down from my presidency, rehired the former president and with Cal's help, drew up an ironclad agreement that insured the man a lifetime position with the company for as long as he wanted. There was nothing my father could do about it."

"Cal did that for you?" She knew Cal thought a lot of Patrick, but he also was very dedicated to Christopher. Still, for some unexplainable reason, she felt like giving a cheer for good old Cal.

"Yes." Pat smiled remembering. "He took one heck of a chance with his own career going against the old man like that but he weathered it out. Dad was either smart enough to know Cal's value to him or else he was too wrapped up in Sylvia to even care what was happening. I also relinquished all rights to any profits from the company for myself and my wife." He laughed again. "Boy was I naïve. I was going to take her, move to another state and get back to the basics...save our marriage and live happily ever after."

"I have a feeling she didn't share your enthusiasm."

"Understatement. You would have thought I had cut off her food and air supply instead of her money...which, to her was the same thing...money, food and air. I think she screamed for one week straight."

"So that's when she left?"

"Not exactly on her own. When she found out *Daddy* couldn't do anything about the money situation, her temper tantrums caused her to fall from his grace. Suddenly she wasn't *suitable* anymore." His tone grew grim. "I guess it takes one to know one because he knew exactly what it would take to get her to agree to a divorce...money."

Janet grimaced and was beginning to see why Patrick was so bitter toward money, but she still believed Christopher was a changed man and that there was hope for the two to reconcile.

"He offered her a hundred thousand dollars to get out of my life. The worst part was...she took it. Kind of an insult, don't you think? With all Dad's millions, she didn't even hold out for a better offer. Just grabbed the lousy hundred thou and ran. Of course she had quite a nest-egg accumulated in all the jewels and furs dear dad had given her." His voice trailed tiredly.

Janet's compassionate nature took over. She reached up and took hold of his hand that was dangling over the edge of the couch. She tugged lightly at one of his fingers, the feel was one mixed with rough and smooth. "Maybe he did you a favor. If she was that shallow."

"Heck, I knew the honeymoon was over long before that, but I guess I was trying to kid myself into thinking maybe if we got away before the baby was born..."

"Christopher obviously didn't know."

"She insisted on keeping it a secret from everyone. In fact, she wouldn't even discuss it...like it would go away if she didn't think about it."

Janet's eyes welled with tears. "Oh, merciful heaven! Didn't she even want your child?" When she thought about

Matt, her heart nearly broke. "I would have been so proud." She stopped short, dropping her hold on his hand.

He reached up and brushed his fingers across her hair. "Thanks for that." His voice was barely a whisper. "I don't know why, but that meant a lot to me."

She leaned her head against his hand, savoring the feel of his touch on her hair. "It's just that Matt is such a great kid."

He twisted a long tendril around his finger and played with the curl as he continued. "Realizing the marriage was over, I had Cal instigate divorce proceedings and, of course, it went through without a hitch, other than granting her another large sum of money. Well worth it. But that didn't alter the fact that she was carrying my child. She disappeared immediately. I had to find her. I was in a panic. I thought maybe she took the money to have an abortion or something, I didn't know. I DID know she wasn't thrilled at being pregnant."

"How did you find her?"

"Luck. Sheer luck."

Janet smiled to herself remembering Matt's account of the incident. He had said it was *fate*.

"I remember her mentioning this place in California where she lived long before I met her. I took a chance on her going there. I was right that she went there, but wrong about her getting an abortion. I found her the very week Matt was due."

"Thank God."

"I don't think God entered into her decision much. She was planning on springing the grandchild on dear *Daddy* as soon as it was born. She was sure he would be very happy to, as she said, *share some of the kid's inheritance with her*."

Janet moaned, "Ohhh, no."

"She didn't get the chance. Since she obviously did not want the baby, it was easy to buy her off and spare her the hassle of trying to get more money from dad. She didn't even hesitate to let me have the baby for a six-figure deposit into her bank account."

"Just can't imagine a mother giving her child away." Janet shook her head sadly.

"All that money didn't do her any good. She died before she left the hospital. She hadn't taken very good care of herself. Kept herself bound so she wouldn't show, didn't eat properly, hadn't even consulted a doctor. I learned she was addicted to Oxycodone among other narcotics. Probably why she never consulted a doctor about her pregnancy."

"I'm truly sorry."

"So was I. I made funeral arrangements for her but didn't stay for the service." His voice was sad and weary, lowering to a whisper. "This is where God did come in. Matt was born healthy. By His grace, the baby and I left California and settled here. I notified Cal I wouldn't be back and I was doing fine on my own. That's when he told me Dad had made me co-owner of his businesses. I told him not to waste the paper on that agreement. I wanted no part of any of it."

Janet felt his hand slip from her hair and dangle lifelessly off the couch. The sound of his slow, even breathing told her he had fallen asleep.

CHAPTER SEVEN

*L*eaning her head back on the divan, she tried to make sense of her feelings for Matt and Patrick...feelings she was having a hard time denying. Was it because they were Christopher's family? Was she feeling a bond with them because of her love for Christopher? Whatever the reason, the feelings were all too real.

She picked up the brownie from the plate on the floor and munched on it while mulling over what had transpired over the last day. Had it only been a day? She smiled to herself. *A day and nearly a night.* At least now she knew the burden Patrick bore, but she still wished with all her heart he could see his father through her eyes. She was sure Christopher was trying to atone for his wrong doings and was suffering as much as Patrick.

Fatigue settled over her as she swallowed the last bite of brownie. She rose quietly and pulled the afghan from her shoulders and spread it over Patrick's long form. Her eyes rested on his slightly parted lips. His peaceful breathing...in and out, in and out...mesmerized her.

Studying his face for a long time, she again marveled at how handsome he appeared to her. As she was questioning her mentality for having more than just a casual feeling about this man, an uncontrollable urge engulfed her...a raging desire to kiss him. Like having an out-of-body experience, she leaned down and very lightly touched his mouth with hers, immediately feeling a warm tingle flow through her entire body. There was no self-control left as she kissed each corner as softly as she could. Like a fool, she closed her eyes and allowed herself one last taste, kissing him fully on his warm, moist lips. She couldn't remember anything tasting so sweet or feeling so wonderful.

Berating herself for such brazen behavior, she lifted her face from his. When she opened her eyes she was startled out of her wits seeing his staring back at her. She gasped and straightened like a shot, her face flushing hot as fire.

He remained calm, his expression unchanged. "What was *that* all about?" he asked, using the same question she had when he kissed her earlier.

"I...it was...something came over me," she stammered, finally blurting out, "I thought you were asleep."

"What's my next move?" His expression bordered on mockery. "Am I supposed to slap you?"

She dropped her shoulders sheepishly. "At least I didn't attack you and try to suck your face off!"

"Oh, didn't you?" he taunted, a teasing smile playing at the corners of his mouth.

A suffocating sensation spread over her. She whirled around and plopped back down on the floor and covered her face with her hands. "Don't look at me...I can't believe I did that."

He reached out and tugged at a strand of her hair. "Hey."

She jerked away. "Don't talk to me either."

He chuckled. "I didn't say I didn't like it." He smacked his lips. "Tastes a lot like chocolate."

"I ate the last brownie."

"Cheater. You ate more than I got to."

"When you snooze you lose."

He laughed out loud and turned her face toward him. "In fact, I think I could get used to those kinds of chocolate kisses."

She finally found courage to open her eyes and look at him. His expression was one of kindness which only made her nervous condition worse. Her skin prickled against the smooth flannel as his hand snaked around her neck, his thumb fondling her earlobe.

"Come here, Pip Squeak," he gently urged, pulling her up to him.

She gladly obeyed. There was not one second of hesitation on her part as he lifted the afghan as an invitation to lie down next to him. She knew she shouldn't let her body melt against his, but there was neither the strength nor the will to stop it. His hand glided skillfully over the flannel shirt seeking hungrily for the bare flesh of her thigh. His palm rested hotly on her trembling leg while his thumb rubbed softly back and forth. She shuddered with delight.

His fingers splayed across her skin and pulled her closer to his rigid form, all the while their eyes locking passionately with the wonder of it all. He moved his mouth to hers, barely touching as another helpless moan escaped. Her lips tickled as his voice rasped against them. "You're so lovely."

Her response was wordless. It came as a tightening of her arm around his neck, pressing her lips to his and wetly tracing her tongue along the curve of his mouth. The feather-light touch of his tongue to hers made her quiver and squirm closer. He was so tender and loving...nothing like he had been when he kissed her before. She knew at this very moment that there would be no way she could ever be able to walk away from him and pretend she had never met him. Her life could never be the same even if she had only known him for a day.

She caught herself holding her breath, trying to stop

the incessant quaking that was tormenting her body as the slow motion of his tongue swept over her mouth from corner to corner again and again. She finally fell limp against him when his lips nibbled over her face, across her eyelids and back to her mouth.

An uncontrollable sob-like groan trickled from her throat as another round of shivers scampered down her spine. He shifted his weight, taking her more fully into his arms, cradling her face against his neck while he stroked her long hair.

"Shhhh," he whispered, soothing and comforting her shaking, turning the heated sensuality of the moment to one of tenderness. Her body was still aflame, burning with unfulfilled passion, but she silently thanked him for stopping something that could have gotten completely out of hand. Something so confusing to her, it made her head swim.

She snuggled contentedly against him, breathing in his wonderfully distinctive masculine smell. A hot tear spilled from her eye just before he tilted her face up with one finger. His thumb traced a circling pattern around her lips before he kissed them again...just one soft, tiny kiss. Her emotions at the moment puzzled her. The feeling that washed over her was something like deep gratitude, respect, admiration... It was almost like falling in love.

LOVE! How absurd. More like lust, although she had never considered herself a lustful person. She had been madly in love with Mark and had thought she had experienced all there was to experience about loving someone, but now she doubted if she had even touched on the real emotion of love. Something told her there was a world of loving sensations she could learn from Patrick Mayhew. That is, if she ever had the opportunity which was doubtful. They were worlds apart. He wanted nothing to do with her life with his father...a life she could not forsake.

"I'm afraid of you," he said out of the blue, breaking

into her thoughts.

She raised her head to look at him, puzzled by his remark. "Afraid of me? Why?"

He let his breath out slowly. "I don't exactly know. I guess just because you're here, because you're so beautiful, so soft, so..."

"Vulnerable?"

He waited a moment before answering. There was a pained look on his face and she watched the reflection of light from the fire flicker in his eyes as they looked into hers. "Yes, vulnerable." He hesitated a second. "Don't you know how easy it would be for me to have made love to you?"

"Why didn't you?"

"It couldn't be just a casual thing with you. You're not the casual type. You need...no, you DESERVE much more."

She took a deep breath and let it back out. "Well, thanks for that at least. I take it you don't think I've come here for some ulterior motive anymore?" She let out a half-laugh. "Ironic, isn't it? Half my time here I spent trying to convince you I was Miss Goody Two Shoes and the other half offering you my body and soul." Her face heated again with embarrassment. "I didn't waste much time, did I?"

He smiled. "Don't be so hard on yourself."

"But I haven't even known you twenty-four hours."

"There's no timetable for...I guess you could call it romance. It just happens. It's not something you always plan."

"Well, you're right about me. I *would* want to know it was more than just a casual weekend fling."

"Some sort of a commitment?"

"Yes."

"That's something I couldn't give you. I've spent a number of years avoiding that sort of thing."

"And I've spent a number of years searching for that

sort of thing."

"You're husband hunting?"

She raised up on one elbow. "Is that what you think?" She laughed. "Hardly. But if I were, this is an unlikely place for me to look for one." She lay back down. "No," she continued jokingly, "in the dim light I mistook you for a nice guy who might be fun to neck with."

Laughing, he squeezed her affectionately and kissed her forehead. "I think it's about time the nice girl in you goes to bed...before I turn into that savage you find so disgusting."

She gave him a half-lidded gaze, tilting her head back cockily. "And you think I couldn't handle him?"

They exchanged a subtle look of amusement. "You'd *better* get to bed, Squirt, before I decide to play your silly game."

Her face grew serious as their eyes locked for a brief moment. "Maybe it's not a game, Pat," she said softly, dropping her eyes thoughtfully, admitting to herself that her feelings for him went far beyond games. "Maybe...maybe it's fate."

He took her hand and brought it to his mouth to kiss the tips of her fingers. "You've spent too much time with Matt, I see. Don't let him sucker you in on that we could use a *woman's touch* around here. Don't get me wrong. You're very desirable. You're also very NICE. Now go to bed!"

Her eyes clouded as she looked longingly at him for a second, taking her hand from his and brushing the back of her fingers along his jaw, feeling the stubble of his unshaven face. "I really do like you."

His eyelids closed slowly, fighting thoughts of forgetting this nice-girl business and giving in to his desires. He pulled her hand from his face and squeezed it, stating emphatically, "GO-TO-BED!"

A Woman's Touch

*****

SOUTHERN CALIFORNIA

"Did you get your old lady's money for our trip, Max?"

"Where you been all night?"

Ruby shook a plastic Ziploc half full of pills in the air and did a little dance around Max's chair. "Look what I got us from some guy. Feel-good pills."

"For crying out loud, Ruby. Are you crazy? What guy?"

"A guy I met at a bar. He thought I was going to get a room somewhere so he gave me these pills along with a couple hundred dollars." She giggled a drunken hiccup. "While he was in the men's room, I hurried out of there. He's still waiting to hear from me about the room."

"You stupid woman! You're going to get us killed before we get out of town." Max grabbed the bag out of her hand. "We need to keep a clear mind. I've got some leads I need to check out."

Ruby squealed. "You found him? I knew you could."

"Quiet. You'll wake Mama."

"Ooooo, don't wanna disturb the Mama. How would you know if she was disturbed or not? She don't know nothing."

"What runs through your veins, Ruby? Ice water? You're livin' in my Mother's house, livin' off her money, eatin' her food. I'm trying to help you for old times' sake. How can you talk about her like that?"

"Don't get your shorts in a twist. I'm just excited about getting out of here and our hands on the Mayhew money. Now tell me, did you find him?"

"I found a Patrick Mayhew living in Montana. Could that be him?"

"Did you find a Mayhew company in Montana?"

"No, but I don't think he works for Mayhews or any other company in or around St. Louis. The best bet is Montana. I'll do a little more searching and see what I come up with." He yawned. "First I need to get some sleep."

"Want some company?" She tried to sound sexy but only slurred her words.

"You're drunk."

"So what's wrong with a guy buying a girl a few drinks when the girl can score? If you don't want to party with me then give me the pills back."

He held the Ziploc up. "Do you even know what they are?"

"The guy said they were Oxy."

"The guy said." He eyed her. "You're pathetic. You take some yahoo's word for what he's giving you. You could wake up dead for all you know."

"You're such a party pooper anymore." Ruby pouted and collapsed on the couch.

"Another thing I've been thinking about while you were out selling yourself to the highest bidder is that we can't take my Mother's car. We could be traced too easily if anyone questions why we skipped town and the car is gone."

"So who's stupid now? What are we supposed to do? Take a bus?"

"As soon as I pinpoint where this Mayhew character is, we fly there under assumed names, rent a car, get the kid, hide out until we get the money, give the kid back, leave the car somewhere and fly to wherever we need to."

She bolted upright. "Whoa, hold on there. Give the kid back? Give the kid back?" She emphasized each word. "And have him identify us?"

"He don't know us."

"He could describe us to the police. We're *not* giving the kid back," she stated flatly. "If it wasn't for that brat, my sister would still be alive."

"You're talking crazy."

"My sister was going to take me to Hawaii with her. She was going to hook us up with some rich dudes she met. We were going to have it all."

"Get some sleep, Ruby. You're talking out of your head. This is the first time I've ever heard of you going to Hawaii with anyone."

"I'm telling you, I was going."

"Okay, okay, you were going, but now you ain't. We're going to Montana, find your sister's ex, grab his kid and—"

"Did you get the gun?"

"You don't worry yourself about the gun. You're not going to get your hands on it. I'll be the one taking care of the gun business if it's necessary. It's just for insurance, remember?"

She closed her eyes and smiled. "Yeah, I remember," she said sleepily as he left the room, then whispered to herself.

"I'm *not* giving the kid back."

CHAPTER EIGHT

MONTANA

Janet yawned and stretched herself awake, feeling a very distinct lump on her foot. When she raised to see what it was, the lump was staring back at her with his yellow eyes and Janet's smile was greeted with loud purring.

"Good morning, Carlyle," she said kindly, reaching to give him a loving stroke across his arching back.

The cat rose, stretched and then stepped gingerly as if walking on eggs until he reached the warm pillow, then curled up against it. Janet laughed softly. "I thought you didn't like any other human beings except Matt?"

Carlyle answered with an affectionate, "Meow."

"Well, I like you, too." She picked him up and put him on her stomach. She lay back down and glanced around the room, taking a better look at everything in the daylight. It was all very masculine. The wall décor consisted of one muzzle-loader shotgun hanging above the bureau. A school picture of Matt sat on top of the dresser along with a hair brush. Not exactly a decorator's dream but still comfortable.

She felt puzzled. Why should she feel anything about this place...comfortable or otherwise? Everything about her stay so far in Montana was a puzzle to her. She certainly had not been herself last night. Last night! She moaned and snuggled deeper under the cover as if she could hide from herself, wincing slightly as she reflected on last night. Her kissing Pat. Pat kissing her. Despite the tingling sensation she felt just thinking about it, she was totally aware of how foolish she had been.

Carlyle's purring raised in pitch, bringing Janet's thoughts back to earth. She let out a low chuckle. "Wise old Carlyle. I'll bet *you've* never made a complete fool of yourself."

He nudged her hand for another pet and gave her an understanding "Meow."

"Man of few words, huh? You're smart. I should take a few lessons from you and learn to keep my big mouth shut."

Carlyle's ears perked at the sound of someone coming up the stairs. Janet's smile broadened when she saw the top of Matt's brown head appear over the stairwell. She watched him walk toward her in his flannel pajamas with pictures of horses and cowboys on them.

"Hi, punkin," she greeted, holding her hand out for him to join her on the bed.

The boy gave her a bashful smile. "The last thing I thought I'd ever want to be called is *punkin.*"

"Sorry."

"That's okay. From you it kind of sounds...nice." He leaped on the bed nearly bouncing Janet out. "I knew you were still here."

"Why?" She playfully mussed the boy's hair. "Because your dad was on the couch?"

"No, because your underwear and pantyhose is draped over the shower rod in the bathroom. No one goes out in this weather without their underwear."

"That's ARE draped, not IS draped," she corrected, blushing slightly at his boldness. "I'm glad you reminded me. I forgot I rinsed them out last night." She started to get up. "I'd better get those out of there before your dad gets up."

Matt grabbed her arm. "It's okay, he's dead to the world. Besides, they look good there. Sort of gives the place...you know...a *woman's touch.*"

She fell back on her pillow. "You'd better not let your dad hear that."

"It'll be our secret."

"Yeah, I think that would be best. He's probably had about all the *woman's touch* he can stand." She lifted the cover. "Come on, get under here before you freeze. Is it always this cold in Montana?"

He scooted under the blanket. "No, it's real nice in the summer. You should come back then."

She gave him a wary glance.

"I just thought maybe you could give me some tutoring on my grammar. You know, are and is, sit and set."

"I don't think you need much tutoring in any department, you little con artist. In fact, you could probably teach me a few things." Carlyle settled comfortably between them, stretching out his full length. "I somehow get the impression this house belongs to Carlyle and he lets humans use it."

Matt giggled and gave the cat a sound pat on the stomach. "He likes you and he's a very good judge of character."

"Oh, really?"

"I like you, too." He hung his head, looking a little embarrassed.

The smile on Janet's face faded as her eyes misted. Something about the sincerity in the boy's voice stabbed at her heart. She had to be realistic about this. When she returned to St. Louis, she was going to have to erase him from her mind. Could she do it? *Oh the heck with it!* She put her arm around the boy and kissed him on the forehead.

She'd worry about forgetting him later. "And I like you, too, Matt. Very, very much."

Carlyle raised his head and meowed loudly, causing Janet and Matt to giggle.

"I think he wants a kiss, to," Matt said.

"How about settling for a hug." She gave the cat a big squeeze.

"You're fun, Janet. You're nice to talk to. I'll bet you know a lot about my Grandpa," he added hurriedly, hoping to catch her off guard.

"Huh, uh. You know how your dad feels about that subject. I've done enough damage in that area already."

"Please, please. Tell me just one thing about him." His big brown eyes looked pitifully sad.

"Cut it out, Matt. Do you want to get us both thrown out on our ear...or some other part of our anatomy?"

'Okay, then tell me about St. Louis. Tell me about the big arch. I saw it on TV."

"It's unbelievably gigantic." She saw no harm talking about St. Louis. "You can go up in it and look out over miles and miles."

"WOW! Would you take me up there when I come to St. Louis?"

"Matt," she cautioned.

"When I'm twenty-one I mean."

She grinned, letting him know she was aware of his tricks. "When you're twenty-one you won't need me to take you."

He settled back against her arm. "You smell good...like a mother should smell."

"Matt, I'm warning you." She poked him in the ribs.

"If Dad wasn't so stubborn, we could go to St. Louis and see the arch." His mouth formed a pout.

She wanted to say she agreed his dad was stubborn, but thought better of it. She pictured how much fun it would be taking Matt to the zoo and other places. "We've lots of wonderful things to see and do in St. Louis." She stopped herself from getting too enthusiastic. "But, of course, I'm sure you have lots of wonderful things to see and do here in Montana, also."

"Sure we do, but...I'll make a deal with you. I'll get Dad to show you our fun stuff and you get him to let me go to St. Louis." He giggled.

"Why you conniving little...." She started tickling him, their playful antics causing Carlyle to move to safer territory at the foot of the bed. Their laughter drifted delightfully through the air and Janet felt very much alive and happy, never wanting the fun to end. But the pain of it was just as intent as the joy and she felt compelled to make things clear...as much for herself as for Matt.

She fell back on her pillow, catching her breath from laughing so hard. "Matt, you do know I have no right to interfere in your lives?"

"You're not interfering."

"But, I would be if I tried to convince your dad to bring you to St. Louis."

Matt sat up. His face was solemn as he looked sadly into her eyes. "Then answer just one question for me. Does my Grandpa have white hair?"

She let her breath out, her brow knotted. What could she do? He had wormed his way into her heart. "Yes," she answered, fighting desperately to keep from telling him every detail he wanted to know about his Grandpa.

"Does he have a fat belly like Santa Claus?"

"No more questions. You said only one." She rolled over. "It's time we get up."

"Does he?"

"No, he doesn't," she spat out, adding, "Well, maybe just a little paunch. Now, get up and no more questions."

"Does he wear glasses?"

She clamped her hand over his mouth. "I said no more questions."

Just one more," he mumbled through her fingers.

"No."

"Just one."

She shook her head and mouthed, "N.O."

He dropped his shoulders resolutely and she took her hand from his mouth. "I was only going to ask if you knew how to make French toast."

"You little twerp," she said while laughing. "You were not. You just made that up.:

He shrugged. "Well, do you?"

"Yes, as a matter of fact, I do. I happen to be the world's champion French toast maker and it's making my mouth water thinking about it. "I'll need milk, eggs, bread of course, and the way I usually make it would take vanilla and cinnamon...oh, and butter for frying. Do you have all that?"

"Yep, I think so. Doyne cooks over here for us sometimes so we have a lot of weird stuff."

She chuckled. "That *weird stuff* is what makes it good. Do you have syrup?"

He wrinkled his nose. "No. No syrup."

"Do you have brown sugar?"

"I think so."

"Then I can make syrup."

His mouth dropped open. "You can *make* syrup? Fantastic!" Matt acted like he was in awe. "It's got to be fate...sending us someone who can *make* syrup."

"Oh, shut up," she laughed, giving him a shove, "and get out of my bed so I can get dressed."

As soon as she said it, it dawned on her she only had her good suit to put on. She would just get breakfast in her nightshirt instead. Before she could say another word, Matt offered to get her a pair of his jeans and a T-shirt.

"Matt, no, wait. I don't think—"

"They'll fit. You'll see." He flashed her a cocky grin, reminding her of his father. "Would fate send us a woman the wrong size?"

She jumped out of bed and chased him down the stairs. They both clasped their hands over their mouths when they heard a mournful groan coming from the couch.

"What in the world is all the racket about?" Pat's gruff voice rang through the cabin.

"I'm so sorry, Pat. I guess Matt and I got carried away."

Matt turned and with exaggeration tiptoed into his room.

Pat pulled himself to a sitting position and looked over the back of the couch at the tiny form standing near the stairway. His shirt hung loosely over her slender shoulders and she looked more like one of Matt's schoolmates than the *grown woman* she insisted she was. She may not look like a grown woman, but he was fully aware of just how much woman she was. The memory of her in his arms would be etched in his mind for a long time...maybe forever.

Her skin prickled as she watched his perusal of her, while memories of last night crept deliciously to her mind, flooding her with a soft warm feeling. She smiled and nodded a good morning, afraid she had no voice. Even though he was in dire need of a shave, he still looked very tempting to her.

"Your feet are going to freeze," he finally said watching her toes wiggle up and down.

His words weren't exactly the most romantic ones she had ever heard from someone she had kissed a few hours ago, but the sound of his voice sang a sweet song in her mind.

"Uh...." She pointed toward Matt's room, sounding like she was attempting a foreign language. "Matt is getting me some clothes and he gave me some booties to wear. I left them in the bathroom and uh..." She couldn't quit stammering, feeling very imbecilic. Taking a deep breath, she gathered strength to bring up the subject they both had on their minds. "Before Matt gets back...about last night."

"Forget it."

Forget it? She couldn't forget it. She didn't even plan to forget it. As stupid as she felt about kissing him, it wasn't something easily forgotten. "I just feel I owe you an apology is all."

"No need."

Her eyes darted up to meet his. She wondered if their kiss had meant as much to him as it had to her. She was torn between hoping it had and wishing a hole would open up and swallow her.

His broad mischievous smile broke the spell. "It sure beat the heck out of smoking."

That answered her question. It obviously did *not* mean the same thing to him. "Well, at least it wasn't a total waste of your time then," she shot back, a hint of sarcasm in her voice.

"Not at all." His teasing fed her annoyance. "I've spent a lot worse evenings."

His laughing eyes gave him away and even though she knew he was joking, she still felt a little miffed at how easily he could dismiss the whole thing. "Name one," she retorted snidely. "I'll bet you'd be hard pressed to think of one. You probably can't wait to buy a pack of cigs just in case it should ever happen again."

He laughed at her and she knew she was acting childish, but *dumb* had been her middle name since she met Patrick Mayhew.

"Speaking of cigarettes...I still have a bone to pick with my son." He came to a full stand. "Matt!" His voice was very deep and authoritative.

Matt entered the room and, seeing the stern look on his father's face, turned sharply around. "Uh, I think I forgot something in my room."

"No you don't, young man. You come back here."

Matt turned slowly, glancing toward Janet for protection.

Her aggravation with Pat made her brave. She pulled Matt into her arms, squared her shoulders haughtily and glared at the tall man towering over them. "You lay one hand on this boy and you'll have both of us to whip. After all, he's just a child."

Pat's mouth dropped open in disbelief for a second before he broke into laughter. The sight of two tiny people huddled together was ridiculously funny. "You're right. He IS just a child, but he has quite a lot of trouble remembering that."

Matt held his hand to the side of his mouth and whispered to Janet. "What did I do?"

She put two fingers to her lips and made a puffing motion. "Couldn't find his cigarettes."

The boy wilted. "Oh, that."

"Did you..."

The boy nodded yes.

"Good for you," she whispered, looking even more defiant at Pat.

"If you two don't take the cake! I could whip you both at the same time with one hand tied behind me, but it wouldn't be worth the hassle. I'm tired, I'm grimy, I need a shave and I'm starved to death...and that's just for starters," he said, walking past them, mumbling, "and I desperately need to use the bathroom."

"Wait!" Janet held her hand up. He stopped and turned to her. "Could I get in there first? My...I mean, I rinsed out a few things and they're hanging on the shower rod."

Pat slapped his thighs. "Sure, why not. Nothing else has gone my way since I met you. Why should I think I could use my own bathroom?"

Janet took the jeans and shirt out of Matt's hands and scurried into the bathroom, making record time at dressing, brushing her teeth and combing her hair. She pulled on the furry house shoes, grabbed her things off the rod and padded back to the main room. She laid her things across the back of a chair so she could use both hands to tug and stretch the T-shirt Matt had given her to wear. One amusing thought quickly crossed her mind. *Fate* had missed by about one size in the shirt category but, she shrugged, maybe no one will look past the faded picture of a rock star on the front.

"It's all yours," she said brightly to the tall irritated man pacing back and forth.

He tossed her a quick assessment of her attire. "It's about time." She heard him spout, "Women!" as he closed the bathroom door.

Matt came out of his room, having dressed in jeans and a sweatshirt. "What a grouch!"

"Some people just don't like their routines upset," she called out loud enough for Pat to hear. "It's a sign of old age," she added, grinning impishly at Matt.

Just before they reached the kitchen to start breakfast, they heard loud and clear, "You're both asking for it!"

CHAPTER NINE

 Ɓy the time Pat finished in the bathroom, breakfast was ready and Janet and Matt were setting it on the table. The smell of food made him forget he was irritated with them and was all smiles as he sat down at the table.

"Smells great." He reached across the table and took their hands. "Janet, I'm sure you would like to say Grace."

Clearing her throat, she began, "Dear God. Thank you for the food on this table."

Matt's eyes darted upward to hers and she gave him a conspiratorial wink.

"Now dig in and eat all you're able."

Matt snickered and Janet covered her mouth with her free hand to keep her own giggles back.

Pat refused to let go of their hands and squeezed them tighter. "You know, I could snap your fingers like twigs if I wanted to. You and Matt have spent entirely too much time with each other."

"Don't be mad, Dad. That's what friends do," he explained using the same words Janet had used the night before. "They tease each other."

"Who said we were friends. Right now you're both a pain in the neck."

Janet pulled her hand from his and smiled sweetly at

him. "The pain in your neck will feel a lot better after you fill your belly."

Pat looked at first one then the other and then to the food before him. "Hmmm, break fingers or eat."

Matt pulled his hand free and forked a couple slices of French toast. "I say eat."

They all did just that, and if Janet did say so herself, she had done an outstanding job making breakfast. The bacon was nice and crisp and the toast was a beautiful golden brown beneath the melting butter and homemade syrup.

"Boy, I wouldn't mind having Janet fix this *every* morning for us, would you Dad?" Matt's eyes cast a fleeting glance toward his father before focusing back on his food. He made a big deal out of smacking his lips, then turned to Janet. "You ever think about getting married?"

Pat's fork stopped in mid-air. He glared at his son, then to Janet. "You don't have the corner on persistence."

She gave Pat an indulgent smile and put another bite of toast in her mouth.

"Well," Matt continued, "she isn't getting any younger. I just thought..."

Janet sputtered and nearly strangled on her food.

"Sure, look at the pitiful old maid now," Pat said dryly, "choking on solid food. Probably needs her false teeth relined." He slowly and methodically laid his fork down and wiped his mouth with his napkin, all the while staring a hole through his son. "I am only going to repeat this one more time." His voice held a no-nonsense tone. "Knock-it-off."

*****

Breakfast was finished with a minimum of conversation. However, when Pat wasn't looking, Janet gave Matt a reassuring smile, letting him know nothing he said had upset her in the least. Pat's grim expression let her know Matt had probably embarrassed as well as exasperated him with his constant matchmaking and she sympathized with him. But at the same time she adored Matt and found his little games extremely amusing.

"Dad, I promised Janet you'd take her over to Vernon's to see the horses."

Janet came to an abrupt halt as she carried dirty dishes to the kitchen, this being the first time she had heard of such a plan. She turned her head and stared openly at Matt, wondering who in the heck Vernon was and, at the same time, amazed at how an eleven-year-old boy could relentlessly carry on with his determined plan to *snare* a woman for his dad. This was a bit too far, even for Janet's taste. She opened her mouth to say something, but Matt interrupted.

"You remember my telling you about Doyne's dad, Vernon?"

His big round eyes looking at her so pitifully caused Janet to quickly relent. Not wanting to get the boy into any more trouble than he was with his dad, she mentally crossed her fingers for the lie that was about to come out of her mouth.

"Of course...Vernon...the one with the horses."

"That's right." Matt breathed a sigh of relief. "There's just one hitch. I promised Roger and Josh I'd help put that motor together on the model plane they're building, so I guess you'll just have to drop me off at Roger's on your way to Vernon's. You might as well plan on staying a long, long time because we'll probably be working that silly old motor—"

"Cut the crapola, Matt," Pat warned. Janet's face flushed, realizing Pat had seen through Matt's scheme from the beginning. His eyes dropped to meet her embarrassed ones. "As for you, young lady...I don't need you encouraging him."

"I didn't mean...I'm sorry."

He waved his hands in the air, dismissing her explanation. "I'm going to get some wood in." He grabbed a jacket off the coat rack.

Just before he walked out the door, he turned to her, his features not as grim as his tone of voice had been. There was even an apologetic gleam in his eyes. "Breakfast *was* delicious, Janet. Thanks."

She stood motionless for a long time after he left. Just a simple *thanks* but the look on his face and the soft tone of his voice brought back the memory of last night when he held her so gently and spoke in the same soft tones. She felt the familiar glow slowly creep over her body. It felt wonderful...maddening, but wonderful.

"I think we're making some headway with him." Matt's voice brought her out of her stupor.

"Headway!? He's about to kill us both. Matt, you've got to quit this. You can't continue trying to play matchmaker for your father."

"But you're perfect for us."

"But I'm not. And besides, don't you think your father and I have some say about it?"

"Don't you like Dad?" Before she could answer, he rushed on. "He really IS a good guy, Janet. Really he is."

"I know, Matt. I *do* like him." She wanted to add, really, *really* like him, blushing at her foolish thought.

"Then what's the problem? Why can't you..."

"You've got to understand," she cut in, "my life is in St. Louis. I will be leaving soon to go back to that life...back to your Grandpa." Her voice trailed off sadly, reminding her she needed to make her phone call. "But even if that weren't a fact, *you* can't pick out someone for your father. That decision has to be up to him."

The boy looked dejected, dropping his head. Janet pulled him to her and gave him a hug. "It's too bad your father feels like he does about your Grandpa, but he does and we can't change it, nor can I change my feelings. So you see, I would be the last person on earth your dad would ever consider."

"Does that mean *you* would consider him?"

She let her breath out hastily. "You haven't listened to a single word of my sterling advice." She laughed. "No, that's not what I meant...well, yes, to be honest—" She stopped. The boy was even smarter than she gave him credit for. Of course, she would *consider* Pat. She'd be lying to herself if she didn't admit he certainly sparked a romantic feeling in her, but there were just too many obstacles to overcome, not to mention about a million ifs. IF she would give up her life in St. Louis and be content to be a *cowboy's woman.* IF she could forsake her strong ties to Christopher...what was she even thinking about? Patrick Mayhew had given her no reason to believe he cared anymore about her than someone sent here by his father to upset his life. She didn't know if she had fully convinced him that she could be trusted. That was the biggest IF of all. IF he could ever trust her...then maybe...no, it was all too far-fetched.

As if reading her mind, Matt said, "IF he weren't so stubborn." He raised his head, his huge brown eyes looking at her hopefully.

She draped her arms over his shoulders and smiled at him. "I'll be honest with you, Matt. I've taken a very strong liking to you and I sense the feeling is mutual, but sad as it may be, we have to face reality. If it weren't for a freak accident of nature, I would have never met you."

"Fate."

"Accident," she insisted. "After I go back to St. Louis, I'm going to have to forget you exist. It breaks my heart to say this, Matt, but we can't even be friends. I promised your father I would abide by his wishes. Now, you're going to have to help me keep that promise." Her voice became thick as the reality of the situation penetrated. She pulled him back to her, hugging him affectionately as her words faltered. "I desperately need your help, Matt. Don't make it any harder." She held him for a silent moment longer, then gave him a shove back. "Now, no more matchmaking. Okay?"

He looked at her with big brown eyes, his expression never giving a hint of an answer to her question. "You want me to help with the dishes?"

"You're impossible. No, you make the beds and clean the bathroom. I'll clean the kitchen and living room. That's the least I can do for making your dad sleep on the couch. When we finish, I'll have your dad take me to the motel. I need to make some phone calls." She glanced at the clock. "As a matter of fact, I'd better call the airport and cancel my reservation for this morning."

"Sure," Matt offered brightly, "make your calls from here. You don't need to go to a motel. Stay here." His eyes widened. "It would save Dad a trip to pick you up for the dance tonight."

"Matt, I'm not going. Your father hasn't even asked." She stopped. "You're doing it again, aren't you?" The boy grinned. "I am going to change into my suit and go to the motel as soon as I tidy up this place. Do I make myself clear?"

Matt didn't say a word as he walked up the stairs to the loft to make the bed, but she could tell his mind was reeling trying to think of something to make her stay.

*****

SOUTHERN CALIFORNIA

"Wake up, Ruby."

"Hmmmm? What time is it?"

"What difference does it make? You've slept most of the morning."

"Then what day is it?"

"Oh, for crying out loud. Get your sorry self off that couch and get cleaned up. Me and my hacker friend I met in the pen finally pinpointed that Mayhew guy in Montana."

"Your hacker friend?"

"Yeah, we kept in touch. He owed me a couple favors."

Ruby sat up, stretched and smiled. "That's why I picked you to help me with getting the money. I knew you knew more about computers than anyone. Of course, if you get caught again hacking—"

"Shut up and go take a shower."

Max called to her through the bathroom door. "We got a flight to catch in a few hours so pack some things...not too much. I don't have the money to waste on extra luggage at the airport."

"Where'd you get enough money for airline tickets?"

"I'm not too proud of it, but I went to the ATM while you were snoring away and wiped out Mama's savings and most of her checking. Soon as we get the Mayhew money, I'll pay her back."

Ruby laughed. "Of course you will. Wouldn't want *Mama* to think badly of her little boy."

"I swear, Ruby, you say one more thing about my Mother and I'll—"

Ruby opened the door with a bang. "You'll what!? If it wasn't for me, you wouldn't even be *getting* any money."

"Calm down. We need to keep our wits about us." He eyed her up and down. "Change your clothes. I'll take you out to get something to eat on the way to the airport and we can discuss our plans."

She stripped down to her underwear in front of him then sashayed into the bedroom while running her hands down her body from her breasts to her hips. "If you *ever* want any of this again, you'd better watch your tongue with me. There are other fish in the sea, you know."

He mumbled to himself, "If I didn't need the money so bad, I'd—"

"Are you talking to me?"

"No! Just thinking out loud about our trip. Hurry up."

"I'm hurrying! I'm thinking about the trip, too." She came out of the bedroom wearing a skirt much too tight and a red satin blouse.

"Couldn't you have worn something a little more conservative?"

"Tell me fashion guru, how are we going to get a gun through security?"

"I've got that covered. My friend who owes me favors will have a gun waiting for us in the motel I've booked in that town near where that Mayhew kid lives. By the way, we are now Wilbur and Madge Brown. Here's your new driver's license."

She looked at her picture on the card. "How'd you do this?"

"I spent time in prison for this sort of thing. It didn't wipe out my memory on how to do it."

"Can your hot-shot friend score us some blow or maybe meth? And where's those feel-good pills you stole from me?"

"I flushed them down the toilet. They didn't look like Oxy to me."

"You flushed them!?"

"Quit whining. We have to be clean and sober to pull this off. After we get the money, you can snort it all up your nose or shoot up your veins and get as high as you want."

"Yeah, all that money. I can do anything I want." She swayed and closed her eyes as in a dream. "I can't wait to get my hands on that snot of a kid."

"You promised. No one is going to get hurt."

Her eyes snapped open. "Blah, blah, blah. Let's go.

I'm hungry."

CHAPTER TEN

MONTANA

"Look who I found outside," Pat announced as he came back into the room with a load of wood with a young blond-haired boy trailing behind him with kindling in his arms.

"Josh!" Matt ran to take some of the firewood. "Where's your Dad?"

"He's coming. He's gathering up the airplane stuff. We thought we'd work on it over here. Some of Doyne's lady friends are giving her a baby shower and Dad said we needed to get out of the way."

Josh glanced toward Janet who was drying her hands on a dish towel. Matt walked to stand beside her. "This is Dad's friend, Janet. Janet, this is my best friend I told you about."

"Nice to meet you, Josh. Yes, Matt has told me a lot about you."

Josh looked her up and down and then turned to Matt. "She looks more like one of *your* play dates."

Pat placed the wood on the hearth and laughed so loudly, Janet wanted to crown him with one of the logs.

"Maybe it's *not* nice to meet you," she told Josh.

"Friends tease each other," Matt reminded her.

"I know." She chuckled. "I've gotten this *are you a grown woman* quite often while I've been here." She wrinkled her nose at Pat.

Pat finally stopped laughing at her and said, "I don't want to seem totally inhospitable, considering you *did* make a fabulous breakfast and I see you've tidied up the place."

"I made the beds," Matt chimed in.

"Getting him to do that is a miracle in itself. Anyway, before I was so rudely interrupted, maybe you *would* like to see some of our country. I really do need to go over to Vernon's to see about the horses. That is if you even like horses."

"Of course, she likes horses," Matt volunteered. "Who doesn't like horses?"

"What about your friends, Josh and Roger?"

"They're going to be working on the airplane. I'm of no help to them with that. So, you up to seeing the horses?"

She held her breath and stood perfectly still for a moment. The fact was, the closest she had ever been to a real live horse was the pony she rode in a park one time as a child. Of course, she saw the Budweiser Clydesdales in a parade once. "I've always been fascinated by horses," she blurted out, surprised at her own words. Did *fascinated* mean the same as scared? She WAS excited that Patrick was inviting her to share a part of his world. Should she? Did she even WANT to get more involved? A little voice nudged her mind. *Of course you do, stupid!*

"I'm just sorry I won't be able to ride," she stated as calmly as she could, showing bravery above and beyond what she felt. "Matt was good enough to loan me these jeans, but my shoes leave a lot to be desired for horseback riding." She laughed again. This time a slight nervousness appeared. "It's either high heels or these sheepskin booties."

Pat eyed her skeptically, a grin spreading across his mouth. "I don't think you need to worry. We won't be riding in this weather, but we will need to do something about shodding you properly. Vernon might need help with feeding or something."

Shodding me? How romantic. He thinks I'm one of the horses.

She heard a loud thud at the front door. "I think someone is trying to kick down your door."

Pat hurried to open it and Roger stepped in with his arms full of boxes and sacks full of their supplies. "Hope you don't mind us using your house for this."

"Not at all," Pat said, taking some of the things out of his arms. "Roger, this is Janet. I've told you why she's here."

"Yeah, Doyne said you got weathered in. Sorry about that."

Janet smiled. "Can't be helped. It's been okay. Matt and I have had a good time."

As Roger, Josh and Matt spread out their things on the table, Janet excused herself and went into the kitchen to finish her chores.

Pat followed. "You've done enough. Leave the rest. I'll take care of it."

She watched his amused grin turn seductive as his eyes surveyed the curves under the tight jeans and T-shirt. His lips parted as if he were about to say something else, but didn't. She was standing close enough to be able to see the tip of his tongue sliding along the edge of his teeth, and a slight quiver scampered down her spine as a waft of fresh-smelling aftershave embraced her nostrils.

Her eyes dropped to the open V of his western shirt and dwelled on the curly wisps of reddish hair that peeked back at her. She was thankful the others were behind her in the other room. It made it a little easier to control the foolish urge she felt creeping up on her. She wanted to touch those manly wisps of hair with her lips. She wanted to kiss the coarse edge next to the hollow of his neck, feel the virile brush against her mouth, then work her way up to feel his lips on hers and taste the tip of his tongue.

A knot rose in her throat and she swallowed hard. She was so lost in her thoughts, she hadn't noticed him staring openly at her admiring the view. Explosive currents surged through her as she ached to touch him, to have him touch her. She knew she shouldn't...even worse, she knew she couldn't. It was like looking at a mouth-watering treat through a plate glass window. Look all you want, but don't touch. This is crazy! Her heart was hammering against her chest, drowning out all other sounds in the other room.

Pat's gaze settled on her heaving chest, reminding her that the T-shirt was too tight. She unconsciously pulled down on it to stretch out the material, but all it did was give him a better view of her well-rounded breasts cushioned snugly against the faded picture. Realizing what she had done, she let go of the shirt immediately.

His thoughts were running all over the place. She pleased him. Pleased him too much. Even though his fingers ached to touch her face, her lips, he knew not to. He was fighting the longing he felt for her...longing mixed with the familiar anger he felt every time it dawned on him that she belonged to another world. A world he hated. A world that could destroy his present life as it had destroyed his past life. *Why? Why had she come into his life?* Even more puzzling to him, why did he have these feelings for her?

She was totally entranced by his nearness and was barely aware he was calling out to Matt. His eyes never left hers, nor hers his. It would have taken a blowtorch to separate them.

"Matt, go find those snowmobile boots you outgrew." His voice trailed to a whisper as his gaze penetrated hers deeper. As if coming out of a dream, he jerked his head to see around her. "Bring several pairs of thick socks to wear in them. They'll be too big," he ended in a normal, sensible tone of voice.

Now she knew how the heroine of a romance novel felt. Her pulse quickened, her knees turned to jelly and her heart beat so rapidly it nearly choked her.

"Pat...I...uh..." She stopped and breathed deep. "I can't talk when I'm nervous."

"Do I make you nervous?"

"Yes." Her eyes dropped to examine her fingernails.

"Why?" His voice was quiet as he reached out and tilted her face up with one finger.

Her eyes lifted to reveal no protest as his thumb traveled the outline of her lips as she spoke. "Because I think I'm beginning to like you...too much."

He chuckled, dropping his hand from her face and rubbing the back of his neck. "Crazy, isn't it? This whole thing is just plain crazy."

"It's not that I didn't like you before. It's that now I...oh, I'm not making any sense."

"Yes you are, little one. I was determined I *wouldn't* like you. That nothing you could do would MAKE me like you...but—"

"But?"

"You know nothing could become of this."

"I know."

He stepped closer, his voice thickly passionate. "Now that we have that settled, kiss me."

"I thought you'd never ask."

He lifted her to him at the same time her hands smoothed upward over his chest and locked together behind his neck. "We'd better make this quick before Matt gets in here."

She smiled against his lips. "That's all we need is for him to see us kissing. He'd *never* give up on that *woman's touch* thing he thinks you need so badly."

His strong tendons flexed as his mouth captured hers in a sweet, mind-shattering kiss. The pressure of his lips increased heatedly as he pressed her against his length. His kiss was forceful, yet exhibited a sweet tenderness that made her quiver.

As quickly as it started, it ended. "I think I hear Matt close by." He gave her quick kisses at each corner of her mouth and eyelids and then let her slide back down so her feet were touching the floor.

"Funny," she whispered, catching her breath, "that didn't exactly feel like *nothing could come of this*."

"Kissing elves can be habit forming."

"Ooooo, a fate worse than death."

He grinned, but there was a sad seriousness in his eyes. "It could be. It could very well be."

"Here're the boots," Matt announced, plopping them down on the floor and running back to the other room.

"Thanks, punkin," Janet called out, then turning to Pat. "He hates to be called punkin. But that's what friends do. They tease each other."

Pat just shook his head. "You two. Just no explaining it."

She sat down in a chair and began putting on the boots.

"Here, let me help you." Pat knelt on one knee and pulled off one bootie.

"I...I shouldn't have told you how I feel.' She kicked the other bootie off. "For some reason I don't feel like we're strangers, even though we are. I've heard about you through the years at Mayhew's. I've heard Cal speak of you often and a few times from Christopher, but still I never thought in a million years that I'd...never mind. It puts you in an awkward position. You probably feel obligated to say something like...I like you, too...or I hate your guts...or something."

His expression didn't change. The same seriousness

bathed his face. "It's not exactly one-sided...whatever it is between us. You surely know what you do to me. You're not that naïve, are you?"

She flushed. "Would you rather just take me to a motel?"

He laughed. "Lady, you say the darnedest things at the darnedest times!"

"You know what I mean."

"Is that what you want?"

She was silent for a moment. Her sensible side was screaming yes, but her heart won. "No, I'd like to spend the day with you...feeding horses or whatever."

If he had less control of himself, she would have been able to see the delight her answer brought him, but he remained quiet and unemotional. He knew what a disaster any kind of romantic involvement with her could be, but he was also sure he could control the situation. He was sensible enough to know there could never be anything long-term between them. Just a few casual kisses and that was all. He learned the hard way that he could never *share* another woman with his father. Even if Janet's relationship with his father was in no way like Sylvia's, there was still that same strong bond between them. Just not a bond of money this time, but something much more dangerous...loyalty, moral obligation, genuine love and respect. The mere thought of her devotion to Christopher Mayhew brought hot bile to his throat. He rose abruptly and turned.

Janet was puzzled by his sudden behavior. Would he rather take her to a motel and out of his life?

"Pat, if you'd just as soon I go—"

"No," he answered, his voice controlled, "there's no point in your spending your time here locked in a motel room. We're both adults. I think we can surely spend a couple of days together without letting things get out of hand."

"Oh, I agree completely." She *did* agree. Why then did she still have this undying urge to kiss him again?

"I know you want to make your calls, so go ahead. I'll get you a coat to wear. We'll leave as soon as you are finished. The kids can work on the motor with Roger in peace." He glanced at her, smiling broadly. "I don't mean to brag...well, maybe I do mean to...but my kid's an electronic genius. If it's wired, he can take it apart and put it back together."

Janet raised an eyebrow. "Electronics?"

"Yeah, why?"

"Just odd." Her brow knitted. Maybe fate *was* knocking...nah!

"No, why would you be interested in Matt's electronic ability?"

"I'm not...it's just that...well, you remember my telling you that Mayhew Enterprises was in the middle of some negotiations when your father had his attack. Things that had to be settled right away?"

"Yeah, that's why you're here."

"Yes, well, we're negotiating for a chain of manufacturing companies whose main product is..."

"Let me guess. Electric motors."

"Right."

"For Heaven's sake, don't tell Matt. He'll think it's fate for sure. He'll think he's destined to take over the company...when he's twenty-one."

"Are you so sure it isn't fate?"

"Don't you start."

Matt came bounding into the room. "Did the boots fit okay? I wondered about the one where a mouse chewed up the inside."

"A mouse!" Janet stomped up and down. "It's still not in here is it?"

Matt pulled a ball of gray fuzz from his pocket and tossed it to her, yelling, "There it is!"

She screamed bloody murder and leaped into Pat's arms.

Matt went into hysterics as Pat gave him a scornful look, at the same time giving his son a mental thanks for causing her to flee to his embrace. He put her down and joined in the teasing.

"Ooooo, don't want to take the chance of fuzz bite. Very dangerous."

"Okay, okay, you two. How can you possibly laugh at a woman who is on the brink of having a heart attack?"

Matt gave her a hug. "That's what friends do—"

"I know, I know," Janet cut in, "they tease each other. I'm regretting I ever told you that." She hugged him back. "Now go back with your friends and pester them."

She followed him into the other room. "Roger, you have a sweet wife."

"I think so. She said almost the same about you."

"When is the baby due?"

"Actually, when WAS the baby due? Last week."

"Wow. Do you know what it is? A boy or girl?"

"Girl. We're excited."

"Poor girl." Pat chuckled. "As soon as she gets old enough to print her name, Roger will have her sign an affidavit that she won't date until she's thirty."

"That's right," Roger stated emphatically. "Especially if there are guys like you still around."

She saw the proud look on Roger's face. "I think I can understand your concern." She then turned to the boys. "I would love to be here when she puts the two of you in your place when you start teasing her."

Josh put down his piece of the wing he was painting. "Janet, Matt sent me an e-mail yesterday saying that you were cool and a lot of fun. He said friends tease each other..."

"Seems I've heard that quite a lot lately." She gave Josh a friendly punch in the shoulder. "I don't get mad...but

I *do* get even." She smiled at both boys. "I hope I get a chance to challenge you guys to a game of Texas Hold'em."

"Righteous!" They both yelled together.

"My rules this time."

The boys looked at each other and rolled their eyes.

*****

Janet made all the calls she needed to do, cancelling her reservations with the airline, calling Cal who wasn't in so she left the message that she was being detained due to weather and could be reached in an emergency at Patrick's number. She then made the most important call to the hospital. Christopher was still in Intensive Care on a respirator. He was stable, but had not improved as much as the doctors had hoped.

She could not conceal the worried look on her face even though she turned her back on everyone.

Pat walked to her and turned her to him. "What is it? My father?"

She glanced at Matt who was watching and listening. Not wanting to cause anymore worry than necessary, she stated as calmly as she could. "He is still in ICU," adding quickly, "but stable."

"Dad?" Matt's voice was a little shaky. "Is Grandpa going to die?"

Janet held her arms out to him and he came to her. As she cradled his head to her, her eyes linked with Pat's. "I'm sure he is not dying, Matt. He's in God's healing hands. But he's really sick and we need to pray for him. He would love knowing we are praying for his recovery."

The muscle flexed nervously in Pat's jaw as he jammed his hands into his jeans' pockets. "As big as St. Louis is, you'd think they'd have a *damn* doctor who could do something!"

"Dad! Watch your language. There's a lady in the house."

Tears sprang uncontrollably to Janet's eyes. Patrick cares. He cares a lot.

She held her arm out to him and he wrapped his around her and Matt, the three sharing one special moment together in mutual concern.

CHAPTER ELEVEN

"Your father. He has not improved as much as the doctors had hoped. They're worried, which makes me worried."

As she and Pat walked down the hill to the Jeep, she conveyed the details about his father's diagnosis to him. It saddened her even more when she saw the grave expression on his face.

"Your world would end if you lost him, wouldn't it?" he finally asked.

"We would *all* lose a lot." She tried to keep her emotions in check. "Yes, he means the world to me. I lost my own parents in a house fire when I was very young. I was shifted around to a lot of foster homes...some good, some not so good, until I graduated from high school. I went to work as an intern at Mayhew Enterprises and Christopher took me under his wing. I never had anyone care as much about my well-being as he did. He agreed to let me work all the hours I needed to around my college schedule. That was very helpful."

"I'm sorry about your parents. I didn't know." His voice was soft and caring. "Didn't you have any other family to take care of you?"

"My little sister was all I had. We were separated and I never saw her again until...you don't want to hear all this."

"Of course, I do."

"Well, let's get in the Jeep first. My teeth are chattering."

After several moments driving down the bumpy road, Pat turned to her. "Your sister. You were about to tell me about your sister."

"Jeanie. She was only five. Like I said we were put into different homes and I never saw her again until I graduated from college." She pulled a tissue out of her pocket and blew her nose. "Are you sure you want to hear everything."

"Why not?"

"You never seem to want to hear nice things about your father and frankly that's all I have is nice things to say about him."

"Go ahead. I'm a big boy now. I think I can take it."

"Well, as I've told you I came to work for Mayhew Enterprises to make some extra money for college. There are many reasons I'll be forever grateful to your father but the main one was Jeanie. When he discovered I had a sister I had not seen since the death of our parents, he left no stone unturned until she was located." Tears stung her eyes every time she recalled their reunion. "Your father hosted a graduation party for me and my gift was Jeanie."

Patrick's eyes softened. "Somehow I just can't picture him..."

"It took him a long time to find her. She had been adopted, her name changed and by the time he located her, she was married and living in New Jersey with her husband, Rob. They have two children, Danny who is five and Stacey three." She smiled thinking about them. "Without your father's efforts finding Jeanie, I would never have had the opportunity to be a proud Aunt."

"From the way you interact with Matt, I'll bet you're a super Aunt."

"I love children." Her gaze traveled back to Patrick

who still looked a little disbelieving. "Christopher has been the best father a girl could have, and I love him dearly."

Pat shifted nervously and raked his fingers through his hair...something she noted he did when he was deep in thought.

"I'm not through. A few years ago I had a disastrous affair with a man and had sunk to the pits of hell. Your father was so understanding and patient, giving me a shoulder to cry on. We read the bible together and he pointed out passages that made me feel better about myself...regain my self-respect. I don't know what I would have become."

He stared at her for a long time. For one thing, he couldn't imagine anyone having a *disastrous* affair with her. An affair with her could only be beautiful in his estimation. Secondly, it was hard to imagine his father being *understanding and patient* without an ulterior motive.

"I don't even presume to know the hurt you feel at the hands of your father, but that man is not the man I know today." She sat silent for a long moment. "This is totally none of my business to say what I'm about to say and you may want to throw me out of this Jeep, but—"

"I hate *buts.*"

"Just listen with an open mind and then I'll never mention the subject again." Clearing her throat, she went on. "You're hurt and you want to lash out at your father and hurt him too. Well, you've succeeded. He lives in a world of remorse and would never ask your forgiveness because he doesn't feel he deserves it. He can't even forgive himself, but if you could only see him as he is today and open your heart and let forgiveness in, I think you'd learn to love again. You're not only hurting your father, you're hurting your son."

"I love Matt more than life. I want the best for him."

"I know you do. I've grown very fond of him myself, but he's so curious about his Grandpa. He begged me to tell him everything I knew about your father but I held fast and told him I would abide by your wishes. That didn't stop him. He asked question after question until I finally put a stop to it."

"You're right. It's none of your business how I raise my son."

"What happened to listening with an open mind?"

"Do you ever let up?"

"No."

"I didn't think so. Go on. I presume there's more."

"It saddens me to think about Christopher lying in the hospital near death. If only you could find it in your heart to at least let him know you're praying for him." She shook her head. "I know you won't do it, but if he knew there was even a chance of seeing you again and knowing he had a grandson, he'd have a reason to fight for his life."

They drove for what seemed like silent hours but in reality it was only a few minutes.

"Are you through?"

She wiped tears from her eyes. "Yes."

"Blow your nose. We're almost there."

After wiping her nose she looked at him. "Did you even hear a word I said?"

"How could I not? You're not more than a foot from me."

"Just one more thing."

"I was afraid of that."

"No, it's not what you think. I want you to know that I think you are a wonderful father and I've seen the softer side of you so I know you are a superb human being. I know you care about your father's well-being. I saw the look on your face after I made the call to the hospital. So did Matt. You can't make me think otherwise." She blew her nose again. "Pat, I care, Matt cares, you care. Now please let your father know you care. I'm not suggesting Sunday dinners and family vacations, just a word from you that you're praying for him...something!"

He pulled the Jeep into Vernon's lane, stopped and turned to her. "Who are you really? A female Dr. Phil?"

"Just a concerned citizen."

He took his hat off and raked his fingers through his hair and around the back of his neck.

That deep in thought gesture he always does. He's thinking. That's a good start.

Not a word was spoken for a long time. Finally, Janet reached across and laid her hand on his. "What are we waiting for?"

"You. You're *one more thing* seems to go on and on. Are you through reading me my rights, counselor?"

She patted his hand. "Yes."

He turned his face straight ahead to avoid looking at her any longer. Her pixie face glowed with the chilly bite of the day giving her an even fresher allure. Her dark hair was bunched up around her face as she snuggled her head deeper into the parka. He could close his eyes but he still couldn't erase the picture of her big round eyes pleading with him to contact his father.

"You remind me of Matt. Relentless."

She smiled. "I'll take that as a big compliment. I adore Matt."

A wide grin spread across his face. "I get the impression, if I wanted to spank Matt, I'd have to spank you first to get to him."

"I just stand up for what I feel is right." She gave him a very pointed look. "And I never give up."

"You're a little spitfire."

"When I need to be...but I have my softer moments." She gave him a flirty wink.

He leaned back in his seat and let his breath out slowly. "I know. I remember a couple of those moments." And what *moments* they were! He could have taken advantage of her last night but it was hard to shake the compulsion to keep her safe from all danger, to fend off dragons, to shield her from all harm. He almost laughed out loud at himself. What a stupid thought. Who needed protecting from whom? Who was going to protect HIM from HER? Finally snapping out of his stupor, he opened his door and came around to help her out of the Jeep.

"Come on. Let's get Vernon. The horses need tending to."

As they walked toward Vernon's house, Pat took her hand to help over the rough path. Her eyes were big as saucers as she took in the huge white house that reminded her of an elegant old hotel. While admiring the view, Pat's voice broke the silence.

"You...you want to go to that dance tonight?" Before she could answer, he rushed on. "Might as well. There's either that or play cards with Matt."

She couldn't control a grin that spread across her face. "My, my, you really know how to sweep a girl off her feet. How could I refuse such a gracious invitation?" She thought a moment. "Will my suit I wore here be okay for the dance?"

"No, but we'll take care of that on the way back to my place."

"What do you mean?"

"Western wear. You need *cowgirl* clothes. My treat for causing you to get stuck here for an extra day."

"An extra day? I thought I was staying two extra days...until Monday."

"I know you're anxious to get back. You're consumed with worry over my dad." He raked his fingers through his hair. "I'll sign the papers. You can leave in the morning if you want to."

She stood staring at him, her mouth dropping open. It WAS what she wanted. Why then did she feel a stab of sadness? Maybe HE wanted her to leave. "Perhaps I could leave today." She tried to sound indifferent. The blood began to pound in her temples. Why did the thought of leaving feel like the end of the world?

"And perhaps you couldn't." His tone had an air of authority demanding obedience.

Her eyes darted up to meet his. The set of his chin showed his stubborn streak which triggered her own defiance. "And just why not?"

He cupped her chin with one strong finger. It was only when she saw a lazy smile start to form on his lips was she able to relax.

"Because you promised to go to the dance with me."

They exchanged a subtle look of pleasant combat and her heart felt relief. He obviously wasn't all that anxious to get her out of town.

She raised her head to look him in the eye. "That, and the fact that you're so darn stubborn. You could have signed those papers yesterday—"

His laugh cut her off. "I like to think of myself as cautious, not stubborn."

She took hold of his wrist, pulling his hand from her face and studied him with mock intent. "Mmmmm, no, I've seen cautious and I've seen stubborn. You're definitely stubborn."

"Why you..." He grabbed for her but she scrambled out of his reach with lightning speed through a round of giggles.

They were still laughing when a spry elderly man greeted them at his opened front door. "I thought I heard some racket out here." He looked Janet up and down then turned to Pat. "Who you got there, Buck? I thought for a minute it was Matt, but see now it's not. You picking on this little girl."

"Hardly. She's picking on me."

Vernon cackled. "And you look like you hate every minute of it."

Pat shook the man's hand. "Vernon, I'd like you to

meet Janet Raye. She works for my father in St. Louis. She's here on business and I'm showing her a few aspects of our life in Montana."

"Nice to meet you, Janet. Come in. I've got a pot of coffee just waiting to warm you up."

"We'll take you up on that." Pat put his hand on Janet's back and ushered her into the inviting interior of Vernon's house.

"What a lovely home you have, Vernon. So comfortable."

"I owe that to my sweet Myrtle May. She was the best wife a man could have. She passed on to heaven several years ago and I haven't changed a thing in this house. She wouldn't have wanted me to."

She saw Vernon's eyes begin to mist. "I'm so sorry. You must have had a wonderful life with her."

The old man smiled and glanced around the room. "I still do. She'll always be with me."

Janet envied love like that. She prayed some day she would find her soul mate she could love until the day she died and, if Vernon was right, even in the hereafter.

"I met your daughter. I'll bet you're anxious for your granddaughter to get here."

"Oh, you know my Doyne? She's a sweetheart. Just like her Mom."

Vernon poured them each a cup of coffee and offered the cream and sugar which they both declined. "You staying long, Janet?"

"Not long enough, I'm afraid." She made a sweeping gesture over the vast land she saw out the window. "Your *ranch* as Pat referred to looks almost as big as St. Louis. It would take me days to see it all."

"That's true." The old man laughed.

Janet noticed he had the same delightful accent as Doyne. She couldn't put her finger on it. It was almost like Swedish. Whatever it was, she loved hearing it.

"Well, what I see is breathtaking."

"Why do you think Montana is nicknamed the *Treasure State*?" Pat said softly coming up beside her and putting his arm around her waist. "You want to go with me to check on the horses now?"

"What's your hurry? Finish your coffee. You want something to eat?"

"Oh, no," Janet replied quickly. "I don't want to intrude."

"What you mean intrude? Since when's a friend of Buck's been an intrusion?"

"Thanks anyway," Pat interjected, "we can't stay that long. Matt, Josh and Roger are at my house putting together an airplane and motor and I'm sure Roger doesn't want to stay too long. Not with Doyne this close to delivery."

"How many grandchildren does this make you?" Janet inquired pleasantly.

"Well, actually only two. Josh and the new one, but Matt makes three."

"Matt?" She looked up into Pat's face. "Our Matt?" *Our* Matt! It was out of her mouth before she thought.

"Sure." Vernon started speaking before Pat could say anything. "When Buck came to us back in...how long's it been, Buck? Over ten years, I guess." Pat nodded. "Anyway, he was carrying this little round-faced baby no more'n a couple months old, if that." The old man's eyes twinkled as he recalled the facts. "It's cold out there," he blurted out in the middle of his story. "Let me get a warm coat and I'll go with you to the barn." He disappeared into the other room.

Pat pulled Janet tight against his side. "Shucks! I was hoping to get you in the hay alone."

"I'll bet!" She squeezed him back playfully. "You'd probably scare off faster than you did last night."

He smiled down at her and she could feel his warm, clean breath fan across her face. She snuggled against him.

He was looking an awfully lot like that *nice guy she'd like to neck with* again.

"Yes," Vernon chuckled, coming back into the room, still reminiscing. "He might have been tiny, but it didn't take him long to show us who was boss around here. Remember that, Buck? One little whimper and we all snapped to attention."

"Remember?" Pat laughed. "He *still* thinks he's boss."

"You mean you lived here when Matt was a baby? I just assumed you and Roger lived together along with Josh."

"That came later. I came here from California not long after Matt was born. Someone told me about a job as a ranch hand here on Vernon's ranch. We stayed for a few years."

"Best hired help I ever had."

"I was glad to get the job. Not many would have taken in a man and his baby."

"Don't let him kid you," Vernon interjected. "You'd of had a fight on your hands with Doyne if you took that baby somewhere else." He shook his head and laughed again at his thoughts. "Doyne was about Matt's age now, but she took to mothering like a duck to water. Bless her heart. She had just lost her own mother a couple years before."

"Spoiled Matt is what she did," Pat informed in a scolding tone bringing Vernon out of his melancholy.

"No more'n we all did, son. You know that."

"Why'd you leave? I'd think it would be hard to leave such a beautiful place."

"I met Roger and he was in about the same condition as I was. A young son, no wife. The boys were about to start school. It made sense to move in together."

"Oh, yes, Roger the Ranger we called him." Vernon chuckled. "Remember that, Buck? Roger the Ranger." He cackled again to himself. "Anyways, when Roger told Buck they needed some more good men Buck thought he would put his talents to better use as a Ranger."

"I'd have stayed if you needed me, Vernon. You know that."

"I was just jerkin' your chain, son. I know you would. I had cut back on my livestock and had plenty of help, so I wished him luck and sent him on his way." His voice grew low. "Sure hated to see him go, though." His tone brightened again. "Then before I knew it that scrap of a kid of mine grew up right under my nose, fell in love with Roger the Ranger and the rest is history as they say. Sure got lonely around here 'til I got used to the quiet."

"Doyne's your only child?"

"Now, she is. If Myrtle May and I hadn't gotten started so late in life, we'd of probably had a dozen, but we just had the two." There was a note of sadness in his voice. "Our son, Bobby, died of pneumonia the winter before Buck joined the team." He sniffed and wiped his nose with the back of his hand. "Would have been thirty years old last February." His voice trailed off thickly and Janet was close to tears herself.

The old man straightened suddenly and squared his shoulders, letting out a loud cackle as if all thoughts of his son had vanished. "Yessiree, the day Buck showed up with that baby was something else."

Janet instinctively put her hand in Pat's wanting to be as close as possible...to touch him...to feel him. She sensed her chances of convincing him to have anything to do with her life in St. Louis were rapidly diminishing. With friends like these, she wondered if she even would WANT to try to persuade him. The thought saddened her greatly. She tightened her grip on his hand and grasped his sleeve with her other.

He looked down at her, his brows raised. "Cold?"

She couldn't speak. She only shook her head. No, she wasn't cold. She suddenly felt very lonely and had an overwhelming outpouring of love for him at this moment.

She knew it was crazy. You don't fall this desperately in love in a day. Then she remembered something Pat had said about there being no certain timetable for...*romance*. Well, obviously there was no timetable for love either, because that was exactly what it was. She knew deep down that it was more than just romance. In fact, as much as she would enjoy a romantic interlude with him, she knew there would have to be much, much more. If she ever made love with him, she definitely could never let go.

She leaned her head against his arm, still clinging to him like it would be their last walk together.

Dear God. Please help me. I'm so confused. I'm afraid my heart would be broken to leave all that I feel for Patrick and Matt behind, yet my heart would break if I had to forsake Christopher. I so desperately need your guidance, dear merciful God.

CHAPTER TWELVE

Although Janet kept a cautious distance, she loved the beautiful animals and was awed at the size of everything. The barn looked as large as a stadium with its indoor workout track and numerous stalls all very clean boasting of excellent care and attention. There was a separate grooming room where a hired hand was currying one of the horses and she was amused thinking it could be rented out as a ballroom when not in use. It was that huge.

"I'm overwhelmed." She turned to Vernon. "Are *all* ranches out here this big?"

"A lot of them. We have quite a bit of wide open spaces out here." He pitched some fresh hay into one of the feeders. "I guess you're used to people living a little closer together?"

"Well, yes. I guess you could say that." She smiled. "I live on the fifteenth floor of a high-rise apartment building. I can see for miles from my balcony but it's miles of city, people, parks, buildings. It's beautiful too, but in a very different way."

"I'll bet. Never been to St. Louis." He cackled again. "Never been anywhere much. You see, my ancestors were some of the first settlers here in Montana way back in the early eighteen hundreds. My great grandpa started this place, then my grandpa took over, then my dad and me. I always planned on Bobby—" He stopped short. "Well, I guess it'll be divided between Doyne and Roger and Buck."

Janet raised her brows.

"Didn't he tell you? He's bought a partnership in this place. I got good help here and all, but I'm getting old. I'm tickled to death Buck wants it. He's always been like a son to me." He went quiet again and turned back to his chores.

Pat pointed behind them. "You can't see it from here but there's a beautiful spot a few miles south that I plan to build on. Someday when Matt's older we're going to move out here and run this place along with Roger and his family." A wide grin spread across his face. "The way we have it figured, since Doyne and Roger say they plan on five or six kids, we'll have all the farm hands we need. That right, Vernon?"

The old man nodded happily.

Janet smiled weakly. She felt so far removed from all these glorious plans. It was impossible to think she could even remotely be a part of all this...to supply her own little farm hands. She had her career in St. Louis. She had Christopher. Her thoughts saddened even more. Poor, poor Christopher. So ill. So alone.

"You okay?"

She smiled. "Yes. I was just thinking about how proud Christopher would be knowing you're so happy with your life here. He's miserable not knowing if you're—"

"You just never quit." Pat went to a nearby stall and began mucking it.

Janet followed, making sure Vernon was out of earshot of them. "No, I don't. He needs you and I think you need him. During a conversation with your father not too long ago, he was in an unusually melancholy mood and told me I was the only family he had now...that I was a *daughter* to him. He asked me never to leave him and I told him I never would. But, Pat, I can't take your place in his heart."

She grabbed hold of his arm and made him turn toward her. "I never had an inkling when I left St. Louis that I would have feelings for the estranged son and grandson of the man I vowed to never forsake. Do you know how hard it will be for me to pretend I never met Matt or forget how I feel when we kiss?"

"But you have to." Pat's voice was soft and she noted a touch of sadness in his expression.

As they left the barn to return to the Jeep, she hugged Vernon and told him how nice it was to be able to visit his ranch and how she would never forget the overwhelming vastness of it.

"To give you some comparison, little girl," his *little girl* caused her to roll her eyes at Pat and grin, "one of the reasons you don't see as many people out here as you do in Missouri is because there aren't all that many. Montana is close to a hundred and fifty thousand square miles and Missouri probably has thousands more people in it at half the space."

"Really?"

"Really," Pat emphasized. "There's probably five million people in Missouri." He grinned. "Of course, today there's only four million, nine hundred ninety-nine thousand, nine hundred ninety-nine." He hugged her to him. "You're here. Probably seems awfully quiet in Missouri without you. Can't imagine how some are getting along without your advice. You know, that advice no one asks for but gets it anyway."

She glared at him but the quirky smile on his face told her he was teasing.

"Yep," Vernon went on absently as he followed them to their vehicle, "we got a lot of room to stretch our legs out here."

Just before she stepped up into the Jeep, she threw her arms around the gray-haired man again and hugged him tightly. She would undoubtedly never see him again and it would certainly be her loss.

He didn't say another word, just gave her a fatherly pat on the back and helped her into her seat. He was still waving to them as they drove out of sight.

"What a nice person," Janet finally said, after thinking over all that had transpired while they were on the ranch.

"I like to think we're *all* nice here."

"You are...most of the time." She stared out the window for a moment, her voice turning serious. "The country really is beautiful. Makes it hard to leave so soon."

"It's your choice." His voice was almost a whisper."

"I know."

The rest of the ride to Kalispell was exceptionally quiet with only a faint sigh that escaped her lips when she thought about how wonderfully loved Pat made her feel when he kissed her earlier this morning. The feel of his hands, the warmth of his arms...how was she ever going to forget? She reached over and brushed one finger along his stern jaw. Without taking his eyes off the road, he turned his head just enough to rest a soft kiss on the tip of her finger.

"Do you have any idea how hard it will be for ME to forget I ever met you? Right now I'm fighting the urge to just run away with you. Just keep driving."

"What about Matt?"

"Matt who?"

They both looked at each other, then burst out laughing. They didn't know what was so funny, but it caused a welcomed lift of spirits.

They were still laughing when they entered the small dress shop in the center of town. A very attractive red-headed lady glanced up from behind the counter.

"Buck!" She came around and gave Pat a bear hug. "Long time no see. How have you been?"

Janet chewed on her bottom lip, keeping her twinge of jealousy deceptively concealed as the red-head chatted gaily with Pat, telling him how *good* he looked. However, she couldn't resist letting her disgust show in the sickening smile she pasted on her face when Pat glanced her way. His look was one of amusement as Janet turned sharply and began flipping through the rack of ladies' western shirts.

"Do you have anything in a size three?" Janet tried to keep from sounding curt but knew she failed.

"Oh, I'm sorry. I didn't even see you there."

That was obvious, Janet thought hotly.

"She is rather hard to see." Pat chuckled teasingly. "Being a little *short of leg* as they say."

"Some are short of leg and some are long of mouth," she hissed back giving him a scornful curl of her lip.

"Where's your manners, Buck?" The lady exchanged a polite smile with Janet. "I'm Sharon Pearson." She held her hand out in a friendly gesture while displaying a dazzling white smile.

In Janet's estimation Sharon's beauty was breathtaking. She couldn't help from being captivated by the woman's genuine warmth.

"Janet Raye. Nice to meet you."

"You're not from around here, are you?"

Her smile was infectious. Janet could see how easy it would be to like her. "Is it that obvious? She smiled back at the lady as she looked at her own attire.

"It's your accent. It's like Buck's. Are you from Missouri, too?"

"Why, yes." At first she felt a little surprised Sharon would know so much about where Pat came from but on second thought not so surprising after all. It was obvious by the woman's greeting that she and Pat were good friends. Probably *very* good friends. "Yes," she repeated, composing herself. "We're both from Missouri, however we only met yesterday...I mean we're not friends...*old* friends that is...or anything...just met...yesterday...hardly know each other."

Pat laughed. She was floundering and she knew it. All she was trying to do was make it perfectly clear that she wasn't trying to infringe on anything Sharon and good old *Buck* might have going...or was she?

Sharon was kind enough to take the situation in hand, gracefully changing the subject. "I have a beautiful lavender shirt I think will fit you, Janet. It would go perfect with your eyes." She pulled a very becoming western-cut blouse from the rack and held it up next to Janet's face. "Of course, we can't tell much with that big coat on."

"It's not mine. It's Matt's." Janet shrugged out of the jacket and handed it to Pat. "So's this." She tugged at the too-tight T-shirt."

"How IS Matt," Sharon asked conversationally holding the shirt up to Janet's shoulders.

"He's great," Pat answered as he thumbed through the jeans. "He's helping Roger and Josh put together a motor for a self-propelled airplane they're building."

"That boy's an electronic wizard," Sharon whispered to Janet.

"So I've been told." She felt miffed and didn't know why. *Oh, yes, she did! I don't want this woman knowing all about Matt. It makes me wonder what intimate facts she knew about Pat.* She mentally shook herself. Her behavior was disgusting. She had no claims on either Pat or his son.

"You got any jeans to fit an elf?" Pat's voice was on the brink of laughter.

"Buck!" Sharon cautioned him in a reprimanding tone as she pulled a couple pairs of designer pants from the rack and ushered Janet into a dressing room.

"Pay him no mind, Janet. If he couldn't tease, he'd have no reason for living. My husband used to say Buck was the biggest tease there was when they'd all be out on a rescue mission."

Janet hurriedly pulled the T-shirt over her face to hide the look of delight at hearing Sharon was married. After slipping into the lavender shirt, she exclaimed, "I like it. It fits perfectly."

"You have a lovely figure for western wear."

"I've been meaning to buy some. It's very popular in St. Louis."

"How long will you be visiting here?"

"Oh, I'm not visiting." She didn't know how much about Pat's life in St. Louis Sharon knew so she gave no explanation why she was here. "I'll be going back tomorrow." Then a very childish urge took over and the words came tumbling out her mouth. "I would have gone back today, but I promised Pat...Buck...that I'd go to the dance at the Legion with him tonight." It was immature she knew, but she said it just in case Sharon had any kind of designs on Pat. If it bothered the lady, it didn't show in her expression, nor in her voice.

"Wonderful!" Her excitement made Janet feel like even more of a fool. "I'll see you there."

"Oh, are you and your husband going to the dance?"

"I lost my husband three years ago." Her voice grew quiet. "I'm a widow."

Janet let out a gasp. "The mountain?"

Sharon shook her head no. "Car wreck."

"I'm so sorry." Janet really meant it and promised herself to never again act so childish.

"It's okay. We had a lot of wonderful years together." She looked down at Janet's snowmobile boots. "You could use a pair of cowgirl boots to go with your new outfit."

Janet had almost forgotten about shoes. She shrugged and laughed. "Might as well go all the way. Lead me to the boots."

Janet decided to wear her new purchases and had Sharon put Matt's *loaners* in a sack. Much to her dismay, Pat insisted on paying for everything, restating that it was his fault she needed the clothes.

Janet was still arguing with him when they reached the

outskirts of town, heading out into the wide open spaces again.

"You *are* stubborn, Patrick Mayhew! I would have never agreed to buy all these things if I had known."

"Consider it my good deed for the day."

"Good deed?"

"Yeah, for that rock star on that T-shirt. He was in quite a strain."

She glared at him. "You're not only stubborn...you're dirty-minded too."

He gave her a lecherous laugh. "I should have put the fire department on alert."

"What?"

"There's a smokin' hot cowgirl struttin' her stuff around town."

"Pull this car over and park it!"

"What are you going to do? Walk back?"

"Stop this car!"

He pulled into the nearest shoulder and turned to her. "I'm just saying, you've got the figure for tight jeans and cowgirl boots. Mmmm, yum, yum!"

"Patrick? SHUT! UP!"

"Make me."

She literally yanked his head down to hers and gave him a long, wet mind-shattering kiss, took a breath and gave him another one only longer and wetter."

"That works for me." He took a deep breath and let it out.

"Okay, fire up the engine and let's get out of here."

"Wait. I feel like I'm going to speak again. You'd better stop me before I say something tacky."

She looked at him out the corner of her eye, then turned his face to hers again. This time the kiss was softer with a lot of little nibbles across his lips before whispering against them. "How did I ever mistake you for a *nice guy*? You're the devil himself." She gave him one last loud smacking kiss then leaned back in her seat. "I kind of like that in a guy."

This time he *was* speechless.

CHAPTER THIRTEEN

𝒯o keep their minds off what had happened while parked, Pat turned on the radio to a music station.

"Oh, I love this song." Janet began singing along and Pat joined her with a baritone harmony.

"You have a beautiful voice, Pat. You may have missed your calling."

"Thanks. You *ain't* so bad yourself."

Another favorite of Janet's came on and she and Pat harmonized on that one and then another and another. By the time they neared the road leading to the cabin, they had sung every duet they knew and some they didn't know so well.

Janet shrugged her shoulders and sighed. "You DO sound good for a devil disguised as a nice guy."

"What makes you such an authority on devils who look like nice guys? How many could you have known in your young life?"

Her mood grew suddenly serious. His teasing question caused a painful time of her life to surface. "Besides you, just one other comes to mind."

He turned to look directly at her, surprised by her deadly serious tone and expression. "Oh?" He turned his attention back to the road.

"I met him while touring with a musical theatre group."

"That *disastrous affair* you spoke about?"

"Yes." Her voice was barely a whisper as she turned her attention to the beautiful snow-capped mountain in the distance. The weather was still very brisk, but the sun had obliged to shine and was already melting the ice that had frozen on the branches. Instead of remote and desolate as she had once thought this country to be, it appeared comforting and peaceful.

"Is that the mountain where you were last night?

"Uh, huh, in that vicinity."

"How does Doyne stand it? I don't think I could live through sitting at home worrying about my husband while he was out fighting the elements of nature. The mountain, the weather...it's just too dangerous."

He chuckled. "So's St. Louis traffic."

She laughed with him. "You have a point." She turned back to the view. "It's so very beautiful."

"So are you."

"Don't start it."

"Start what?"

"Do you want me to make you shut up again?"

"You do that to me one more time and my vocal chords would be locked up for life. We'd never be able to sing another song." His teasing manner became serious. "Speaking of singing, you were about to tell me about the group you toured with."

"It's not a pretty tale. You don't want to hear it."

"Yeah, I do."

"Well, this troupe came to St. Louis and I tried out and was chosen for one of the minor parts. I asked your father for a leave of absence that summer to *follow my dream*, as I had theatrically told him after being picked for the coming tour."

"You mean he *willingly* let you...actually let you do

something that wasn't for the *good of the company*."

"Oh, stop it, Pat!" She let her breath out in a huff. "Really! Sometimes I don't think we're even talking about the same person. Christopher has always encouraged me to spread by wings, so to speak."

"Go ahead with your sordid tale about the *devil of a nice guy*. You met him in the group. What was he...one of those dancers who leaps around in tights with that bulge between their legs?"

"You're disgusting! That's a guard they have to wear to keep from getting kicked in the...well, where it hurts."

"I know...but they still strut around like it's actually part of their body."

"They do not! Oh, what do you know." She turned to stare out the window. "Besides he wasn't a dancer. He was the stock player for secondary leads...male leads."

"Well, that's nice to know. At least he played the MALE leads."

She let her head fall back on the seat and rolled her eyes toward him. "Do you want to hear this or not?"

"I don't think I do. I was never much on pillow talk when I wasn't involved."

She turned to look him straight in the eye. "I wasn't going to give you a detailed description—" She stopped, leaned back and spoke in a much calmer tone. "It was much more than just pillow talk...on my part anyway. I fell in love. Or so I thought at the time." She sighed dreamily. "He was so sweet to me and oh so handsome."

Pat let out a disgusted snort.

She transferred her gaze to him adding, "Looked nothing like you, by the way." She had to stifle a giggle.

"Thanks. I'm more the female lead type anyway."

"I suspected as much. I'll bet you'd look super in a tutu...knobby knees."

"And I suppose Mr. Leading Man's knees were perfect?"

"Sculpted by the Gods!"

"I was right. I don't want to hear about it."

She paid him no mind and continued her tale. "It was the summer I graduated from college. In fact, he went to my party your father had for me. I thought I had died and went to heaven...reunited with Jeanie after all those years, a handsome stage performer at my side..." she turned her head toward Pat to eye his expression, "...who doted on my every word, who answered to my every whim, who charmed the socks off everyone..."

"Who's making me sick."

She smiled to herself. "His name is Mark...Mark Wilson. Doesn't that just sound like a matinee idol?" She mischievously made her voice sound like a star-struck child.

"Sounds phony to me."

She laughed. "How right you are. Oh, the name was real. He wasn't." She sighed and rested her head against the back of the seat, staring into space, not really seeing anything. "I guess I have a lot to thank him for, though."

"How's that?"

"When I knew him, I was suffering from the vine-covered cottage syndrome. You know, the happy wife in the ruffled apron, kissing the happy husband in his three-piece suit goodbye in the morning, handing him his briefcase as she sends the happy children off to school after feeding them a nourishing, well-balanced breakfast."

"Sounds like you've been watching old movies."

"Yeah, only old movies always had a happy ending. Mine didn't."

"And for that you're thankful?"

"Well, he showed me that life is *not* like the movies."

He glanced her way. "You don't seem to be too shaken by the breakup."

"Oh, I was at first, my dear man. It really knocked me to my knees, but thanks to your dad's help I've managed to pull myself back up. Besides that was a few years ago."

"It doesn't hurt anymore?"

"No, surprisingly enough, it doesn't." She studied for a moment. "I had quit performing with the troupe after my leave of absence was up and went back full time at Mayhew's, but Mark took an apartment in St. Louis and was there a lot. He actually wanted me to move in with him, but that was against my religion." She let out an ironic laugh. "The way I've been acting with you, I guess you think I've lost my religion all together."

"Hardly. It's taken two to tango. It's not all been you."

"Anyway, it's all over now."

"What exactly happened?"

"It was just a freak thing...fate as Matt would say."

"Everything is fate to Matt."

"My best friend at the time was a buyer for women's wear and was supposed to go to this fancy luncheon on the top floor of a popular department store to see some of the latest fashions being modeled. Her date cancelled at the last moment and she didn't want to go alone so she talked me into going with her. I thought, what the heck, it was my day off and Mark had called to say he was sick and needed to stay in bed all day."

"Without you? Must be a jerk."

She pretended to ignore his remark. "Well, I nearly fainted when I saw him at the luncheon." She grimaced. "I can still feel the embarrassment I felt. What a fool I was!"

"What?"

"There I was all smiles walking toward him ready to say something cutesy like, *Well, out of the death bed into the salmon mousse,* when I noticed he wasn't exactly alone. If I thought I was surprised to see HIM there, you can imagine my surprise to meet MRS. Mark Wilson who was hanging on his arm. She was one of the models hired for the fashion show." She turned to look at Pat. "You would have liked her...she was tall."

"You mean you didn't know he had a wife up until then?"

"No. Dumb, huh? For months he fooled me. Months! I guess he could have gone on fooling me for years since they actually lived in Chicago. She travelled as a model and he travelled in the theatre group so I guess there were no questions asked when they were apart for several weeks at a time. Thank the good Lord for saving me. I still can't believe I was so stupid."

"It WAS stupid."

"Thanks for your understanding!"

"I hope you kicked him *where it hurts.*"

"I didn't do anything but cry my eyes out every time I thought about it."

"Whatever happened to the perfect-kneed idiot?"

"He's still around."

He eyed her suspiciously.

"Yeah, he's still with the troupe. They perform in St. Louis a few times a year. He called me a couple of times."

"What!? The bastard has the guts to—"

"Watch your language! Matt would be appalled."

"Sorry."

"He tried to explain that he and his wife had an *open* marriage and he'd still like to see me. I hung up on him the second time he called."

"I can't believe he'd have the guts to even ask."

"What is it to you? You didn't even want to hear about it."

Why *did* he care? He couldn't answer that. All he knew was that he was furious! The thought of some creep taking advantage of her...kissing those sweet lips...holding her warm body. His rage got the better of him and he pulled off the side of the road and slammed on the brakes.

"Surely you've got more sense than to take up with him again?"

She stiffened. "Give me a little credit for having some

brains! Anyway, you don't tell me who I can see. It's a cinch *you've* not lived a life of celibacy!"

His brow shot up.

"It was very obvious you and Sharon were a lot more than mere acquaintances...but then, I suppose that's none of *my* business."

"You're right! It isn't!" he bellowed.

"Well, Mark Wilson is none of yours either," she bellowed back.

"What the hell do Sharon and I have to do with that bastard whose only claim to fame is charming socks and everything else off stupid young girls!?"

"I'm not a stupid young girl anymore, Pat!" She sank down in her seat. "Why are we yelling?"

"I don't know!" he yelled, catching himself. "I don't know," he repeated softly, his voice fading to a hushed stillness as his troubled gaze met hers. "I'm sorry for cussing, but this whole thing infuriates me. Maybe it brings back unpleasant memories. My wife had an open marriage, I didn't. I remember how that hurt me, so I sympathize with your heartache. I really do. I'm so sorry." The bitterness was gone, leaving way to confused concern. He pulled the Jeep to the side of the road. "What's happening with us?"

She suddenly pretended to be busy with the zipper on her coat...anything to avoid his compelling eyes gleaming with a desire she knew so well. She had seen it just before he kissed her. Her fingers pulled frantically at the loose threads caught in the zipper, her body vibrating with her own desire.

Her fumbling was stopped short as one huge hand covered hers impatiently. "Janet." It was more like a moan than actually speaking her name.

She couldn't remember turning to him, but all at once her arms were wrapped tightly around his neck with her thoughts reeling wildly, spinning a web of anticipated ecstasy. The sharp, hungry ache of wanting to feel his lips on hers stabbed at her. She willingly surrendered her mouth to his, yielding to the burning sweetness only his kiss and his alone could give her.

He pulled away a fraction, their breaths mingling for a brief second before she was drawn back into his embrace. She moaned his name over and over. His tongue searched skillfully for hers and finding it brought another spur of molten fire shooting through her veins. Her fingers threaded their way through his thick hair on the back of his head, clasping it in her fist. She couldn't get enough of him...couldn't get close enough.

When she opened her eyes, she impatiently searched for the V of his shirt and unbuttoned the top two closures. Her eyes riveted to the wisps of hair matted against his tawny skin. A moan escaped her lips as they kissed the path her fingers made through the curly mass, lingering to feel the soft tickle against her face. She found her way to the hollow behind his ear, then pulled the lobe with her teeth. "I wanted to do that this morning." She murmured as her mouth sought out his, delighting in the taste of it.

"Janet." His voice was thick and husky. "We've got to stop."

Stop? How could she stop when there were sensations bursting inside her she never knew existed. She couldn't give up the heated pleasures he had introduce her to. "Please, no...not yet."

"We *have* to."

"Are you trying to tell me you didn't want to kiss me?"

"Good heavens, no. You're wonderful...so warm...so loving."

"Then what's your problem?"

"You *know* what the problem is." He took her hand and kissed the back of it. "It's one thing to keep it fun and games, but another when it feels like it could get out of hand. I don't want you to have regrets."

She hung her head. "You're right, of course. It *was*

getting out of hand."

"This can never go any further than this weekend."

"I know, but it makes no sense to me. You can't deny you have feelings for me and there's no mistake about mine for you."

"I have other things to think about besides my feelings. There's other considerations."

"If you're talking about Matt, you know I love.—"

"Him *and* the fact we live in two different worlds."

"And never the twain shall meet?"

"Something like that."

She took his face between her hands and looked at him intently. "Patrick, go back to St. Louis and see your father."

He pulled her hands down and pushed away from her. "Don't start it."

"No, listen to me. When I have a problem with someone, I talk it out."

"There's nothing left to talk about, Janet." His voice was becoming testy.

"All that happened a long time ago. If you would just.—"

"Stay out of it!" His eyes turned apologetic as he placed his hands on her shoulders. "I know your heart is in the right place but I can't take any chances...not with Matt. He's my whole life!"

She breathed a defeated sigh and began buttoning his shirt back up. "So that's final, huh?"

"That's the way it *has* to be."

"You're stubborn."

"*You're* stubborn."

"You make me sick."

"I do not."

They exchanged a brief look of amusement, then burst out laughing.

*****

INFLIGHT TO MONTANA

"Are all flights this bumpy?" Ruby's knuckles were white from holding onto the arm rests so tightly.

"Quit griping. I'm trying to formulize our mission." Max made a few more notes on his tablet.

"I'm going to puke!"

He grabbed the barf bag out of the back of the seat in front of her. "Here!" He thrust it into her lap. "Puke and shut up, Ruby."

"I'm Madge remember? Madge and her *loving* husband Wilbur." She gagged but nothing came up. "Good old Wilbur and Madge Brown. Couldn't you have chosen more exciting names for us...like Tyrone and Celesta Summersmith? Sounds more like the rich people we're going to be."

"We don't need to be drawing more attention to us than you already have with your constant moaning, griping and asking for drinks and snacks that they don't have."

"You really are a definite Wilbur. An old fuddy-duddy." She pouted and looked out the window into the night sky. "Look down there at the lights!"

He glanced over her shoulder.

"Is that where we're going?"

"Not yet. That's just another city we're flying over."

"Looks like little lightning bugs. How much longer? And after we land, how much longer will it be before we have the brat in our hands?"

"I'm trying to figure that out now if you'd leave me alone. We go to the motel first, get the gun and map my friend says he has to where the kid lives. We'll have to stay out of sight when we get to their house and keep an eye on their comings and goings. Then we find an opportune time to nab him. We need to wear the wigs and glasses I packed so he won't be able to identify us after we release him."

As if forgetting she was sick to her stomach, she began to hum a song and smiling. "Okay, here's what I'm thinking. We tie him up and take pictures like I see on TV. You can e-mail them from your laptop. Him holding today's newspaper. Maybe a bloody nose to make it more urgent they get the money pronto or a cut on his head with the blood dripping down his cheek—"

"Shut up, Ruby. Like I'd know their e-mail address."

"Make the kid tell you."

"They'll be no bloody anything. We are *not* hurting him. It's a matter of catch and release. What part about that don't you understand?"

"Think about it. It'd be so easy to dump him in a river or something. We'd be in the clear."

"That is *not* an option. How many times do we have to go over this? I'm not having murder on my conscience."

"Oh, yeah, your precious conscience. Wouldn't want *Mama* to think badly of her little boy."

"Leave my mother out of this. We're *not* harming the boy in any way. *No violence!*"

"Easy as pie. Piece of cake," she said in a sing-song manner. "If he's not around to identify us, then I don't have to wear that dorky wig and glasses. They make me look old and frumpy."

"You're sick!!"

"Yada, yada, blah, blah, blah."

CHAPTER FOURTEEN

"You're a trouble-maker." Pat laughed as he pulled up in front of the cabin. "A very lovely trouble-maker," he whispered, tilting her face up with one finger.

She lifted her eyes to his, swallowing hard to force back the ache her lips were feeling. She wanted to be kissed again...again and again and again.

"We'd better go in." His voice was a murmur.

She wrinkled her nose. "I was afraid you'd say that."

No more words were spoken as they walked up the path to the cabin door. When it was Doyne who opened the door, they were both surprised.

"What are you doing here?" Pat gave her a welcome hug.

"What's even more important, what is that heavenly smell?" Janet hung her parka on the coat rack.

"Lasagna. My friends dropped me off here with all the leftovers from the party. They brought enough to feed an army. I knew my boys would be hungry and hoped you would get back in time to help eat it up."

"I don't know about your *boys* but I'm starving." Janet patted her belly.

Doyne smiled a big open smile. "Boy, you look nice, Janet. You must have stopped off at Sharon's Boutique. I recognize the shirt. I was wishing for one just like it in my size the other day." She laughed. "That is, my original size." She looked down at her stomach. "If I *ever* get it back."

"Any signs yet?" Pat asked.

"No." She moaned disappointedly. "I told Roger, this baby takes after me. Always late. I'm never on time." She sniffed the air. "Whoops! I smell the garlic bread. Better get it out of the oven before it burns up. I thought we'd eat before we went to the Legion. You ARE going, aren't you?"

Before they could answer, she disappeared into the kitchen.

As Janet started walking toward the boys at the table, Pat stopped her. "Wait. Back up."

Why?"

"You look like Minnie Pearl. And don't tell me you don't know who she is." He took his nail clippers out of his pocket. "You've got the price tag still sewn to the back of your jeans."

"What were you doing looking at the back of my jeans?"

"I'm no fool. Hold still while I snip it off...the price tag, that is."

His hand lingered on her backside a little longer than necessary. When he was through, she leaned back against him and sighed. "Are you sure there isn't another tag."

"Watch it!" His voice sounded stern, but Janet felt his hand snake under her arm to her stomach to press her against him firmly. He bowed his head and nuzzled her hair. "Do you have a permit to possess this body, lady?" She arched and planted a moist kiss under his chin causing him to whisper. "I'm about to go out of my mind."

"I already have." She pretended to swoon.

He played along with her game, catching her and scooping her up into his arms. "You weigh about as much as my cowboy hat. How could someone small as you cause so much damage to my life?"

He was joshing her she knew, but her face grew serious. "I don't want to cause you damage, Patrick. I really truly don't. All I want is for you to be happy...and I'll do anything it takes."

"Whew! He put her down and nervously raked his fingers through his hair. "Don't get all serious on me. That I *can't* take!"

Doyne's voice calling out that supper was ready interrupted their conversation and suddenly caused a stampede into the kitchen. The young boys first, then Roger with Pat and Janet hurrying along.

"Hold it! Hold it!" Doyne cautioned. "Take it easy. There's a pregnant woman here."

They all stopped, giggled, and then scrambled for chairs, Matt making sure he sat next to Janet.

"Did you have fun today, Janet?"

She patted Matt on the hand. "A lot...did you?"

"A lot." He spooned a healthy portion of lasagna onto his plate, then very gentlemanly put some on Janet's. "It does a boy good to get away from his dad for a while. In fact, you'd be doing me a big favor if you would take him to the dance tonight."

She clamped her hand over his mouth. "He's already asked me to go and I said yes. Now, just eat and don't get us into trouble again." She could feel his mouth smiling under her fingers and before she lifted her hand, she planted a kiss on his cheek.

"Dad, we're just about finished with the plane. Tomorrow after Sunday School can we go to that open field next to the church and fly it?"

"Don't know if we'll have time. I need to get Janet to the airport in the afternoon."

Matt's face dropped. "I thought you were staying until Monday."

Just looking at him broke her heart. "Sweetie, I need to get back. Sorry."

Matt put his fork down and left the table, calling out, "I need to do a little more work on that motor."

*****

Later while Janet helped Doyne with the dishes the two chatted about the day's happenings.

"Matt thinks an awful lot of you, Janet."

"He's playing matchmaker."

"No, it's much more. He talked a lot about you before you got back."

Janet swirled the soap around in the water with her finger, her thoughts not on the dirty dishes at all. "Doyne? Can I talk to you? I mean...really talk."

Doyne studied her a moment. "Of course, you can. Come on, let's sit down."

"No, it's not THAT serious." Janet laughed nervously and started scrubbing a dish mercilessly. "First of all, before I get into anything too deep, I want to tell you what a wonderful father you have. He's a delightful gentleman."

"Why, thank you. I think so, too. I'm glad you had a good time there today. He loves company. Someday when Roger gets *rangering* out of his blood, we plan to move back."

"Yes, that's what I hear. Doyne?"

"Yes."

"Something happened to me out there...well, I guess it started happening before that, but I realized just how much. She stopped. "This is sounding crazy."

"No, it doesn't. Go on."

"This can't be happening to me. I feel like I've fallen in love with Patrick. I love him, I love his son, and I love this land."

"It happens. I think there's something on his part, too. I

can see it in his eyes...and there's no mistaking Matt's feelings. I hope things can work out. I know Buck has no desire to ever go back to St. Louis or to have his father know about Matt. He was hurt too deeply."

"I know, but you see, the Christopher Mayhew I know is a wonderful man. Since I've known him, God is a big part of his life and decisions. I'm sure he's not the same person he was in earlier years. I owe him a great deal and I'll never forsake him. I just couldn't live with myself."

Doyne picked up a dish, dried it and put it in the cabinet before she spoke. "I'm afraid I don't have any magic solution."

"I know. I guess I just needed someone's shoulder to cry on." She smiled. "I usually call my sister, Jeanie, when I need a sympathetic ear."

Doyne put the dishtowel down and laid her hand on Janet's arm. "Thanks for using mine. I'm glad I was here for you. I care a great deal for Buck and Matt myself. They're my family. I don't ever want to see them hurt and I know you wouldn't want to see them hurt either." She shook her head and sat down at the table, putting her feet up on the other chair. "Complicated, huh?"

"Very."

Janet finished cleaning the dishes by herself, surmising Doyne was worn out from the long day. "All done." She draped the dishrag over the edge of the sink and turned. Her smile quickly faded when she saw Doyne's paleness. "Doyne? You're white as a sheet. Are you all right?"

"Whew! I must have eaten too much lasagna. Something's not setting too well on my stomach."

"Do you think it's the baby?"

"I don't know. It could be, I guess. I've never had a baby before, but—"

"Patrick? Roger? Come quick. I think Doyne's—" She breathlessly spit out the words, feeling very hyper, like she should be boiling water or sterilizing surgical instruments or something.

Pat and Roger were in the kitchen in two giant steps, one on each side of Doyne...Pat rubbing her shoulders and Roger wiping her forehead vigorously, brushing her hair back from her face with heavy frantic strokes.

"For crying out loud, guys, leave some skin on me!"

Roger called out to Josh. "Call the doctor. You know the number. Buck, start the car. Get it warmed up. Make sure it's running smooth.

"We can take my Jeep."

Doyne moaned.

"No, we'll take the Bronco. It's more comfortable. Just do it, man!" Roger was extremely anxious. "Follow us in the Jeep and stop by the house and get her suitcase out of the hall closet. It's already packed. You know where the key is to get in."

Matt's big brown eyes searched Doyne's whole body. "Is the baby coming now?"

Doyne shook her head. "Not right this minute, Hon. But soon, I think."

"Righteous!"

Everyone went about their duties in a strictly business-like manner and soon they were on the road with everyone deciding the baby could never be born without all of them being there.

Matt sat in the back seat behind Pat and Janet. "Boy, this is exciting, isn't it?" He wiggled like a worm.

"Almost too exciting," Janet returned nervously, feeling a little wiggly herself.

"Won't you be glad when you have a baby, Janet?"

"Matt," Pat warned, "now is not the time."

"No, I'd like to answer that." She looked toward Pat, her eyes brimming with honesty. "I can't think of anything more beautiful than to share the joy of childbirth with the man you love."

She was silenced by his somber expression. He

frowned, his eyes level under his brows. He said nothing. His thoughts raced back to eleven years ago to another time...another birth. One where the mother didn't look upon childbirth as beautiful. A mother who had paid dearly for that observation.

When Janet saw the frown set into his features, she sensed what he was thinking and sympathized with him for the pain he must feel fathering a child with a woman he loved, but who didn't return that love."

"They're going to name the baby after you, Dad. Doyne told me they were."

"Buck for a girl's name?" Janet laughed.

Matt fell into fits of giggles. "No. Patricia. They'll call her Patty." He laughed harder. "Buck for a girl! Janet's funny, huh Dad?"

"A laugh a minute."

*****

Patty arrived exactly three hours and fifteen minutes after arriving at the hospital. Doyne and Roger Murphy became parents to a seven pound, six ounce, bald-headed baby girl. Mother and child were doing nicely, but they nearly lost the father. Roger had paced the floor like a Boston Marathon runner until the nurse gave him a calmative. Unfortunately, he was asleep when the actual birth took place. Pat stood in for him and viewed Patty, counting fingers and toes when the doctor brought her out.

The staff of the small hospital were so kind, they allowed Matt, Josh and Janet to view the baby through the nursery window later. Matt and Josh placed their noses against the glass as Janet stood behind them with her hands resting on their shoulders.

"Do you think she can see me?" Matt gave the baby a little wave.

Josh snickered. "Why would she want to see you?

She's *my* baby sister."

"I doubt she can see either of you yet." Janet smiled to herself. It's going to be fun watching these two vie for her attention over the next few years. "She looks like she's sleeping anyway."

"Kind of cute for a kid with no hair, don't you think?" Matt quirked his head sideways and punched Josh in the shoulder. "A lot cuter than her brother."

"Dork." Josh punched him back.

Janet hugged both boys against her side. "She's beautiful."

"Well," came Pat's deep voice from down the hall, "I thought I'd find you all here. Roger's awake now. He's in with Doyne." He laughed. "I think he's going to make it after all." Pat peeked in at the newborn, then at all the rest of the babies. "She's the cutest one in there...notice that?"

Janet chuckled. "You probably think *all* women are cute."

He bent down to whisper in her ear. "Only teensy, weensy ones."

The next sound he made was a painful grunt when her sharp elbow thudded against his ribs.

*****

OUTSIDE A MOTEL IN KALISPELL

"Has your friend here got anything, how shall I put it, recreational?"

"Get in the room and sleep it off while I talk to Zeb about our plans." Max gave her a nudge toward the motel door.

"Listen, Mama's boy, you don't talk about OUR plans without me." She fluttered her lashes at Zeb. "Besides, we got time for that. If you've got anything in your pockets we can share, I'll make it worth your while."

Zeb looked her up and down and then to Max. "I kept my end of the deal. There was nothing said about drugs. Besides, I don't deal in that anymore. I've been clean since I got out of the slammer."

"So that makes you better than me?" Ruby's hands shook as she adjusted the collar on her coat.

"Pay her no mind. She's a coke head coming down from her last fix."

"Pay me no mind!!? Why you punk." She shook her fist at Max. "You wouldn't *have* a deal if it wasn't for me."

Zeb quickly handed Max a paper bag and a piece of paper. "Here's the map to the Mayhew place and the gun you wanted, serial filed off in case you get fingered."

"No one's going to get fingered," Ruby spit out. "There won't be anyone to finger us if I have my way."

"I'm outta here, Max, before that keg of dynamite of a woman you brought with you blows. You said the gun was only for scaring, not killing." Zeb turned to go and Max took hold of his arm.

"Thanks, Buddy." Max handed him a hundred dollar bill but Zeb handed it back.

"I say we're even now. I don't owe you nothin' and you don't owe me nothin'." He then looked at Ruby. "All I ask is if this goes sour, you don't know me and I don't know you. Understand?"

"Know you? When I get my hands on this money, the likes of you wouldn't be in my league. I wouldn't spit down your throat if your guts were on fire!"

"Money?" Zeb smirked. "When I was checking on this Mayhew guy, I discovered he doesn't have any money to speak of. So good luck, Bitch!"

Ruby lunged at him. "You're lying. The Mayhews have millions, maybe billions."

"Max, we were pretty good friends once and you did good by me, giving me an alibi to help me get out of the slammer, but as long as you have her tied to your tail, you can forget we ever met." He looked Ruby up and down again. "Where'd you *ever* find this piece of garbage?"

Ruby grunted and got up in Zeb's face, poking him in the chest. "Don't you have somewhere you have to go? Like back under the rock you crawled out of."

"That rock is a palace compared where you're going to end up."

Max pulled them apart. "Don't worry, Zeb. There's not going to be any violence."

"I just hate to see you go back to prison over the likes of her going off halfcocked. If I were you, I'd keep an eye on that gun around her."

"I can handle her."

Zeb walked away and Ruby picked up a pebble and threw it at him. "You'd better keep an eye on your own back, loser!"

"What in the world are you doing, Ruby? He's the last person you want to make enemies with. He has connections."

"I'm Madge."

"You're Madge only for identification around strangers. You got the D.T.'s. Get in the room and sleep off your shaking. You'll feel better in a few hours."

"I'll feel better when I get the money and I can buy my own damn crack or anything else I want and no one can stop me."

"What are we going to do if Zeb is right about Patrick Mayhew not having any money?"

"His old man has. Patrick can get it from his father. I'm sure the old man wouldn't want to lose his grandson."

"No one is going to *lose* anyone."

"My sister died giving that brat life. None of those rich bastards gave a rat's ankle about her. Why should that kid live to enjoy all that Mayhew money."

"You can't hold that against the boy. He did nothing wrong."

She grabbed at the paper sack. "Let me see the gun."

He jerked it back. "You're in no shape to be handling weapons."

"You don't tell ME what shape I'm in. After this is over, I could just as soon blow your head off along with that snot-nosed kid's and have ALL the money."

He opened the door to the room and pushed her in. "Listen to yourself. If that's how you really feel, then I'll just leave and you can do what you want...by yourself! You've stepped on my last nerve!"

"Oh, Maxie, I'm just fooling with you. I couldn't pull this off without your help."

"Then keep a clear head. I mean it. No one is going to get hurt. Not me, not the kid. If I didn't need this money so bad to make sure Mama was taken care of the rest of her life, I'd not even be here."

"Mama, Mama, blah, blah, blah."

CHAPTER FIFTEEN

HOSPITAL, KALISPELL

*P*at smiled down at Janet. "Sorry about the dance."

"I don't think it could have topped what we've been through tonight."

Roger came up to them. "I'm staying here tonight with Doyne."

"Is something wrong?" Pat's brow wrinkled.

"She's experiencing a little bleeding and they want to keep her for a few days."

"You want us to stay with you?" Janet asked.

"Oh, no. You guys go home and get some rest. I would like for you to take Josh with you."

"Sure. He can have a sleep-over. He and Matt probably have a lot to talk about having a new little person in their lives." Pat chuckled.

Roger shook his head slowly. "I still can't believe it...a girl, Buck. We got our girl!"

"Try to get some rest, sport. We'll brag about her tomorrow. The boys and I will drop by the hospital tomorrow afternoon after I take Janet to the airport.

"Ohhhh," came a wail from the younger set. "Please don't leave." Matt whined.

"You promised to play poker with us," Josh chimed in.

"I have to." Janet cradled both boys against her.

"Just one more day. Please, please, pretty please."

"Let's go," Pat ordered gruffly. "You know she can't stay forever. Now, I don't want to hear any more about it."

Janet hoped his grumpiness might be a cover up. Maybe...just maybe he didn't want her to leave either. It was just as well she didn't know for sure. It was a bittersweet thought. Nice to think he didn't want her to go, but his knowing she had to. The fact that she had no other choice didn't make her parting any less painful...it only made her life more complicated.

After the bumpy ride home and the climb up the hill to the cabin, all were ready to just relax a moment before going to bed.

"How about some ginger ale?" Matt offered, patting Carlyle who had greeted them.

"That would be great." Janet took Matt's coat and hung it on the rack alongside the parka she had worn. "I'll help you. How about you, Patrick, Josh? You guys want some?" She tried to sound cheerful to see if she could perk up Pat's somber mood. She didn't want their last hours together to be sad.

"Not me." Josh yawned. "I'm going to bed."

"Wimp!" Matt called to him as Josh disappeared into the bedroom.

"Might as well have some." Pat wadded up papers and got sticks of wood to start a fire.

"I can get it, Janet. You help Dad."

Dad, of course, didn't need or appear to want any help from her so she sat down on the couch and tugged at her new cowgirl boots. After a couple of grunts, she gave up.

"Hey, cowboy! Would you give a lady a hand here?"

"Huh?" Pat seemed distracted.

"My boots. She stuck her foot up. "I haven't quite got the hang of it. I can't get them off by myself."

"Oh...sure." He smiled weakly as he effortlessly pulled each one off.

"I guess you're just going to have to go home with me after all. If I ever wear these again, I'll have to have you to pull them off."

He held one of her feet against his stomach, absently rubbing the arch. "Did you know all along we wouldn't stay strangers?"

She stared at him blankly, feeling the warmth from his body against the sole of her foot. Her gaze drifted away from him. She felt stupid talking about such serious matters with her foot stuck in the air.

"I had no intentions of falling in love, if that's what you mean."

"I don't know if it's love or not, but...brother! I'm thirty-eight years old and I feel like a high school kid."

"I think there's always been a kid in there." She pressed his stomach with her toes.

He dropped her foot and she curled her legs under her. "Honestly, Pat, I don't know if it's love either, but it sure feels like the start of something very similar."

He turned back to the fire, deliberately avoiding looking at her.

"Anyway," she continued, "thanks for today. It's been wonderful. I loved every minute of it...even the horses."

"Don't think anything of it. It's part of the FIESTA tour package we offer stranded Missourians."

"Just part? You mean there's more?"

He turned his head to look at her, his tall figure almost god-like silhouetted against the native stone of the fireplace. The miffed tone in his voice was gone, the rich tones seductive, matching his gaze. "There could be."

This time it was she who looked solemn. The teasing all gone. She couldn't think of any reasonable reply. She wanted him so much, but not love him tonight and leave him tomorrow.

"I don't think I could...and then just forget it ever happened."

"We'd have to forget. It couldn't be any other way. I know you have to go back. Your life in St. Louis is important to you. I know that. I've come to terms with that."

"You're important to me, too. As crazy as it seems, I think I AM falling in love. I want time for us to get to know each other better."

"It just seems like love. It's just a strong physical attraction. It feels so urgent because we only have a few hours together."

"That's just it. We have only a short time. How can we possibly know for sure?"

"We can't." He breathed deep and walked toward her and eased his long frame onto the couch beside her. He picked up one of her hands and toyed with her fragile fingers. "I guess a lot of guys are cut from a different mold than me, but I found out a long time ago that I don't need to be bit by the same dog twice. I don't like to share my woman or my life with Dad. The more distance I keep between him and me, the happier I'll be. I can't...I won't...ask you to share those feelings. I just ask that you understand."

"We can't just forget each other."

"I can."

"Well, I can't. I won't!! I can't run away from what's started between us. You feel it as much as I, don't you?"

"It would never work between us, believe me."

"Don't throw it away, Patrick. Don't be stubborn. Your father's ill. He needs you. Talk to him before it's too late. You're alive, he's alive barely. There will always be a tie. You can't make a clean break from your father any more than you could make a clean break from Matt."

He studied her features one by one, then with unexpected swiftness rose to his feet. "What in the world makes *you* so smart?!" He was visibly shaken by the intensity of the moment. He jammed his hands deep in his pockets, calling out tersely, "Matt, are you bringing those drinks or not!"

"Just a minute longer. I'm making something special."

Pat turned on his heel, picked up the poker and stabbed at the logs in the fireplace. "I'm sure you mean well, but you're wasting your breath."

She didn't think so. Nothing worthwhile was a waste of breath. "I guess when you have parents, you have a tendency to take it all for granted. When you don't have parents, you long all your life for someone to...to hold you on their lap...to sing lullabies...to like you when you're not too likable. In other words, to have someone who is uniquely yours"

"Is that what *Christopher* did...hold you on his lap and sing lullabies?"

She sprang to her feet and marched to his side, pulled on his shirt sleeve and told him in no uncertain words, "Listen to me, you overgrown cowboy, I thought we had this all settled once and for all about my relationship with your father!"

"We did." He let his breath out. "I'm sorry."

"You're never going to be able to give yourself fully to someone as long as you're carrying around anger and resentment for him. You don't have one hundred percent of yourself to give." She took his hand, her anger subsiding. Just the touch of him could work miracles on her disposition. "Let it go, Patrick. Whether I'm ever part of your life or not, I want you to be happy, but no one can be happy harboring all that bitterness. Turn it over to the Lord. All things are possible with Jesus in your life. Let Him handle it. He's got broader shoulders than all of us."

"You don't understand."

"Your father's dying, Patrick. Who cares who's right or who's wrong? You're still family. The woman you're fighting over is dead. For all that's Holy, are you going to carry this grudge to your own grave?"

"Is that what you think?" He was angry and surprised at her accusation. "Do you think I'm still hung up on Sylvia?"

"I don't know what you think. I only know I can't fight all that hate you carry in your heart for your father."

"No one's asking you to!"

They glared at each other. Janet's eyes brimmed with hot, stinging tears.

He immediately drew her to him. "What am I doing to you!? You have nothing whatsoever to do with my resentment, yet I'm taking it all out on you." He hesitated a moment. "Listen to me. I'll try to explain. My one and only concern is Matt. You may think you know my father...and maybe he's been nothing but wonderful to you...I really hope so, but I know him, too, and I know what he's done in the past and what he's capable of doing. He has an uncanny ability to manipulate people into his way of thinking and to get such a strangle hold on their lives that they can never be free to be themselves."

"You said it. That was the past." Her voice was muffled against his shirt. "It happened so long ago."

"It can happen again. It's a price I'm not willing to pay." He pushed her gently back to look at her face. "All I have to do is look at you to see what a hold he has on you. There's really no point in our arguing over this. It won't change a thing. I guess I can't expect you to understand. Even though we're never going to see each other again, I would feel much more secure in the knowledge that you understood. That way I would know you'd never divulge Matt's existence."

"I told you I wouldn't." She traced her finger along the worry line on his brow. "Whether it's me or who it is, try to take people at face value. Don't be so wary of their motives. Wariness makes these little tiny lines up here turn into caverns. You'll look like an old man before your time."

He laughed, his expression smoothing to one of amusement. "My face has never been one of my great concerns."

"Well, it concerns me. So take care of it."

He tapped the end of her nose lightly. "Everything concerns you. You've got to be the world's champion crusader."

"Okay," Matt called, "here I come, ready or not."

Janet turned to see the boy carrying in a tray with three wine glasses full of ginger ale, slices of cheese carved into heart-shaped pieces, corn chips, and Oreo cookies on a party tray and a huge half-used candle burning in the center of it all.

"This must be the rest of the FIESTA package your Dad spoke about. Nice touch," she added, pointing to the Santa Claus napkins.

Matt grinned sheepishly. "Those were the only colorful ones I could find. In fact, it took me a long time to find all this stuff. The plate and glasses were way back in a cabinet we never use. Oh, yeah, Dad, I found some more of these." He held up a pack of cigarettes, then tossed them in the fire.

Pat glared at his son and Janet quickly spoke before he had time to do anything rash. "I think everything looks perfect." She popped a corn chip into Pat's gaping mouth. "Delicious, huh?"

Matt ordered them to stay seated on the couch while he handed them each a glass of *champagne*, as he called it, and they all three clinked a toast to the new baby..."our Patty." He then filled their glasses back up and ordered, "Now, you two wrap your arms together and take a sip."

"Like this?" Janet tried to get her small arm around Pat's muscled one. "Come on, Pat, give me some help. You've probably seen this a million times in your old Humphrey Bogart movies."

"I like old movies. Don't be making fun of them." He intertwined his arm with hers and gazed romantically into her eyes. "I think I'm supposed to say something like, *Play it again, Sam.*"

"What a sweet-talker you are, cowboy." She took a cautious sip of soda. Her mouth could hardly reach her glass when Pat bent his arm to take a sip from his glass. They all three began to laugh at their own silliness, exchanging light-hearted banter and thoroughly enjoying the next hour or so.

Finally, after everyone was laughed out, Matt nestled in close to Janet with Carlyle squeezed between them. Matt yawned and laid his head on her shoulder. "I'm glad to know you, Janet Raye."

"The feeling's mutual, Matthew Mayhew."

Carlyle raised his head and meowed loudly.

"Carlyle says he's glad to know you, too."

Janet turned to Pat and whispered, "Carlyle likes me and I've been told by a very reliable source that he's a very good judge of character."

Pat smiled down at her. "That cat's never been quite right."

"That make us even. Neither have I."

Pat threw his head back and guffawed. "So I've noticed."

"I notice something else." She nodded toward the sleepy boy on her right.

"Yeah, better get Ace here to bed. This has been a pretty late night for him, but since it was a special occasion and your last..."

"Don't remind me." She didn't want to even think about it.

"Come on, son. Time to go to bed."

The boy rose slowly and started toward his room, then turned back and hung his head. "Janet, you can...well, you can kiss me goodnight if you want to."

She had to choke back a sob. "Oh, Matt, I can't think of anything I'd rather do. Thank you." She kissed his forehead and each cheek. "Goodnight, sweetie."

He returned a kiss on her cheek. "You can call me *punkin*."

She smiled through her tears. "Goodnight, Punkin."

CHAPTER SIXTEEN

It took her several minutes to regain her composure. The short time she had known Matt might as well have been a lifetime. The boy had made an indelible mark on her heart. She couldn't think more of him if he were her own child. She watched the fire flicker for a long time before she finally spoke.

"Patrick?"

"Hmmm?"

"Are you sure I only just met you. Were you and Matt ever in another life with me?"

He chuckled softly. "I doubt it. I think I would have remembered you."

She rolled her head toward him. "I wish we were in another life together now. It's going to be hard to get Matt out of my system, let alone his dad."

He pulled her to him in an act of sheer possessiveness. She could feel his heart pounding in his chest. "Janet..."

"Wait, Pat. I need to say this right up front. I can't make love to you. I can't trust my emotions. I'd end up saying all sorts of mushy things. I'd make a complete idiot of myself, but most importantly, I couldn't live with the shame that I made love with a man that wasn't going to be in my life forever. I'm sorry, but that's the way it is with me. It sounds prudish, I know, after all the *necking* I've done with you, but necking and making love are entirely different. I'm falling in love and I know it would be the most magnificent thing for you to make love to me, but for sure I could never just walk away without a struggle."

He leaned back against the couch, still holding her but not quite so aggressively. "I don't know about falling in love, but you're right about making love. It would be magnificent but it wouldn't work out. If I got close enough to you to make love, I'm afraid I'd lose what scruples I have left."

"You *are* close enough."

"No, we're a million miles apart."

She raised her head. "Boy, how things change. When you thought I had been sent here as an *offering* by your father, you were ready to take me up on it."

"That was a hundred years ago seems like."

"What about all that big talk about my not being the first woman who didn't like you...then changed her mind?"

He laughed, clearly embarrassed. "That's all it was...big talk. I think I heard that in an old Humphrey Bogart movie. It sounded so macho."

"You ARE macho."

"I am? Is that good or bad?"

"Mmmm." She studied his face. "On you it looks good."

"Thank you. I think."

She settled back in the crook of his arm and laid her head against his shoulder. She breathed in, savoring his manly smell and kissing his arm through his shirt.

"Are there other women? Never mind. You don't need to answer that. That's another one of those stupid questions that comes out of my mouth without thinking first. None of my business." She kissed his arm again.

"Well, there have been, yes." He waited a moment. "But not right at the present. There hasn't been for a while."

Since he didn't seem to mind answering her stupid questions, her curious nature took over. "Ever any serious?"

He sucked his breath in slowly. "I don't know...what do you mean by serious? Did I go to bed with them, or did I ask them to marry me?"

"Both."

"Yes and no. Yes, I went to bed with a few and no, I never wanted to marry."

The next question she thought about but asked it anyway. "Was Sharon one of them?"

There was a long pause. Longer than she would have liked.

"Yes." He became very quiet.

"I thought she was...maybe still is."

"Was." He looked down at her. "What is this? The third degree? Are you jealous or something?"

She pouted her lips and shrugged. "Maybe a little."

"Well, don't be." He squeezed her up close and rubbed her arm affectionately, then bowed his head to give her a long, leisurely kiss. "You taste good. Kind of like ginger ale and Oreo cookies."

"And you kiss good. To think I thought you were just an annoying cowboy."

"And now?"

"I think you're just an annoying cowboy."

He laughed.

"No, seriously, Pat. Beneath that stubborn exterior beats the heart of a sweet and tender, caring—"

"Oh, stop it. You'll ruin my reputation." His fingers traced a pattern on her neck and along her jawline. "You feel good for an—"

"If you say elf or little person, I'll break your face"

He laughed again. "I was just thinking if anyone saw us right now, they would think I was molesting a child."

She sat up and turned to him. "Yep. You *are* an annoying cowboy and I AM going to break your face."

"No, you won't."

"Yes, I wi—"

Her words were stopped by his lips on hers. His mouth toyed and sipped its pleasure without resistance, her hands clutched the front of his shirt.

"Come closer." He pulled her onto his lap. She scooted into a comfortable position causing an ardent gasp to escape his lips. "You scoot real nice, lady." His hand skimmed over her hip to her waist and started upward to the curve of her breast.

She grabbed hold of his hand to stop him. "Let's not start something we're not going to finish."

His hand returned to her waist.

She pulled back, trying to muster up some sensibility. "We really should get some sleep." She allowed herself one last nibble at his lips.

"I agree." He sounded just as sensible but his tongue ran along the perimeter of her open mouth as he spoke. "I don't want to let you go right now. Do you understand that?"

"No."

"I don't either."

"Maybe you're getting soft."

"Hmmm, I don't think so. I'm punch-drunk on ginger ale." He pulled her close to him again and pressed his lips to hers while his hands caressed her shoulders, her back and around her waist.

She surrendered completely to his expert seduction, pulling him closer. She moaned aloud with erotic pleasure as he breathed hot, moist kisses on her sensitive neck. Waves of ecstasy throbbed through her very soul as his lips teased a warm love path over her throat to her mouth. He shifted her weight and stretched his length out beside her, taking her hand and kissing the palm. Love flowed in her like warm honey as her passion nearly exploded.

"Patrick, please." Her body squirmed beside his as she cried out for some compassion. If she were honest with herself, she wanted him over her, under her, around her...she could never get enough of him.

Throwing caution to the wind, she started her own exploration. Her hands travelled over his face, down his chest and around his waist and back to his neck. The real world was spinning, ricocheting off a thousand other planets in a starburst sky. The feel of him heightened her own passion and her body melted to his touch and had he asked her for the world at that moment, she would have gladly given it to him on a silver platter. But he didn't ask. He wanted nothing from her but her hands on his body.

"I love your touch, Janet. So innocent, so soft. Your fingers are like a million feathers fluttering over my skin."

She gasped in ardent agony when his hand slid torturously over her stomach and down her thigh. She loved the excitement and thrill of the moment and fantasized an even greater ecstasy as passion crept through her veins. But fantasy is all it could be.

"Patrick?"

"I know. This can't go on, but for the life of me, I can't stop." He gave her one more mind-drugging kiss, his mouth opening fully over hers, her body engulfed completely in his embrace. "You make me feel like I've never been touched by a woman...like I've never known the feel of a woman's lips, her skin. The taste of you, the smell of you. It's like you were created for me alone. It's crazy."

"No, it's not. I feel it too. I feel that way about you."

"That's the magic of it, but too bad there's a reality too. This feeling is wonderful, but maddening. Happy but sad."

She heard a sob escape her throat. "But I want you so badly."

"I know. Oh, mercy, how I know." He held her tight.

"And I want you with every inch of my body."

"Then why?"

"Can you leave it all behind you?"

Her body fell limp. "I want to say yes so you'll make love to me tonight, but I have to be honest with you. No, I can't. When I remember I can't have you...really have you...everything turns black. My world stops and I can't see beyond despair." Her eyes misted as she gazed longingly into his. "I can't live like that all my life. Making love to you under those circumstances would only imprison me. I don't even know if it will be possible to forget you now, but so far I've only loved you in my mind. If we gave our bodies to each other..." She moaned helplessly, aching from unfulfilled passion.

He pulled himself up and leaned over her before getting off the couch. "I'm sorry, Janet. You'll never know how sorry I am." His gaze dropped to her mouth. "I want to kiss you again so badly I can taste it. I feel like someone has played a cruel, cheap trick on me sending you here, letting me know the wonder of you, the warmth of you, the innocence, then just snatch you away."

If he weren't so stubborn, Janet thought. They could have it all. They could seek out the pleasures of each other, get to know everything there was to know, but there was no use belaboring the point. He would never see things her way, nor would she see things his.

"I guess this *fate* of Matt's isn't always what it's cracked up to be." There was a note of sadness in her voice.

He rose to a sitting position and pulled her up with him. "Whew! My body feels like it's been run over by my Jeep. I probably don't have to tell you, but I've got an ache...where it hurts...like I've never felt before."

Her face reddened. "I know. I would have to be paralyzed not to be aware of your...ache. I'm sorry. I know that can be rather difficult for a man."

"Difficult? Funny choice of words. More like

excruciating."

"I said I was sorry."

"Don't be. At least I know that part of my body is not dead."

She raised an eyebrow. "You mean there was ever a question?"

"It's been a long, long time. My life has been devoted to making sure Matt has a good life and trying to be the best father I can be. I've not had much desire for...well, for passion."

"Well, rest assured you have done a fine job with Matt. He's the most enjoyable, smart, amusing..."

"Okay, okay, now you're giving me the big head. Let's get our mind on something else. Are you sleepy?"

She shook her head. She couldn't sleep. Not after this. "Are you?"

"No. I need to unwind."

She looked at her watch. "How about a cup of coffee. I'll fix it."

"Sounds good."

It was no task to fix a couple mugs of instant coffee and she was back with them in a matter of minutes.

"I'll be leaving in a few hours."

"I know."

"Will you forget me?"

"Probably." He grinned.

"Creep."

He took a sip. "Maybe *Perfect Knees* will call."

"Maybe. Jealous?"

"Humph!"

"You ARE jealous. Good, that's what I was going for."

"I am not jealous. I'm worried. Worried that you won't have sense enough to kick him in the crotch!'

She nearly choked on her coffee. "Well, Patrick! How gross!"

"Well, you'd likely let anybody take advantage of

you."

"Even you?" She peered at him over her cup.

"We're not talking about me!"

She took another sip, slurping loudly on purpose. "Does Sharon have perfect...knees?"

A grin twitched at the corner of his mouth. "Sculpted by the Gods!"

"Who asked you?" Her eyes followed the coffee cup as she lowered it to her lap. "I don't think I want to talk anymore."

Without a word, he sat his cup on the coffee table, rose and turned on the radio sitting on the corner table. She kept her eyes deliberately glued to her coffee as the sound of a good old boy singing a song about not letting your babies grow up to be cowboys floated to her ears.

Pat walked back to stand just in front of her. She felt, more than saw, his unnerving presence. She mindlessly fidgeted with her cup, swirling the coffee round and round, nearly sloshing it over the rim.

He took her cup and sat it on the table. His voice was low and soft. "I seem to recall a certain young lady promising to go dancing with me. I hope you like oldies but goodies country. It's my favorite station."

She rose and her body flowed effortlessly into his arms and began to sway to the beat. The familiar warmth and smell of him permeated every inch of her being as she wrapped both arms around his middle and laid her cheek against his chest, wanting to get as close to him as humanly possible.

He held her to him, locking her in place with his powerful hands.

Sleep would be a stranger to them. They danced 'til dawn to the country music, the local news and weather...even to static when the station went off the air. It made no difference to the only two people in the world. Everything was just one long, beautiful love song.

*****

"Wake up, Ruby!" Max shook her hard.

She raised her head. "It's still dark out. What's going on?"

"I've studied the map Zeb drew for us and there's only one way out and one way in to where the kid lives. I figure we'll sit at the bottom of the road out of sight and wait until they leave."

"What good's that going to do?"

"We'll follow them and wait for an opportunity to nab the kid."

"Why can't we just go up to their house? We've got a gun. What can they do?'

"Don't be stupid. His dad could have a gun, too. Do you think he's just going to let the boy come with us voluntarily?"

She yawned and rose from bed and went into the bathroom. Gagging and choking was all that Max could hear.

"You okay?"

"Do I sound okay? I'm hurting, you nut job."

"Well, you'll just have to hurt. You know we couldn't take a chance on you bringing any drugs on the plane. You're just going to have to tough it out until this is over. And don't call me a nut job. I'm just about one more sarcastic word out of your mouth from walking out on you and going back to California."

The bathroom door banged open. "You walk out on me and I'll track you down and when I find you, your precious *Mama* won't recognize you."

"To quote you, *Yada, yada, blah, blah, blah.*"

CHAPTER SEVENTEEN

In the early morning, Janet stepped out of her dream world and into her best alligator sandals and changed into her business suit. She pondered dazedly as she ran a comb through her hair. Was it two days or two decades she'd been here? She was taking home a lifetime of memories.

Her reflection stared back at her as her thoughts scampered wildly through her mind. She dabbed lipstick on the lips that tingled in remembrance of his kiss. She sprayed a scent of perfume on the neck his lips had touched. Her body heated recalling the smoldering passion he had shown. Oh, Patrick, she almost said out loud. Can I ever forget you? Can I ever forget Matt? Would her mind always burn with the memory of what might have been?

"Janet?" His voice was soft and low, but she jumped at the sound of it. She was so caught up in her emotions, she didn't hear him coming down the hall to the bathroom door.

"I'm dressed." She opened the door. "Do you have a bag I could put my new things in?"

He left as she neatly folded her jeans and blouse and sat her boots on top of them. She picked up the furry slippers Matt had given her and hugged them to her chest. Tears sprang close to overflowing just as Pat returned with a shopping bag.

He watched her clutching the slippers, a look of finality on her face. "I think he meant for you to keep those. That is, if you want them."

Choking back a sob, she could only nod as she stuffed her belongings into the bag.

"I'll make us some coffee," Pat offered. "You hungry?"

"Just coffee for now. Thanks."

He took her bag and sat it by the front door, then pulled the papers from the manila folder and briefly scanned the text of each page before picking up the pen and signing his name.

Pat handed the papers to her. "This really should be notarized, but Cal can take care of everything should there be any question."

She breathed a long sigh. "I hope this works."

"Why wouldn't it work? It gives you the authority you need."

"I'm not a Mayhew. There's something in the name that's magic to stockholders' ears."

"That's foolish."

"I agree, but tell them that, and, well, it doesn't matter. It's not your problem. It's mine."

"What?"

She hesitated a moment, then went on. "I sometimes have a hard time convincing people of my authority at the conference table." She smiled, "Being *short of leg* as you say."

He smiled back. "Just tell them to call me if they want to know just how tough you are."

She looked at him seriously. "Am I, Patrick? Tough, that is?"

"The toughest I've ever run up against."

"Then why haven't I won the fight?"

"Are we fighting?"

"You are...you're fighting me. I don't want to just walk away and pretend I never met you. Pretend I never knew Matt."

"Janet, please, we've been all through that a million times. You'll forget."

"Will not."

"You will, Janet. You're being impetuous. You're letting your feelings run away with themselves."

"That's because I only have a little while left. I don't have a lifetime to cultivate a relationship with you." She looked at her watch. "I have exactly four hours and thirty-six minutes to convince you that you can't live without me."

He threw his head back and closed his eyes, chuckling softly. "Janet, what am I going to do with you? I swear you're worse than Matt. You just don't know when to give up."

"I warned you."

"I'll get the coffee made." He looked at his own watch. "You now have four hours and thirty-three minutes to convince me...less than that if you want to do it before the boys get up."

"I can do it...if you let me have my way."

"Ohhhhh, no. That ain't happen', lady."

"You're such a buzz kill."

They both sat down at the table and Pat put a couple of mugs in front of them. "I'm going to miss our kidding around."

"Me too." She then blurted out. "I don't want to leave!"

He dropped his shoulders. "And just how long do you think you would be able to stay?"

She sat silent for a moment, her eyes wandering everywhere except to his. "You're right. I can't stay. Staying would only prolong the agony."

He rose and poured them each a cup of coffee, then

took her hand and squeezed it affectionately. Did she for one minute think it was easy for him to let her go? But what right did he have to ask her to stay? Could he guarantee her the commitment she wanted...deserved? Could he ask her to give up everything she loved...to uproot herself just on the assumption that they might have a life together? And what if it didn't work out. He would have destroyed *her* life, HIS life and *Matt's* life. No, it was best this way.

"This was just something that was new and different to you, Janet." He wasn't even convincing himself, but continued. "There's always excitement in something you can't have. You'll forget about me before you land in St. Louis."

She stared at him sullenly. "I don't want to forget you. I want us to get to know each other."

"It's not possible."

"It might be. I happen to think it could be the greatest thing since the invention of sliced bread." She lowered her voice. "I don't know if these feelings I have for you is love, but if it isn't it sure should be. I'd hate to think I'm hurting this badly over something less."

"Janet...don't make it harder."

"I wish we'd made love. I wish we'd kissed more. I wish we'd done a thousand things together." Her eyes filled with tears. "We didn't have long enough."

"Dad?"

They both looked up and saw Matt and Josh standing in the kitchen doorway.

"Did you do something to make Janet cry?" Matt was scowling at his dad.

Before Pat could answer, Janet shook her head. "No, Matt, I took too big a swig of your Dad's coffee. That can certainly make your eyes water."

Matt and Josh both giggled. Matt walked over to Janet and hugged her and took her cup of coffee to the sink and poured it out. "I'll make us some hot chocolate."

Pat threw his hands up. "All right!! You win. I can't cook and now you think I can't even make coffee."

Josh chimed in. "You got that right. Dad says for someone so good at a lot things, you sure should just cut the kitchen off your house. It's no good to you."

"I know. Roger has told me a million times I need a wom—".

"Woman's touch," Matt finished.

*****

"Keep your eyes open, Ruby. Watch any cars that might come down this road with a man and kid in it. Do you remember what the Mayhew guy looks like?"

"I saw my sister's wedding picture but that was years ago and briefly at the hospital when my sister died, but I didn't hang around long that day. He didn't even see me. As soon as I saw him I left. I hated the Mayhews. Still do. I'd have my sister if it wasn't for them."

"Well, I don't think many live up this road so just keep an eye out."

"Do you at least have a cigarette you could let me smoke or are you off those too?"

"Yes, I threw them out."

"You're worthless." She laid her head back on the seat. "I've got a headache." Her shaky hand rubbed her forehead. "I guess you don't even have an aspirin."

"You're right. I don't."

"You're less than worthless. You're scum."

"Ruby, if you only knew how much better you'd feel without all that poison in your system..."

"Oh, Mr. Hoity Toity. Suddenly you know everything there is to know about me." She moaned and looked out the window. "Do you know how much I hate you at this moment?"

"I can imagine. I've been where you are, Ruby. Coming down is no picnic, but I'll tell you this. When this is over, you go your way, I'll go mine."

"Quit calling me Ruby. I'm Madge, Mr. Wilbur Brown. Madge Brown is going to be living high on the hog in Hawaii and everyone will be feeling so sorry for the widow Mrs. Brown having lost her husband Wilbur at sea off their yacht in the Bahamas." She turned her head toward him and snickered. "You would have loved the Bahamas had you lived long enough."

Max felt the gun in the left side of his belt to make sure she couldn't get her hands on it. "In a lot of ways, *Madge*, being dead is a lot better than living with you."

"Blah, blah, blah, Mama's boy!"

CHAPTER EIGHTEEN

After finishing breakfast, Pat, Janet and the boys piled into the Jeep and started down the hill toward church.

Matt leaned forward from the back seat. "I wish you could stay to see the airplane fly, Janet."

"Yeah, stay, Janet," Josh chimed in.

"She can't, boys. Now quit begging."

"I'm sure it will be spectacular," Janet assured them.

Matt slammed his body back on his seat and pouted. Josh poked him in the ribs. "Wonder if Patty remembers us?"

Matt finally grinned. "She'll remember me. Your ugly mug probably scared her."

"Take that back!"

They started wrestling and bouncing all around the back seat.

"Okay, you two, settle down. Why don't you sing a song or something?"

The kids sat upright and began singing, "A hundred bottles of beer on the wall. Hundred bottles of beer. If one of those bottles should happen to fall, there'd be ninety-nine bottle of beer on the wall."

Janet burst out laughing so hard tears ran down her cheeks.

Pat swatted the back of the seat. "That's not a very appropriate song to be singing on the way to Sunday School."

The boys cleared their throats and started, "A hundred bottles of milk on the wall."

Janet turned around. "Why don't we all sing Jesus Loves Me."

"We know that one." Matt started first and Josh came in on the second line with Janet harmonizing with them. Pat brought in a bass tone and by the time they finished, the boys wanted to sing it again.

"I think we're sung out, Son. Besides we're just about to the church."

"But Janet has a beautiful voice."

"She should. She sang professionally at one time."

"I knew it." Matt became really excited. "God brought us a singing star."

"Don't get carried away, Matt." Janet chuckled. "I'm not a singing star. I just like music."

"So do Dad and I. It's fate for sure."

Pat gave his son a dirty look and Janet put her finger to her lips to hush him.

They pulled into the church parking lot, Pat braked but left the motor running. "You boys go on in to your class. We'll meet up with you when you're finished."

"Where you going?"

"Nowhere. I just want to talk to Janet a few minutes."

"Okay. So you'll be here when we get out, Janet?"

She shook her head yes.

"I really wish you could stay long enough to play poker with us." Josh patted her hand.

"Good grief." Pat rolled his eyes. "I don't know who is contributing delinquency to who?"

"To whom." Janet smiled at him. "The correct grammar is to whom."

Pat glared at her. "I'm thinking it's *youm* who is the

delinquent."

Matt giggled and looked at Josh. "She knows stuff like that. I bet if she stayed long enough, I could get an A in English."

"You already get an A, you jerk."

"Maybe I could get an A plus."

Pat snapped his fingers. "Get out of the car."

They did as told and Janet watched the boys skip into the church building.

"They're such a treat to be with," she finally said.

"I'll agree. They're good boys...most of the time."

They sat in silence for a long time. Finally she lifted her eyes to look into his tormented face. "Can I call you?"

He studied her intently for a long moment, weighing her words critically. "No. I'd rather you didn't."

"Then, this is it?

"This is it."

"No, Patrick. You can't just turn your back on what's started between us."

"Nothing's started!"

She was silenced by his dark expression. A muscle quivered in his jaw just before he grasped her hand. His fingers were warm and strong and sent a rippling sensation coursing through her arm.

"You said you wished we had made love and done a thousand other things?" He hesitated. "Well, I have a confession to make. The *rat* in me almost did make love to you. The rat said, take her. What the heck. I'll never see her again."

"I wish the *rat* had won."

"No, you don't."

"Do too."

His smile brought an immediate response from her. She relaxed as her own smile widened across her face. "You're right, of course...as usual. I'm being very selfish. She sighed and traced her finger between his as they gripped his hand firmly. "As much as I would like for us to get to know each other better, I would never want you to leave this beautiful country...this life you've made for yourself and Matt."

"That's what I've been trying to tell *you*." His voice had a compassionate tone. "There's just no way. I would never want you to give up all you have in St. Louis, and I doubt if even the *rat* in me could just love you once and let you go."

"I know." She let her breath out noisily. "After I'm gone, try not to be so hard on Matt."

"Hard on Matt?"

"His poker playing is just fun stuff. He'd never be a delinquent."

"I know."

"I wasn't going to play poker with them. I promise I'd play Go Fish or something you'd approve of."

"I know."

"And give Doyne and Roger a hug from me."

"I will."

"And make the boys be careful with Patty."

"I will."

"And be the best *uncle* you can to her."

"Is there much more? If there is, I need to get a pencil and paper."

She giggled impishly. "Just one thing more."

"There always is *just one more thing* with you."

"If you just CAN'T get me off your mind, you'll call me?"

He opened his mouth to say something, but she interrupted.

"You said I couldn't call you...I didn't say you couldn't call me."

His expression was serious. "While we're on the subject of promises...promise me you won't take up with that Mark character should he call again."

"They say promises are made to be broken." She taunted him, smiling at his somber face.

"Forget about *they*. Just promise me."

"Why should you care? We're never going to see each other again."

"I don't know why," he blurted a little too loudly, then softening his voice. "I just care, dammit."

"Stop cursing or I'll tell Matt on you." She brushed at his knitted brow. "Oh, quit worrying. So far every time he's called since I hung up on him that time, it's just been a matter of, hello, how are you, I'm fine, how are you?"

"Why should he care how you are?"

"He probably doesn't. I think it just eases his conscience to see I survived our *affair*, if that's what it was."

"The guy needs his you-know-what cut off."

"Patrick!! You're horrible. I haven't always picked losers. I've dated some nice men since then."

"How nice?"

She eyed him. "You *are* jealous!"

"Good grief, no."

"Not even a little?"

His mouth twitched. "I just think you need a keeper. I don't know how you've made it to ALMOST twenty-eight."

"What about you? Have you been Tom Terrific in your love life?"

His face grew grim and she could have bitten her tongue off. She had done it again...opened her big mouth and stuck her foot in it. "I'm sorry, Patrick. I didn't think. I didn't mean to bring up memories of Sylvia. I was thinking of your present girlfriends." She dropped her eyes. "I'll be frank. I was thinking about Sharon."

He let go of her hand. "There is *no* girlfriend, as you put it, right now. As for Sharon...she's' a very special friend."

Janet leaned back in her seat. That is what she was afraid of...a very special friend.

He continued softly. "Sharon and I tried, but we didn't make it with each other. For either of us. For one thing, she's still in love with her late husband and he was one of my very best friends. She and I could never be more than friends...more like brother and sister."

"If there is no one else, then why can't I at least call you once in a while? Maybe someday we could—"

"No! Don't even think it. False hopes only complicate things more."

"Okay!" She was a little miffed. "Curl up with your cowboy hat for all I care. All I can say is, GOOD LUCK, BUCK!"

He grabbed hold of her shoulder and roughly, almost violently, pulled her to him. She could feel his muscles tense as his other arm circled her shoulder. She somehow managed to lift her head and face him, straining back against the door. She clamped her jaw tight and stared at him defiantly. By his strong hold on her, she expected to see anger in his face, but there was none. He gazed at her for many long seconds. His calmness was maddening as he memorized every inch of her face.

Finally she couldn't hold back any longer. "I've a confession to make. Don't be mad."

His brows raised. "What now?"

"I didn't cancel my flight for tomorrow, nor did I make a reservation for this afternoon. I want to stay one more day."

His head lowered slowly and there was a fleeting moment of uncontrollable joy that flooded her soul when she saw that he was going to kiss her.

"I take it you're not mad?"

"Shut up."

"Make me."

Their lips met firmly, locking in sweet agony. The

pleasure was pure and hungry. He pulled her so close she felt the two were one and she gloried in it, returning his kiss with all the love she possessed. His tongue traced the softness of her lips slowly and thoughtfully, sending shivers of desire racing through her.

When the kiss ended, she laid her head on his shoulder, her hand on his chest feeling his heartbeat. "I can't believe I've only been here a couple of days. It feels like a lifetime."

"I know," was all he could muster to say.

She let her breath out in a long sigh. "The way I see it, we have two choices...your way and the right way. Your way would be that I go back to St. Louis, resume my life like you and Matt never existed. You stay here, pine away for me, can't sleep, can't eat, become so grouchy no one wants to be around you, take up smoking again, develop a serious lung disorder, die and leave your young son orphaned. Assuming your father survives this heart attack, he being Matt's only living relative, Christopher takes him in but is too old to rear a young boy so I adopt Matt and as a single mother do my best to, as he says, *guide his little footsteps* toward becoming a man worthy of the Mayhew name."

Hearing no response, she continued. "OR my way would be I go back to St. Louis and take care of business and make sure Christopher knows we met and really, really liked each other which would no doubt help him get well. We can call, skype, text as well as visit each other on alternate weekends in order to really get to know we are meant for each other and then figure out how we can be together permanently." She glanced toward him. "Which choice do you think is best?"

"What'd you say? I kind of dozed off just as I was dying of cigarette smoke."

"I would make sure you had a decent burial."

"And what would be an indecent burial?"

"I could leave one hand sticking out of the ground holding a cigarette."

"Nice touch. You just never give up, do you?"

She smiled. "You heard every word. You just can't admit my choice is the one we should take." Before he could say anything, she went on. "Hey, if it doesn't work out, what have we lost? A few weeks of phone calls and plane trips. Big deal." She leaned her head back on the seat. It was a few moments before he spoke.

"I don't skype."

"Matt can show you how."

"I didn't say I didn't know how. I said I don't do it."

"Why?"

"Do you need an explanation for everything?"

"Yes."

"Most of my friends work with me. The last thing we would want to do is come home and stare at each other on our computers."

"That was before you met me. We'll skype."

"Stop talking."

"Make me."

Their lips met and he, indeed, stopped her from saying another word. A soft moan escaped her lips when the kiss ended and she lay her head against his shoulder and savored the moment.

*****

"Well, what do you know?" Max adjusted the binoculars and chuckled. "We thought he had three kids in the jeep with him. Looks like the girl kid is a woman."

Ruby came out of her stupor and stared bleary-eyed in the direction of the church's parking lot. She vaguely remembered following the jeep they saw coming down the road from the cabin.

"What are you talking about?"

"While you were sleeping off your hangover, I watched two boys enter the church while dear old dad necked with the one we thought was another kid. Sure not a kid. Good looker, too."

"Gimme that!" Ruby grabbed the binoculars and peered through them. "How dare her."

"Why you got your panties in a twist? What's it to you?"

"She can't have all that Mayhew money and live the life of luxury. She's living Sylvia's life. Sylvia was going to take care of me."

"You're being paranoid, Ruby. Your sister died years ago. Let it go."

She stared through the binoculars for a few more minutes. "That bitch. Wait'll I get my hands on that kid. Wonder just how much it's worth to them...a mil, maybe two, three?"

"You're being crazy again. Stick to the plan. Five hundred thousand, give the kid back and get on with your life."

"They're not going to get away with cheating me out of Sylvia's money."

"Ruby, I took you in for old times' sake to help you get clean. You don't want to get sober and I don't want to live a life with you. After this we're through. Where were you most of the night, coming in drunk or high, zonked out of your head? We can't pull this off with you acting stupid."

She tossed the binoculars in the floor of the car. "Don't you tell me how to act, sissy boy. I went out and found a little fun at the local bar. This guy took a liking to me and he offered me some Molly and we—"

"Spare me the details. You dropped Ecstasy? Are you completely out of your stupid mind?"

"You watch your tongue or I won't give you one red cent. Your mama can rot in that hell hole you live in while I'm enjoying life in a luxurious resort somewhere."

Max sucked his breath in sharply. "That hell hole has been your home for the past few months. You were living with any man who would have you for the night. You're sick, Ruby. You need more help than I can give you." He retrieved the binoculars from the floor and again watched the occupants in the green jeep while Ruby mumbled to herself about wiping everyone out after she gets the money.

"No one is going to be wiped out. No one is even going to be hurt in any way. You will let me do the talking."

"Blah, blah, blah." She yanked at her wig to put it in place and fell asleep against the window.

*****

Janet sat upright when she heard the boys laughing and skipping their way back to the jeep.

"How was Sunday School?"

Matt climbed into the back seat. "You guys didn't go?"

Pat started the jeep as Josh entered. "No, Janet and I had things to talk about. By the way, she's staying another day."

The boys both whooped and hollered, "Righteous!"

"Soooo," Janet said, "I can see if that plane you manufactured really can fly."

Through giggles and laughter they wound their way to the field alongside the church and got out to enjoy the boys' air show.

Matt hugged Janet around her waist. "I'm so glad you're staying. I was sad thinking about you leaving."

"I know. So was I." She hugged him back. "Now go fly that thing."

Matt started the motor and Josh took the remote control. The plane made several circles then swerved toward some trees quite a ways off.

"Josh, bring it back," Matt called.

"I'm trying. It won't turn."

Matt grabbed the remote and tried to no avail. The plane landed somewhere in the trees and the boys took off in a dead run to retrieve it.

"Hope it didn't wreck too badly." Janet had a pained look on her face.

"If it did, I'm sure the boys can put it back together. Are you cold?"

"A little."

"Come here." He put his arm around her shoulders. "Better."

She smiled up at him. "Much."

CHAPTER NINETEEN

$\mathcal{M}$ax brought the car to a slow stop just past the row of trees and watched two boys tramping through the brush to find their plane. He poked Ruby in the shoulder.

"Wha...what!"

"Shhhh. Time's come. Both kids are in the woods. We don't know which one is which."

They both got out of the car and stood at the edge of the thicket listening to the boys thrashing around. As luck would have it Max spotted the plane in a nearby tree on one of the lower branches.

"Hey guys, you lookin' for a toy plane?"

Josh and Matt hurried toward the sound of the man's voice. "Yes. Did you find it?"

"I'm looking at it right now."

They came through to the clearing and Max pointed up in the tree. He didn't want to miss their chance on nabbing the right boy so the only thing he could think of was, "You look familiar. Are one of you the Mayhew boy?"

"Me," Matt volunteered. "You know my dad or something?"

"Or something." Max pulled the gun out of his coat pocket. "Get over here." He motioned to Matt, then pointed the gun toward Josh. "You stay where you are until we're long gone. Do as I say and no one will get hurt."

Ruby opened the trunk and ordered Matt to get in.

Max shook his head. "He don't have to ride in the trunk. Let him lay in the back seat."

"And have him know where we drive to. Who's stupid now?" She grabbed Matt by the collar and jammed him into the trunk.

Max frowned but went along with her. "If they look for us it would be at the motel. I've got a remote place staked out where no one will find us."

"How'd you know about it? How dare you make plans without me!" Ruby's voice was becoming slurred and more agitated.

"While you were out having your *fun* I was getting things settled in order to get the job done."

She spit in Max's face then turned toward Josh, yelling, "You tell them we want five hundred thousand dollars. We'll be in touch and tell them where to bring the money. They'd better make it snappy or the price goes up and I don't know how long the brat will last in the trunk. *and* no police, you understand?"

Josh had big tears in his eyes. "Don't hurt him. He's my best friend in the whole world."

"Quit sniveling you little creep and do as I said." Ruby slammed the lid down on the trunk. "Do you understand?"

Josh shook his head and repeated, "Stay until you're long gone, five hundred thousand, no police."

Max nodded and wiped the spit off his face with his sleeve. "Good boy," adding sympathetically, "Don't be scared. It'll all be okay."

"Yeah, yada, yada, yada. Get in the car, Mama's boy."

*****

"Where the heck are those kids?" Pat held his hand over his eyes to shield the sunlight. "They've been gone too long?"

"Call out to them. Maybe they'll hear you."

"I'll do that but I'd better try to find them. They may be having trouble finding the plane and knowing them, they won't give up. I'll give them a hand." He looked down at her feet standing in her high heels. "You wait here. I don't think you'd get very far in those shoes."

She smiled. "Be careful."

He took off in a fast pace calling out, "Matt! Josh! I'm coming to help. Yell out so I'll know where you are." His heart began to beat faster when there was no answer.

He tore his way through the thick brush and finally found Josh squatted down with his head in his hands, sobbing. He saw the plane stuck in the crook of a branch and retrieved it.

"No need to be upset, Josh. The plane's not totaled. I'm sure you guys can put it back together." He touched the boy on the shoulder. "Where's Matt?"

Josh raised his head, his eyes red from crying. "They had a gun, Buck. They had a gun. They put him in the trunk. I begged them not to hurt him. The man said no one would be hurt, but I don't trust the woman. She looked crazy."

"Who. What man? What woman? What are you talking about?"

"They took Matt. They said they wanted five hundred thousand dollars and would contact you to tell you where to deliver it. They told me to stay here until they were gone and they said no police." Josh sobbed again. "I'm so sorry, Buck, but they had a gun. I was afraid to not do as they said."

Pat took Josh into his arms. "You did fine. There was nothing you could do." He had to stay calm while his insides were being torn apart. *This can't be happening!* Suddenly he felt he was choking on his heart and swallowed hard. "Did you see what kind of car they had?"

"It was black. A Ford, I think. It all happened kind of quick."

"What did they look like?"

"They looked funny. Like they had a disguise on. The crazy woman kept pulling on her hair and it moved back and forth. I think it was a wig. The man had a big mustache that was a little crooked and hung down too far on one side. Probably fake."

"Come on, let's go. They said no police, but they didn't say no Rangers. I'll radio them for help. I'll drop you off at the hospital so you can stay with your dad. We'll leave the plane at the cabin for when Matt gets home."

"You will get him home, won't you Buck?"

"You bet'cha!" He was boiling but didn't want Josh to know just how worried and angry he was. *Who in the world even knew of Matt's existence!? Janet? It can't be. She loves Matt, I know that for sure. God, please keep my boy safe.*

"I heard the man say they were not going back to the motel. He had a remote place they were going to take Matt."

"Good boy, Josh. That's a big help. Remember anything else?"

"Only that the man was nice and told me everything would be okay but the crazy woman shoved Matt into the trunk and said if she didn't get the money right away, she didn't know how long Matt could last in the trunk. She called him a brat. I hope the man was right and everything will be okay."

"Everything WILL be." *Everything has GOT to be!*

When they came in sight of Janet standing in wait, Josh took off in a dead run and hugged her around her waist. "Matt was kidnapped. They had a gun. I couldn't stop them."

She squeezed the boy close. "What are you saying?" She then saw the distraught look on Pat's face. "What?"

"A man and woman took Matt at gun point." Pat stared at her.

"You don't think I had anything—"

"No, of course not. It's just that they want five hundred thousand dollars. I don't have that much money."

"Yes, you do."

"I'm not getting my father involved in this."

"It's your money. You remember when you refused the profit sharing checks. Well, Cal put your part into an escrow account in case you ever needed it."

He could only shake his head. "I'll get the money on my own."

"This is Sunday. What bank will lend you the money on Sunday? If you won't contact Cal for help, I will."

"You?"

"Yes. Remember you gave me power of attorney. I have the signed papers. I'm going to get the money and I'm going to get Matt back." Her voice cracked and she began to sob. "I've grown to love him, too, Pat."

Pat came to her and put his arms around both her and Josh. "I know, Janet. I'm sorry I was short with you. I'm just going crazy trying to think who even knew Matt existed."

"Well, no one in St. Louis knew, I can assure you of that."

They all walked back to the Jeep and climbed in. Janet put her hand on Pat's shoulder. "The only other person who knew of Matt other than you died giving him birth."

As they drove toward the hospital to drop Josh off, Pat sucked in his breath. "Sylvia." He pondered a moment. "She had a sister. She sent her money all the time. But how would she know where we lived? And why after all these years..."

"I know it's a long shot, but it's all we got right now to go on. Do you remember her name?"

"I'll think of it. I'm a little rattled right now. I need to contact the Ranger station for their help looking for a black Ford in a remote location. If they locate them, they need to stay their distance until after we hear from them. They have a gun and I don't want them to use it on anyone trying to rescue Matt. I want Matt safely in my arms before we try to apprehend the kidnappers."

"I'll call Cal at his home to alert him to wire the money to your account first thing in the morning. We'll get the cash, put it in a suitcase and as soon as we hear from the culprits, we'll get them the money. Now, give me one of your checks so I can give Cal the account number."

Pat knew it by heart and gave it to her while she wrote it on the palm of her hand with her ballpoint, then dialed Cal's number on her cell.

He answered on the first ring. "Janet? Are you okay?

"I'm fine, Cal. How's Christopher?"

"Same. Fortunately no worse."

"That's good I guess." She took a deep breath. "Cal, this is a don't ask, don't tell situation but I need your help. I need you to wire five hundred thousand dollars out of Patrick's escrow account to his bank account here. I can only tell you it is a dire circumstance and we need it first thing in the morning. If you need my signature on anything, I have the power of attorney from Patrick. I can fax you anything you need." She gave him the account number and had him repeat it to make sure there was no mistake.

"I trust you to know what you're doing, Janet. I'll take care of it. I just hope you're not in any danger. You sound a little frantic."

"I'm fine, Patrick's fine. No need to worry." She tried to sound calmer.

"When will you be back?"

"Tomorrow or the next. Call me on my cell if there's any change in Christopher's condition or if you need any further assistance from me on getting the money here in the morning."

"Will do. See you soon."

She said her goodbyes, slowly put her phone back in her purse and turned to Patrick. "Done." She then promptly broke down in tears from the strain. Patrick put his arm around her and silently shed a few tears himself while Josh put his hands over his face and sobbed loudly.

*****

Ruby coughed and fanned the dust away from her face. "Where'd you find this stink hole?"

"It's the best I could do under the circumstances. We needed a remote place that didn't cost much money."

"They should pay us to stay here."

"It's only for one night. You can surely last that long."

She sat on the bed and bounced a couple of times. "Not too bad for a dump."

"I'm going out and let the kid out of the trunk. Put your wig back on."

"Leave him there."

"I'm not leaving him there. It's cold."

"I said LEAVE HIM THERE!!! I'm not wearing that dorky wig anymore."

"You'll have to when you pick up the money. Patrick might recognize you from family pictures of something."

"Yeah, he might, but I'll have that tramp he's taken up with deliver the money. I know she doesn't know me and besides I want to let her have it face to face."

"Let her have what? You're going off the deep end again, Ruby. Shape up."

"You shut your mouth. You don't tell me what to say or do."

"Okay." He took off the scarf he had around his neck. "I'll blindfold the boy so he can't see us, but I'm getting him out of that trunk. I've got some snacks I bought at the convenient store this morning. I'll bring them in. We can eat and he can give us his dad's phone number to let him know where to bring the money.

"Where the *tramp* can bring the money."

"Whoever. I can't wait to get this over with and away from you."

"Ohhhhh, missing Mama? You're pathetic!"

"Pathetic would be a compliment to you."

"Yeah, blah, blah, blah."

CHAPTER TWENTY

At the hospital, Pat filled Roger in on the happenings. They agreed not to tell Doyne. She had a lot on her plate to get well enough to go home with the baby.

"I'll handle all the arrangements with the Rangers, Pat." Roger hugged Josh tightly. "I'm taking Josh to Vernon's. I'll call the school in the morning to excuse Josh and Matt from school."

"Josh said they were taking him to a remote place, not back to their motel. So I take it they did stay in to a motel recently."

"I'll have the guys scout out every motel for a couple who checked in recently and come up with a name. You go home and wait for my call and their call. Let me know when you hear from them...day or night, let me know."

"I will. Thanks, Pal." The two men embraced and Pat and Janet left, still in a daze and both trembling.

During the ride to the cabin, they remained relatively silent except for Pat apologizing. "I'm so sorry you're being put through this nightmare, Janet."

"No, don't be sorry. I want to do anything I can to help."

"You have already. You really take the horse by the reins so to speak. Getting the money. You're something else."

"Yeah," she whispered, "whatever *else* is."

"I *will* pay back the money."

"I didn't expect anything less from you. I know how you feel, but we needed the money now."

"I know and I do appreciate what you did."

Back at the cabin Janet made them coffee and they sat together on the couch staring at the blaze in the fireplace Pat had started.

"This waiting is excruciating!" Pat ran his fingers through his hair.

Janet patted him on the arm. "Try to relax. Everything is being done that can be done at this time."

"Why aren't they calling?" His voice was thick with worry. "I can't stand to think of my boy stuffed in a trunk of a car."

"He's in God's hands. He'll be fine. Let's spend this time praying out loud or silently. God hears us."

Pat nodded. "God in heaven, please watch over my precious child. He certainly does not deserve to be harmed. I'll gladly pay the money to have him back. His life is worth much more than mere money."

Janet added, "One more thing, God."

"You always have one more thing." Pat smiled.

"This is also important. God, let your grace shine on these two unfortunate soles who stole this sweet boy and let them see their unrighteous ways. Let the boy go unharmed and back in the arms of his loving father. We ask this in the name of your precious son, Jesus. Amen."

*****

Darkness set in and still no call. Patrick had paced every inch of the cabin and Janet had finally convinced him to sit down and try to relax. Carlyle was even meowing loudly and running to every room obviously sensing something amiss. Finally, he jumped into Janet's lap. There was no purring like he usually did, just sort of a whimpering mewing. She had filled his water and food dishes but Carlyle had refused them.

"I'm going to walk Carlyle outside for a few minutes. Maybe he'll calm down."

"He has a litter box but he does like it outside. Don't be long. We don't know who might be outside watching."

"I'll be careful and not far from the door."

She had just re-entered the cabin when the phone rang. They both jumped at the sound. It was Roger.

"Does the names Wilbur and Madge Brown ring a bell?"

"No."

"I didn't think it would. They supposedly came in from California but we ran a check on them and it seems they died in a head-on collision three years ago. We have to presume these people are the ones who kidnapped Matt and they have assumed another identity. Any clue?"

"California, you say?"

"That's the address they had on the register at the motel."

"That's where Sylvia was from and she had a sister there. Ruby!" He looked toward Janet. "I just thought of her name. It is Ruby Lewis. Lewis was Sylvia's maiden name. Ruby may have a different last name by now if she married but that can be checked out if necessary. It's *got* to be her. She would be the only person who knew Sylvia gave birth to a son."

"Josh said she was nuts."

"I never knew her but evidently she has used up all of Sylvia's money and is looking for more. Sylvia had quite a huge bank account thanks to me as well as my father."

"We'll check it out. Hang in there, Buddy. Let me know when you hear from the idiots."

"Thanks. I will."

Janet took his hand and kissed the back of it. "Want me to make more coffee?"

"No, I'm fine." He sat quietly for a few moments. "I can't believe if it *is* Ruby that she would harm her own nephew."

"Let's pray she won't."

"But they said she was crazy. Probably a druggie."

"Josh said the man was nice."

"That's all I can think about and hope he can win out over the woman."

When the phone rang again, Pat noted on the caller I.D. that it was Matt's cell number. "Matt?"

"Dad, I'm okay. The man let me call you to let you know that. The crazy woman took the car keys and left. She said she was going to find someone who would have something to make her *feel good.* I think she wants some dope."

"I've been going out of my mind. I love you, son. Are you sure you'll be safe?"

"As long as the man's in charge. He made sure I got something to eat and even let me play a card game on his computer after the woman left."

"Can I talk to him?"

"No. He just wanted you to know I was okay. The woman will call you when she gets back and don't let her know the man let me call you. She gets really, really mad at him for everything. I've got to hang up now, Dad, but if Janet is still there I need to talk to her for a minute." Pat handed the phone to Janet.

"Sweetie? Are you hurt?"

"No, I'm okay. The man says as soon as they get the money, I'll be let go. I'm so glad you're with my Dad."

"I am too."

"I know he's worried to death. He's like that, but please don't let him smoke."

Janet had to laugh at that. "Oh, don't worry. That will

be the last thing I would let him do. Rest assured."

"Thanks."

"One more thing." She heard Pat snicker. "Tell those people we have the money lined up for in the morning as soon as the bank opens. We'll have you home soon. I love you, sweet baby."

"I love you, too. Got to go before the crazy lady gets back."

Janet held the phone to her heart for a few moments. "He's such a brave boy. Makes me feel like a sissy."

"You? A sissy? Hardly."

"He asked me to not let you smoke."

"Oh, brother. You and Matt are definitely two peas in a pod."

"I know. I love that."

Knowing Matt was okay for the time being made it a lot easier to relax for a few minutes.

"I'll call Roger and let him know I heard from Matt and see if he has found out anything else about the abductors."

"While you talk to Roger, I'm going to change into my cowgirl boots and jeans. As soon as morning comes, I'll be ready to go with you to deliver the money."

"I don't want you in harm's way."

"I'm going."

He knew better than to argue with her so he hurriedly dialed Roger. "I heard from Matt. The guy let him call me to tell me he was okay. What have you learned?"

"I'm pretty sure it might be Ruby. I checked her out. She has never married and has been in and out of jail on drug charges and being a public nuisance while she was high several times. In other words, a real loser. No known address, however, but all this has taken place in southern California."

"Sounds like it is definitely her. I'm still waiting to hear from them as to where to bring the money. I'll call you immediately. I guess you've not found where they are staying tonight?"

"Not yet. We're still searching."

"Matt said she had left to find drugs or something. You might check some of the taverns for a woman trying to hook up with someone."

"Will do. Later, buddy."

Pat turned to Janet as she walked back into the room. "Pretty sure it's Ruby. They've taken the identity of some people who died in a crash a few years ago."

"Nothing to do but wait some more. I'm sure they will be calling soon after Matt tells them we have the money."

Sleep would evade them and they both agreed that it was the longest night of their lives but about seven in the morning the phone rang. It was Matt's number on the caller I.D. but Pat suspected it might not be Matt.

"Hello. Patrick Mayhew here."

He heard a raspy woman's voice say, "You got the money?"

"I will as soon as the bank opens."

"Not a minute later. You hear me?"

"Yes. Where shall I bring it?"

"You won't. I want that tramp you're living with to bring it."

"I'm not living with anyone."

"You think I'm stupid? Put her on the phone."

"I tell you, I don't live—"

"You want to see your son again? Put her on the phone."

He handed the phone to Janet. "I think she wants to speak to you."

"Me?" Janet was puzzled but took the phone and put it on speaker so Pat could hear the conversation. "Hello. You wanted to talk to me?"

"You bring the money...alone. Any funny business and I'm not responsible for what might happen to the brat."

"Of course. I'll do anything you ask, but why me? I don't have anything to do with..."

"You don't ask questions. Just do as I say. *You* bring the money."

"Okay, okay. Where do you want me to deliver it?"

"You know the open field by the church where the kids were flying their plane? It's wide open and I'll see if anyone comes with you."

"Patrick will have to get the money out of his account. I can't."

"Okay. He brings you and the money but stays out of sight. Understand?"

"Yes, I understand."

"If I see an inkling of a car or person near you, the deal's off. We'll hightail it out of there *with the kid*. You can kiss him goodbye for good."

"I'll be alone."

"The bank opens at nine. I'll expect you in the middle of the field with the cash no later than nine thirty."

"Right." She hung up the phone and turned to Patrick. "I guess I'll be delivering the money."

"I can't let you do that."

"You have to. You heard her. I don't know why any more than you do, but she was adamant I bring it alone."

"I'll stay out of sight but I'll be near. If anything happens to you—"

"It won't."

Pat called Roger and told him the plan. "We don't know why they want Janet to deliver the money, but she insists to do what they want for Matt's sake."

"Janet is one brave lady. Can't believe you're not going to pursue a relationship with her. You're dumb to let her go."

"Mind your own business. Just make sure everyone stays out of sight until Matt and Janet are safe."

"The guys are ready and set. We'll wait until the coast

A Woman's Touch

is clear before we nab the idiots. I tell you I'm looking forward to seeing them behind bars right after I punch them in the face."

Pat laughed. "Now who's dumb? They are not worth hurting your hand over and don't do something to get sued over when they go to court and plead brutality."

"You watch too many Law and Orders."

"I know you'll do what's right, Pal. Tell all the guys how much I appreciate their help."

"Will do. By the way, we checked out some taverns and she might have been at one. The bartender said there was a woman there who was obnoxious and flirty but left with some loser before we got there."

"Well, we know where they will be at nine thirty this morning."

"Right. We've got your back. Take care."

"You too."

CHAPTER TWENTY ONE

*P*at and Janet were sitting in front of the bank when it opened and walked in with a huge duffle bag. It didn't take long for the bank teller to fill the bag with the cash.

"This is so unusual." The teller spoke in hushed tones. "I hope you know what you're doing? We could issue a cashier's check."

"No, we need cash. I know it's odd." Pat tried to stay calm.

They left and drove to the field where Pat parked behind the church. Janet got out and had to drag the bag behind her. It was too heavy to carry.

Pat gave her a quick hug and kiss. "Be careful. I'm going to see if the church is open. It usually is so people can go in to pray anytime they need. I'll go in there and watch out the window. I'll make sure they don't see me."

Janet lugged the bag through the grassy field and stood waiting trembling with uneasiness. She put on a brave face for Patrick but her insides were churning. Finally she saw a black car careen around the curve of the road and up the hill toward the middle of the field where she was standing.

A man with the fake mustache and woman with a horrendous wig stepped out of the car. The man held a gun but it was pointed toward the ground.

The woman screeched, "Bring me the money."

"Show me that the boy is okay and we'll make the exchange."

"You're not running the show here. I am. I want to see the money first."

Max stepped behind the car and opened the trunk and let Matt out. "See, the boy's fine."

"You idiot! I told you I wanted to see the money before you let him out."

Max patted Matt on the shoulder. "Tell the lady you're okay."

"I'm okay, Janet. Give her the money."

"Shut up!!! Everyone just shut up! I'll give the orders. I'm sick of everyone telling me what is going to happen."

"Calm down *Madge*. Let's get this over with."

"Over with? It ain't over with 'til I say so." She turned her attention back to Janet. "You bitch! You think you can live a life of luxury on the Mayhew money?"

"Keep your mouth shut, *Madge*. You're here to get the money and give the boy back. Get on with it." He guided Matt toward Janet and actually walked him halfway there as Janet dragged the bag of cash to meet him.

As soon as she had Matt in her arms, she turned to run back to safety but the woman called out, "Stop! Not so fast you low-life tramp."

When Janet turned around, she saw the woman had grabbed the gun out of the man's hand and was screaming at the top of her lungs. "If it wasn't for that snot-nosed kid killing my sister I would be sharing in all that money. You, bitch, would be slinging burgers at McDonalds instead of playing suck-face with Mayhew in his Jeep. Don't deny it. I saw you yesterday in the church parking lot."

"You and dad were kissing?" Matt whispered.

"We'll talk about that later."

"Righteous!"

When Ruby raised the gun toward them, Janet pushed

Matt down to the ground and fell on top to protect him and called out loud and clear a passage from the twenty-third Psalm. "Yea, though I walk through the valley of the shadow of death, I will fear no evil; for thou art with me."

Matt chimed in. "Thy rod and thy staff they comfort me."

Janet heard one click. *Miss fire?* Then another click and another. She peeked back at the woman and heard her rant at the man.

"You gave me a gun without bullets. You imbecile!!!"

"I told you no one was going to get hurt. That was the only way I could assure you wouldn't do something stupid."

She threw the gun back at him and he caught it in midair. "I already did do something stupid. I asked you to help me." She yanked the bag of money to the driver's side of the car, threw the bag in as she climbed behind the wheel and started the engine.

"It's over, Ruby. Give the money back. You opened your big mouth. They know who you are."

"Goodbye, sucker!"

Max called out to Janet. "Are you and the boy okay?"

Janet rose and pulled Matt up with her. "We're fine." She saw Pat running through the grass toward them as the woman sped down the hill only to be stopped by a flood of Rangers who had her blocked on all sides. She tried to run into one of their vehicles but she obviously thought better of it when two armed Rangers pointed their guns at her.

Roger climbed the hill and Max handed the gun to him willingly, then Roger called out. "Everybody good here?"

Pat grabbed Matt and kissed him all over his face and head then hugged him so tightly, Matt groaned. "Dad, let me breathe." He let the boy go and did the same to Janet who didn't care if she ever breathed again as long as Pat was holding her.

Roger smiled. "Guess so. Janet that was something you

did falling on top of Matt to shield him. I don't even know what to say. It brought a lump to my throat."

Pat took her face in his hands. "You laid down your life for him."

"That's what people do for the ones they love. Fortunately there were no bullets in the gun."

"But you didn't know that."

"I would do it over again. I knew we were in God's hands."

They watched the Rangers round up the two kidnappers and put them in one of the vehicles to take them to the police station. Roger retrieved the money bag and brought it back to Pat. "I'm sure the police will need this for evidence but I want you to hold on to it so you can put it back in the bank."

Pat slugged him lightly on the shoulder. "Don't know how I'll repay you guys."

"No need. That's what friends are for." He turned to Janet. "When you leaving?"

"Late this afternoon."

"Well, I hope we're through at the station in time. They'll need your testimony as well as Matt's. Again, you're one swell lady." He pointed his finger to Pat, then to Janet, then back and forth again ending with Pat. "I love you like a brother, but you're an idiot. She's a keeper."

Janet gave Roger a hug. "Thanks, dear friend. It's been a treat to know you and Doyne. Take good care of that baby."

"Doyne will hate she didn't get to say goodbye but we understand you have to get back to St. Louis." He walked back down the hill.

Janet sighed. "You are, you know."

"What?"

"An idiot."

"Probably in a lot of ways."

She watched the abductors being hauled off. "We need

to put a good word in for the man. His heart really wasn't in this caper."

Matt added, "He really was nice and made sure the woman did not hurt me. I heard him say he only wanted his part of the money to care for his sick mother and the crazy woman kept telling him he wouldn't see a penny if he didn't do what she said."

Pat nodded. "I'll do what I can but what he did was still a criminal act but maybe he won't get as long a sentence as Ruby."

"What did she mean when she said I killed her sister, Dad?"

"I didn't want to tell you all this until you were older, but after all you've been through, you need an explanation. She is your mother's sister and her brain has been fried by drugs. "Your mother did not take care of herself during pregnancy and died two days after you were born. You had absolutely nothing to do with her death. You were a gift from God. You could have been born addicted to whatever she had been on but you weren't. You were a healthy beautiful baby. I put a large sum of money in her account just before she died which later all went to her sister. I made arrangements for her burial and left California with you and ended up at Vernon's. The rest you know.

"How'd she find us?"

"The internet probably."

"Oh. And I thought the internet was just to learn how to play poker." Matt laughed.

"You twerp!" Pat grabbed him and hugged him again. "Am I the only one traumatized by this ordeal? You're making jokes about poker on the internet and Janet is calling me an idiot."

Janet drew them both to her. "Sorry. It's over now. We can relax. We need to bless God for taking care of us."

The three bowed their heads and gave thanks to their Father in heaven.

A Woman's Touch

The police Captain was very nice to them, giving them coffee and soda. Matt was such an adult through it all, explaining every detail of the abduction.

"Oh, I was scared when the crazy lady put me in the trunk but I asked Jesus to be with me and from then on, I wasn't scared. I don't know where they took me. The man put a blindfold on me while she was there because she didn't want me to look at her. When she left, he took it off and let me eat snacks and play games on his laptop."

"Did they hurt you in any way?"

Matt shook his head. "The man was very nice when the woman wasn't around. He loves his mother even though her mind is gone and she doesn't recognize him anymore. She still recites the bible. She remembers Jesus. I asked him if he read the bible. He said no. He had stopped believing a long time ago when he was living such a drug-filled life. He thought God wouldn't forgive him for things he had done. I told him we had a forgiving God and all he had to do was to ask Jesus to come into his life and he would be saved. I don't know if he believed me or not but that's when he told me to call Dad to tell him I was okay."

"I don't know of another eleven year old who could be so brave in such a dire circumstance." The Captain patted Matt on the back. "You're a hero in my book."

"Janet's the hero. She put her body on top of me to keep me from being shot."

The Captain shook his head. "Just goes to show you. Great things come in small packages."

Janet laughed. "You could have gone all day and not said that, but I appreciate the sentiment."

Pat smiled at the inference to her size. "She's little but mighty. I can never thank her enough for what she did for my boy."

Matt took a sip of his soda. "What's going to happen to the man?"

"Don't know yet. He pleaded with us to let him go back to California to see that his mother is taken care of before he goes to prison. She has Alzheimer's and won't know him, but he said that doesn't make any difference. He still knows her and he needs to make arrangements. Actually, after what Matt and Janet told me how good he was to Matt, I hope we can make it happen for him. He will spend time in prison for his part, but not as much as that nut case he hooked up with."

Matt stood and shook the Captain's hand. "I think he really heard what I told him about asking Jesus into his heart. I'm sure it was Jesus who told him to take the bullets out of the gun."

The Captain patted Matt's shoulder. "What a boy!" He then looked at Janet and Pat. "You two must be very proud him."

"We certainly are." Janet quickly agreed. "We could take a lesson from him, telling those who are in spiritual need about Jesus. I'm afraid a lot of us adults fail to do that when we have the opportunity."

Patrick stood as well. "I guess if we're through here, we need to get to the cabin so Janet can get her belongings. She has a flight back to St. Louis this evening."

"Oh, I thought you two were a couple." *I wish,* he heard Matt whisper.

"No," Pat quickly interjected, "just acquaintances. She got caught up in this horrible situation through no fault of her own."

The Captain raised one brow. "Whatever you say."

They said their thanks for the kindness they were shown at the station and went straight to the bank to redeposit the money. Pat made arrangements for it to be wired back into the escrow account.

Janet touched his arm. "It's your money, you know."

"I don't need or want it."

Back at the cabin, Janet changed into her suit and packed her cowgirl clothes into a bag Matt gave her.

"I'll mail this back to you, sweetie."

"Keep it. You may need it when you come back to see us."

"Matt!" Pat's voice was loud and clear.

Matt just shrugged and walked up beside Janet with his cell phone in his hand and before she knew it, he took a selfie of her and him together.

"Sweet boy, you are going to get us both in trouble."

"Nah. You saved my life. He can't *ever* be mad at you and after all that's happened to his little boy, he'll probably just want to hug and kiss me the rest of the day."

Janet and Matt both giggled at his silliness. "I'm sure going to miss you."

*****

All three stood in the airport terminal waiting for the last call for Janet to board her flight. She had her arm around Matt's shoulders but her eyes were on Pat's. "There's nothing good about goodbyes."

Pat didn't say a word, just kept looking at her.

"You can kiss her, Dad. I know you have before. That crazy woman said she saw you playing suck face with Janet in the church's parking lot. I know what suck face means."

"How do you know that? The internet?"

"No. There's guys at school who talk about stuff. I know a lot of things."

"Spare me."

Janet gave Matt a squeeze just before she dropped her arm from him and raised her face up toward Pat. "We have the okay from your son to kiss goodbye."

He bowed his head to her. His kiss was gentle yet it rocked her very being. She wrapped her arms around his middle and clung to him with desperation.

"Never in a million years did I ever believe I'd fall so hard for someone and his son I just met, but I did."

"Janet be realistic."

"The heck with reality. I've fallen hopelessly in love with you and I'm crazy about Matt. If you find that a problem, then it's just one you'll have to deal with yourself. I know you have feelings for me, but I also know you will not act on them so I give up. We'll do it your way, but don't expect me to forget I ever met you and Matt."

"I don't know what to say. I'm sorry it has to be this way. I owe you more than I can ever repay for what you did to keep Matt safe. If I had lost him, you might as well cover me with dirt because I would not want to go on living."

Matt hung his head down. "That's probably how Grandpa feels."

Patrick looked puzzled. "He doesn't even know you exist."

"I don't mean me. I mean you. He feels he's lost you and he might not feel like living."

Janet held her hand up. "I never discussed that with Matt, but he's right. The boy is wise beyond his years."

"Let's not part on a sad note." He gazed into her eyes which were brimming with tears and leaned down for one last kiss as the call came over the loud speaker that it was time to board. "Goodbye." His voice was thick with sadness.

"Goodbye you two." She gave Matt a kiss on his forehead. "Don't give your dad too much grief. He's been through a lot."

She turned to leave but whirled back around. "One more thing."

"Of course there is."

"Listen to Matt about your father. Don't cling to the bitterness you feel for him. You may not have a chance to make amends and then you'll also be clinging to regret the rest of your life. Turn it over to God. He can see you over the roughest roads you will ever have to travel. Believe me. Been there, done that."

"You have rough roads? Miss Happy Face?"

"Sure. We all have. But we have choices. We can wake up happy or we can wake up miserable. I choose happy."

Pat breathed in slowly. "Janet?"

"Yes?"

"I know how much my father means to you. Go ahead and tell him I wish him well, but please, please don't tell him about Matt." He stepped toward her, stretching his arm out for one last touch. "What I'm trying to say is, if you need help with anything with the stockholders and it's really important...I mean *really* necessary...call me."

She reached to touch his fingertips with hers, a quivering smile fluttering at the corners of her mouth. She nodded. She had no voice. She only had enough strength left to board the plane.

CHAPTER TWENTY TWO

*S*he arrived at the airport in St. Louis surprised to find everything so familiar. She certainly was not the same person who left here and somehow thought the whole world might have changed. Her blue Chevy sat patiently waiting for her in the parking lot. She sat in the driver's seat and laid her head on the steering wheel.

What a weekend this has been. Can I ever resume life as it was just a few days ago?

She stopped by the hospital on the way to her apartment, anxious to see Christopher and tell him she had seen his son and he had offered to help her with the company business if necessary. That was stretching Patrick's sentiments a long way, but perhaps it would cheer Christopher up to know his son still cared. What would really cheer him up would be if he knew he had a grandson, but she had made a promise and she was a woman of her word.

The news she was greeted with at the hospital was not too encouraging. Christopher was still in intensive care and the head nurse told her that he just wasn't responding as well as they expected...that he didn't appear to be putting up much of a struggle to live.

"He's asked for you a number of times. Perhaps

knowing you were here will help. I'll tell him when he wakes."

She left the hospital with a heavy heart and wanted desperately to call Patrick and beg him to reconsider his decision regarding Matt but knew it would be hopeless. The only thing left to do was pray for Christopher's recovery.

With a determined set of her jaw, she squared her shoulders, rejuvenating her fighting spirit. The second best news she could give Christopher would be that his company was on stable ground...that all the plans he had laid regarding the purchase of the electronics firms were moving along smoothly.

As she drove down the street toward her apartment, her mind formulated her strategy. She would put all her efforts into cementing the deal within the next week if possible. With the initial purchase in the bag, she would be free to travel to the various manufacturing sites to meet with the heads of the companies to insure the strict standards set by Mayhew Enterprises were conformed with. She had already outlined certain dictates and had brochures printed which told all about the history of Mayhew's, their company benefits, insurance, bonuses, as well as their future plans and expectations. That much had been accomplished before Christopher's heart attack. She knew this challenge could also serve as her salvation. She wouldn't have time to think about Patrick Mayhew.

Why did he have such a hold on her? Like he said, nothing serious had actually started between them. They hadn't actually made love. Maybe not made love physically, she mused, but all the loving feelings bathed her soul and she felt her flesh heat recalling the tender touches, the way his eyes looked at her, his smile, the softness of his lips. Oh, they made love all right...in a million ways.

*****

After unpacking her few belongings, she took a long hot relaxing bath and put on her lounger. It was all the usual things she did before but for some reason she still felt like a stranger in her own home. Nothing seemed the same. Nothing interested her. She gave herself a mental shake. *I'm acting crazy again. Stop it!* She picked up the phone and called Cal to let him know she was home and the money was back in the escrow account.

"We didn't need it after all. Everything worked out without it."

"I'm so glad. I was worried something really bad was happening." He sounded relieved. "I can't believe you got the papers signed so easily."

"It wasn't all that easy, believe me."

"I'll have to admit knowing the way he feels about the company, I'm surprised he'd even give you the time of day."

Oh, he gave me a little more than the time of day.

"Sorry the weather delayed you but I understand Montana is beautiful country. Did you get to see much of it?"

"Yes I did and what I saw was breathtaking. I can see why he loves it there so much."

"Yes, the last time I talked to Pat on the phone, he was really caught up in the protection and conservation of the forests and wildlife out there."

"And people." She knew her voice sounded a little too proud.

"Oh?"

"What I mean is, he happened to have to go on a rescue mission while I was there to locate a couple of lost hunters in the mountain. He takes his profession as a Ranger very seriously."

"And I suspect he's very good at it. Pat was always a very caring person except when it came to his father. How'd he look? Was he well...happy?"

How'd he look? She pondered dreamily. How could she describe a handsome *annoying* cowboy to Cal? She grinned to herself. "He looked fine, Cal, and he spoke very kindly of you."

"That's nice. We always got along great." Cal cleared his throat. "I don't suppose he talked much about...well, did he say anything about his father or about coming back?"

She winced. "Cal, I don't think he wants anything to do with anything or anyone in St. Louis. From what little he told me, I got the impression he is very bitter. I tried to convince him—"

"I take it he told you his feelings about his father?"

"Yes, he told me." She quickly changed the subject. "What I really called you about is that I want to have a meeting as soon as possible with the principals regarding the electronics firms. I think the quicker we get the ball rolling on this, the quicker the stockholders' minds will be put at ease."

"I agree."

"I stopped by the hospital and there's not much change for the better. I certainly don't want anything to jeopardize Christopher's well-being. A big shake-up in the company could do that. I want to show everyone that the company is in good hands...even if those hands don't belong to a Mayhew."

"I'll certainly do all I can to help. Some of the stockholders are already getting a little squirmy. When do you want the meeting?"

"How about next Tuesday afternoon. That should give everyone time to make their plans. I'll have Peggy get right on it in the morning contacting everyone and making hotel reservations for the out-of-towners."

"Works for me. What time?"

"Two o'clock."

"Good. We'll make it happen."

*****

The next few days filled Janet with mixed emotions. As busy as she was, there still seemed to be a mountain of time left to yearn for Patrick. The memory of him was not fading...it was intensifying. That was the bad news. The good news was that Christopher had rallied enough to be placed in a private room. She spent as much of her free time with him as possible. She seemed to be the only person he responded positively to.

"You're a good girl." He told her that over and over during her visits. "You're the only family I have left and if anything happens to me, I've provided well for you. I had Cal draw up the papers."

"No, Christopher, nothing is going to happen to you. I won't let it. Besides, you have Patrick."

"My son is gone from me. I've pushed him out of my life."

"No, he cares." She hesitated, then decided to tell him. "I saw him recently."

"You saw Pat?" The old man's eyes sparkled for a brief moment.

"Yes. He signed some papers for the company. He cares."

"He's here?"

"No, I went to him." She watched his expression turn to gloom. He was so weak and frail, she questioned her decision to tell him about Patrick. She prayed she hadn't done the wrong thing. "He does care, Christopher. It's just that he has his life there and...but believe me, he does care. We prayed together for your well-being."

She thought she detected a slight smile on Christopher's lips at the mention of them praying.

"I need to go, sweetheart. I'll come back tomorrow. Have them call me if you need me before."

The doctor had insisted Christopher have nothing

whatsoever to do with the business and she avoided any further reference to it...especially about the phone calls she received from irate board members and stockholders who thought the company was going to fold tomorrow. Sighing, she thought about the meeting. Would she be able to pull it off? Would the piece of paper Patrick signed be all the clout she needed to prove the Mayhews' trust in her?

She kissed Christopher goodbye and hurried home. Without rational thought, she grabbed the phone and called Patrick. His phone number was etched in her mind as if she had called him a thousand times. Funny, she thought as she nervously listened to the ringing, how some things are so easily memorized...like his phone number, the lines on his face, the tiny hairs on the top of his fingers...

"Hello."

"Patrick." She choked on his name. *Oh, brother!* She wanted to sound sophisticated and business-like but she choked. "Remember me?"

There was a long pause. She could hear his breathing. "I seem to vaguely recall the voice."

Her smile broadened. At least he didn't hang up on her. "How's Matt?"

"He's fine."

"No bad effects from the kidnapping?"

"When it hit the local news, he suddenly became a celebrity at school. The reporter told how Matt witnessed to a criminal and caused him to take the bullets out of his gun. By the way, Matt gave you honorable mention as the *acquaintance* who literally laid down her life for him."

"What a sweetie."

"Oh, yes, he's a cherry pie."

"How's Patty? Did they get the gift I sent?"

"Yes. Matt's fine, Patty's fine, Carlyle's fine, the weather could be better." His voice was flat and impersonal.

"How about you, Patrick?"

"Me? I'm a lot like the weather. I could be better."

"Me too." She couldn't hold back the note of sadness in her voice. "I was just thinking about a song, 'You're the Reason God Made Montana.'"

He chuckled softly. "The song is about Oklahoma."

"I don't know anyone in Oklahoma. You sing it your way, I'll sing it mine."

"Janet." His voice sounded sterner. "Is this all you called for? I distinctly remember telling you to call only if it was *really* important."

"It is really important.

"Is something...is it my dad?"

"He's out of intensive care."

She could hear his breath let out. "Well, that's good. He must be better."

"Not much. He doesn't act like he even wants to live. He still keeps telling me I'm the only family he has."

"You are."

"I'm not. Patrick, I told him you care."

There was a long silence.

"You DO care. I know you do. When I told him, you should have seen the look on his face. It would mean so much to him if you would..."

"We seem to have had this same conversation about a hundred times before."

"He's going to die if something isn't done!"

There was another long pause. "Okay, tell him I care. Tell him I wish him well...but that's all! You hear me? Don't lead him to believe there can be any more."

She smiled. At least it was a step in the right direction. *Thank you, God.* "I'll tell him I talked to you and you want him to get well real soon." Before he had a chance to speak, she changed to another subject. "I also called for moral support. Think of me Tuesday around two o'clock. I'm meeting with the powers that be to sew up the electronics deal. Some of the major stockholders also insist on being there with their evil eyes glued to me."

"Don't worry about it. All they will be able to see is the top of your head over that big conference table."

"Thanks for your vote of confidence."

"Don't mention it." His voice was very affectedly courteous.

"I'm serious, Patrick. Your father's illness has taken its toll on the stock already so a lot rests on this deal going through. If the stock slips any more than it has already, I'm afraid it would mean financial disaster. Public opinion is that your father is dying and the company will crumble without a Mayhew sitting at the head of the corporate table."

"That's nuts. Don't they know one man hasn't done it all? It's people like you and Cal and all the other dedicated employees who have made Mayhew Enterprises what it is today."

"Thank you. That makes three of us who know that...you, me and Cal. Now tell it to the stockholders...those we have left, that is. Some have already sold out." She let out a long audible breath. "I don't mean to sound like a bleeding heart, but it IS critical. The only real ally I have in my corner is Cal. The rest of them have never quite accepted me as anything more than a kid your father took a liking to. Not the *liking* you think either!"

"I didn't say anything."

"No, but you were thinking it."

"Was not."

"Was too."

They both broke into spontaneous laughter.

"Oh, Patrick, I miss you so much. I miss the fun, the teasing...a hundred things, but you're right, of course. It would never work out between us. If we were together, I could never keep Matt a secret."

"I have to go." He was being blunt, she knew. He

hated to discuss what could have been and why it can't be. "Good luck, Tuesday and I *do* wish the best for dad."

"Patrick! Give Matt a kiss from me."

There was no response. The only sound she heard was the click of the phone disconnecting them. She stared blankly at the receiver before putting it back in the cradle. At least he wished her something she direly needed for the meeting. Luck.

CHAPTER TWENTY THREE

ᛒy one o'clock Tuesday afternoon, Janet had chewed the erasers off three pencils and shuffled and re-shuffled the contracts on her desk until they looked like they had been run over by a truck...and she still had another hour before the meeting. She had never before felt such apprehension about a business meeting...but then she had never before had to shoulder all the responsibility of success or failure connected with a business deal such as Mayhew Enterprises was undertaking at the present time.

She drummed her fingernails on the desktop then pressed the intercom. "Peggy, do you have pitchers of ice water and pots of coffee ready for the conference room?"

The secretary chuckled. "How many times are you going to ask? Relax. You'll do just fine. Where's your faith?"

"That's easy for you to say. You're taller than me."

They both giggled at their private joke. Peggy was also "short of leg" as Patrick would say, but was exactly one inch taller than Janet. Having a sense of humor about their height always lightened her spirits; however, she doubted that laughing at adversity in the middle of the meeting would go over too well with the stockholders.

At precisely one forty-five Janet took her place at the

head of the large conference table and sank into the huge leather chair. Patrick's words whirled madly through her mind about only the top of her head showing over the table. She abruptly pushed herself to a standing position and practiced pacing confidently back and forth. There was nothing more she could do except to shuffle and stack the contracts one last time before the members filtered in.

Cal was the first to arrive and introduced Janet as Acting Chairman of the Board as the others seated themselves around the table, sternly appraising the petite Chairman in the blue linen suit. She smiled politely and sensed a few of the members were accepting her status, but some were still very skeptical about her capabilities and, much to her dismay, was not afraid to be very verbal about it.

"I assure you gentlemen that I would not be standing here conducting this meeting if Mr. Mayhew had not placed his full trust in me. The co-owner of Mayhew's, Patrick Mayhew, has given me Power of Attorney. He has other pressing commitments that prevent him from being here himself. Do you think he would entrust his father's company with me if—"

One skeptic interrupted her. "But can you assure us that the stock will increase again in value after the purchase of these electronics firms. Can you guarantee us that these firms will be profitable enough to—"

"No one can make a guarantee like that," came a deep-timbered voice from the back of the room. "Not even me."

"Patrick!" Janet gasped. She barely recognized him. Only his voice was familiar. What happened to the cowboy she knew? This man was dressed in a dark gray business suit. Janet's heart was pounding so loudly she could hear it as he took his place beside her.

"Thank you, Miss Raye." He sounded very business-like. "You've handled everything perfectly. Just as father would have."

She and Cal were matching gape for gape, their mouths dropping open wider and wider. In a hushed tone, she finally stammered, "How...when?"

"My pressing commitments just got un-pressed."

"Well, I don't care how you got here or why. I never look a gift Chairman of the Board in the mouth."

She turned back to the members. "For those of you who do not know this gentleman, I'd like to introduce Christopher Mayhew's son, Patrick. Fortunately he was able to make the meeting after all and will be glad to answer any questions you might have regarding me or the pending acquisitions."

"Pending?" He whispered out the corner of his mouth. "You mean you haven't *wooed* them into signing yet. Tsk, tsk. You *are* slipping, Miss Raye."

She ignored him. "I now present Mr. Patrick Mayhew." She took a seat at the side of the table next to Cal.

For the next hour, she listened to a most brilliant presentation. She was so impressed. Patrick had been away from the company for years, yet there wasn't one question that he did not answer to everyone's satisfaction. He was quick to tell them that he was not as conversant with every phase of the Mayhew operation as Miss Raye, but was very willing to be of any assistance to her during his short time in St. Louis.

"Does this mean you won't be overseeing this acquisition," one member asked.

"No, I have to leave tomorrow. Miss Raye is much more capable to handle this new venture."

Janet rose. "I thank you for your confidence in me, Mr. Mayhew, but I too really feel it would benefit the company immensely if you could find the time to stay a few days...just to go over the electronic firms' books and make sure everything is in order." He opened his mouth to protest but she raised her voice a pitch. "That way you could convey your findings to the stockholders."

He glared openly at her while she smiled sweetly back at him. She was laying a trap for him and had to bite her cheeks to suppress a giggle.

A faint twinkle gleamed from his eyes as they took on a subtle seduction which caused her heart to pick up an extra beat.

"Perhaps my plans could accommodate a few extra days. I could make a phone call or two." His voice was husky, his eyes never leaving hers.

Her expression slowly changed from cocky to endearing and she wondered if anyone else in the room could see how positively wonderful she felt.

After a round of handshakes, everyone left except for Cal who burst into a loud welcome. "My goodness, boy, it's good to see you."

"You too. It's been a long time."

"Too long. Janet tells me you're still a Ranger. I think you had just joined the last time I spoke to you on the phone."

"Yes. That's been a few years."

"I sure hope we get a chance to have dinner one night and catch up. I'm tied up tonight. Maybe later this week."

"Hope so, but I'm probably going to spend what little time I have auditing these books. I have to get back to Montana as soon as I can. I've got things that need to be looked after."

"If your plans change..." He looked at his watch. "Oh, hey, I've got to get out of here. I'm late for another meeting." He shook Pat's hand one more time and left.

Pat stared at the closed door for a moment. "Same old Cal. Always on the run to some meeting. Don't know how he keeps up the pace at his age. He's got to be old as or older than my father."

"He's two years older. He's sixty-seven. Your father is sixty-five."

"Sixty-five? Where did the time go?"

"Too young to die."

His eyes shot up. "Will you get off my back about that!?"

"Excuse me! Sorry to interrupt your moment of grief!"

"What more do you expect from me? I already told you how I feel. I do *not* wish him dead!"

"Are you going to see him?"

"No."

"Can I tell him you're here? It would mean so much for him to know you—"

"No!"

"Why?"

He let out an exasperated sigh. "Because nothing's changed. My being here has nothing to do with my father."

"But you came here to save the company."

"I came here to save your butt!"

She puffed indignantly. "I beg your pardon. My so-called *butt* was not in jeopardy. I could have survived."

"Ha! When I walked into that room, the first thing I saw was a two pound sack of sass standing in front of a chair four times her size." He looked her up and down and couldn't contain his amusement. "Come to think of it, you weren't doing too bad a job. The looks on some of those old codgers' faces were priceless when you spouted out cost figures as easily as if they were your phone number." He looked serious again. "I don't know if you could have pulled it off by yourself or not, but I hated for you to come this far and fall on your face."

She couldn't stay irritated with him. She knew what a sacrifice it was for him to come here.

"I don't know if I could have pulled it off by myself either. Thanks. Your timing was excellent."

Their eyes met again and they simultaneously became aware there was no one else in the room but them.

Without a word, she took an abrupt step toward him,

holding her breath, waiting for a welcome. Within seconds she was in his outstretched arms and felt them close over her body, wrapping her firmly in his embrace.

She tilted her face up. "You definitely get better looking with age."

"Well, sure. I've aged a lot. What's it been? A week?"

"Feels like years to me."

She watched his expression turn to desire. As his arms tightened, his gaze lowered to her soft lips and in torturous slowness, his mouth covered hers. She went limp in his arms as the wet taste of him swirled on her tongue. She wound her arms inside his jacket and joyed in the feel of the corded muscles across his back.

He released the pressure of his lips only enough to whisper her name, then feather-touched her open mouth feeling her tongue with his. "I promised myself none of this. There ought to be a law against what you do to me."

"There is." She pulled at his lip with her teeth. "We should both be locked up in jail...together. Let's go to my apartment. I'll fix you dinner."

"It's only four o'clock."

"Is your appetite on a certain schedule?"

"I need to get going on these books. I *have* to get back to Montana as soon as possible. Matt's school lets out this week. Vernon is staying at the cabin but he needs to get back to his ranch and I can't impose on Doyne with the new baby and all. What I'm trying to get through to you is, if I'm going to finish my business here, I'm going to be pressed for time so I'd better utilize what's left of today."

"And you were the one who said I was all business."

His look became serious as he pushed back from her and raked his fingers through his hair. "You're right. I'm making excuses. Excuses to not be alone with you. We can't just continue on where we left off in Montana. We have the same old problem. If you want more than just a..."

"One-time tumble in bed?"

"Don't make it sound so gross."

"Well, is that what *you* want?"

He shrugged impatiently. "I'd be lying if I told you I didn't want to make love to you." He smiled. "That's the *rat* in me speaking." He studied her face longingly. "You're so lovely. When I walked into this room today and saw you, you made my throat feel like it was full of sawdust and I half-wished you wouldn't have been here."

Her eyes darted to his. "You surely don't mean that."

"I've had you on my mind constantly since you left. Of course it's hard not to. That twerp of a son of mine put that picture he took of the two of you on my computer as my screen saver. He knows I don't know how to change it. Every time I turn it on, there the two of you are grinning like Cheshire cats."

"Matt's such a good boy." She laughed.

He shifted nervously. "I foolishly thought if I saw you in this atmosphere...a place I hated...I'd get you out of my system."

"Did it work?"

"Not even close."

"Don't you like having me on your mind?" She snaked her hands over his shoulders.

He pulled them down and firmly held them away. "Not when it interferes with my work, my life."

"I hate to say I told you so, but I told you so. Why should we deny our feelings? I'm free, you're free."

"Are we? Are we really free? I don't think so. You have ties here, I have ties in Montana."

She pulled her hands from his, her expression turning somber. "You're right. I made a vow to Christopher I would never forsake him but if I did leave all this and went to Montana, like I told you before I could never keep Matt a secret."

"That's the way it *has* to be, Janet."

"Okay. I'm not going to argue with you. Come on, I'll

show you the ledgers. Perhaps you'll find them better company to while away your time in St. Louis."

They both walked stiffly toward her office past the raised eyebrow expression on Peggy's face. Janet called over her shoulder, "Bring in the last quarter's figures for the electronics firms and the yearly projections I worked up. *Mr.* Mayhew needs to see them." Her voice was short and concise.

"Yes, Miss Raye." Peggy was just as business-like. "Oh, by the way. Here are your calls while you were away from your desk. Mark Wilson called three times. He needs you to call as soon as possible. The music troupe will be in town next week and they are short a singer and wondered if you would fill in. He needs an answer right away."

A stony mask spread over Pat's face. "Sure. Would hate for you to miss seeing *twinkle toes* strut his stuff?"

"Patrick!" Janet was incensed with his childish behavior.

"If you'll excuse me, Miss Raye, I have some books to look over then there's a few of my old haunts I'd like to check out tonight...alone!" He slammed the door of her office, leaving Janet standing in its quake.

Peggy gave her a bewildered look. "Who's twinkle toes?"

"Don't ask. Do me a favor. Call Mark Wilson back for me and tell him no I will not sing with the troupe and I'd like for him to not call me for anything anymore."

"Wow, you're really in a mood."

"Ya think?

She left the office fuming over Patrick's stupid antics. Who said she would have gone with him to his *haunts* had he asked.

Her nerves shattered, she stopped by her favorite Mexican restaurant near the hospital and gorged herself on tacos...a sure cure for cowboyitis.

Completely and miserably stuffed, she waddled to her

car and made her way to the hospital. She stayed far longer than she should have, but Christopher seemed to be in much better spirits and enjoyed her company so she stayed until after he fell asleep.

CHAPTER TWENTY FOUR

She drove through the streets of her neighborhood for a while unwinding from the day's events. Relaxing was hard when all she could think of was Patrick out on the prowl. In the mood he was in, hard telling what kind of trouble he would get into...and with whom!

Finally running out of things to do and places to drive by, she forced herself to go home arriving around eleven. She tiredly turned on the shower, shed her clothes and stepped in, hoping it would soothe her enough to get some sleep. Just as she turned off the water the banging started. She quickly wrapped a towel around her body and ran to the door dripping wet.

"What the—" She looked through the peep hole. "Patrick! What do you want?" Under other circumstances she would have laughed at his appearance. His once tidy crisp business suit was so disheveled the jacket hung lopsided over his shoulder with his tie stringing out of one pocket. He looked like he had been caught in a windstorm.

"Let me in." His voice was almost incoherent.

She flung the door open and yanked him in before the neighbors started complaining about the noise. "Oh, merciful heavens, you're drunk as a skunk. I hope this isn't the beginning of another embarrassing scene. P.U.!!" She held her nose. "Please stand down wind. You smell like cheap booze. Probably very appropriate for the company you were with tonight...from the look of your clothes." She flipped down the corner of his shirt collar which was sticking him in the chin.

He pulled her hand away. "Where have you been? I tried to call you on your cell a hundred times at least. Don't you ever listen to your messages?"

"I turned it off while I was at the hospital and never turned it back on. Sorry if it was important. However, you're certainly in no shape to ask ME where I've been."

"I'm in great shape." He slurred his words. "So great in fact I've been drinking all night and can't even get drunk!"

She let out a laugh. "Well, you certainly do a great imitation." She shoved him toward the couch. "Sit down. I'll get you something sobering to drink." She smirked wickedly. "What'll it be? A raw egg and sardine cocktail?"

His face turned snow white as he put his hand over his mouth to keep from gagging.

"Only kidding. I'm out of sardines."

He flopped on the couch and she went to the kitchen and fixed a very potent cup of instant coffee. As she carefully carried it to him trying not to spill it, she noticed him eyeing her intently. Little droplets of water still clung to her skin.

She handed him the cup. "What are you doing...trying to guess my weight soaking wet?"

His mouth turned up on one corner. "Just surprised to see how—"

"Don't say it!"

"I was going to say, how tall you looked in a towel."

"Oh very funny. Ha, ha, ha...bite me."

"Pick your spot."

"You're a jerk."

"Am not."

"Are too."

She laughed in spite of the fact she was very irked with him and sank down beside him on the couch. "If you spill one drop on my couch, you'll be a dead jerk."

He took a very cautious sip then gave her a toothy grin. He was disgusting and smelled like a brewery, but underneath it all she was very aware he was still her *nice guy*. Each time she was with him, her love deepened and nothing else mattered. The fact that he went out and made a fool of himself tonight left her in no way less enamored with him.

"Here." She spoke in a very motherly manner as she took the cup from him and sat it on the end table. "Let me help you off with your jacket. Then I want you to go in and take a nice long hot shower. If you live through that, I have a new toothbrush I bought to send to you. You can use it and save me the postage mailing it to you. And don't forget the mouthwash!"

"Are you insinuating I have..." He lowered his voice ominously, "...bad breath?"

She gave his sleeve a yank. "Let me put it this way. I'm glad I don't have fresh flowers in the room. They would have wilted by now."

He rose, staggered, then gave her a silly salute. "Which way to the latrine, Sergeant?"

"Left through the bedroom."

She followed, guiding him in the right direction and turned the water on for him. "I don't think I have a shirt that would fit you, but I'll give you a big towel to wear." She pulled one from the linen closet and shoved it into his arms as he went into the bathroom.

She had wanted him to come to her apartment with her but had something like a romantic dinner in mind. But as she returned to the couch she thought, into each life some rain must fall. Nobody ever said it would be a torrential downpour. She had truly prayed his coming to St. Louis meant he had changed his mind, but like he said...nothing had really changed. They still had the same old problems.

He stayed in the shower a very long time and she wondered if he was okay. Then she heard, "Holy mother of God!" She grinned inside knowing he had run out of hot water. He would either have to sober up or freeze to death.

After listening to him brush his teeth and gargle, she watched him walk into the living room tucking the end of the big towel into the flap, smiling sheepishly. "You still here?"

"I never leave a sinking ship. Like some *rats* I know."

"Do I owe you an apology for anything?"

"I'm sure there's something but maybe I can think of something you can do to make amends."

"This is no time for jokes, Janet. If you knew how appealing you look sitting there in the dark with just the moonlight shining across your face."

"Everyone looks good in the dark...even you."

"I mean it. I'm not going to promise the *rat* in me won't win out tonight."

"We could always pretend a little. Pretend there was nothing standing in our way to be together."

"This is no pretense." He grunted hoarsely. "This is real...this is now."

She felt the weight of his knee press down on the couch, his hand resting on her shoulder as he gently pushed her back against the side cushion. His mouth descended slowly, softly, moistly teasing and tantalizing her own. His controlled, patient assault on her lips forced her to hold on to him for support.

His tongue lazily circled the outline of her parted lips. He moaned passionately. There was no hurried clawing and grabbing as she had envisioned it might be if they ever got this close. It was like the slow motion she had felt the night they danced until the wee hours of morning. Everything was torturously slow except for their heartbeats which were pounding mercilessly. Their breathing was ragged, even shuddering at times as they clung to each other tenderly.

She explored the rippling contours of his back with soft fluttering touches as his hands traced the outline of her face following his fingers with warm, wet kisses.

Finally pulling away, he whispered, "Janet, we have to stop."

"Shhh." She touched his lips with her fingers, then took his hand and pulled herself up beside him. They touched each other's finger tips then feather-touched each other's hands and arms, working their way up to their faces, sensitizing every inch of flesh along the way.

She drew her breath in and closed her eyes, drinking in the feel and joy of his touch. When she opened her eyes she met his passion-laden ones. She sat very still for a moment enjoying the tingling ache her body felt for him.

"I love you, Patrick. It's as simple as that...I love you. Forgive me for saying it. I hate the circumstances that's keeping us apart."

He pulled her to him, cradling her in his arms. "Maybe it IS love...oh, how I hope it isn't, but whatever it is, I want you to know you are very, very special to me. This isn't just a casual thing with me, but we have to be realistic."

"I've told you before. The heck with reality. I am hopelessly in love with you."

"Even knowing nothing can ever come of this?"

She nodded. "At least we have now. We have this very moment."

"Oh, sweetheart, knowing you and your convictions, if this went any further than kissing, you would end of hating me."

"I could never hate you, but I am being a foolish schoolgirl with a mad crush that just won't go away. You bring that out in me." The very thought of nearly making love to him made her heady, and she started giggling.

"What's so funny? Haven't you ever seen a cowboy in

a towel before?"

"Hundreds." She planted a wet kiss on his smiling lips.

"I want the names of every one of them. I plan to challenge them to a duel."

"Don't bother. I had them all shot at sunrise for wanting to make love with their boots on."

His grin broadened. "I tried that once but the spurs got in the way." He pulled her onto his lap.

"Mmmm, this is nice but I think we better get some sleep. You are going to have a doozy of a headache tomorrow."

"I deserve it. That's the first time I had that much to drink since before Matt was born."

She brought him a pillow and blanket from the bedroom. "You'll be comfortable here on the couch. I nap on it a lot and it's great."

He took them from her and she kissed the back of his hand. "Goodnight, cowboy."

"Goodnight, ma'am."

*****

Janet floated through the next few days, working alongside the man she loved.

Gloom settled over her late Friday night. She knew without being told that Patrick would be leaving the next day. She had prepared a romantic, candlelit dinner for two and they each tried to keep the conversation light, complimenting each other on a job well done with regard to the electronics firms purchase.

With the stockholders thinking Patrick was manning the whole affair, all was at peace. She marveled how well she and Patrick had worked together but her time spent alone with him was the most special. The news of Christopher's slow, but steady recovery was also a factor in making the last few days Janet's happiest.

She lifted her glass of sparkling grape juice to salute their hard work. "Here's to a great productive week. Thank you for everything."

"Thank you." He clinked his glass against hers and sipped to her toast then covered her hand with his. He massaged the back of her wrist absently. "I can't say it enough. You are a very special lady."

"Stay a little longer." Her eyes pleaded with his saddened ones.

"It would only make it harder to leave, you know that. I *have* to go."

"In the morning?"

He nodded and her shoulders slumped. "I can't leave Matt any longer. Vernon said he couldn't stay past this week. Matt's out of school, I've got a job." He breathed in and out noisily. "I've got to get my life pulled back together again." *My life. Will it mean anything without her? It's got to.*

"Will you stay with me tonight?" She reached to touch his cheek and he cupped her hand to his mouth to draw warm wet circles in the palm with his lips. "If you leave, I'll have you shot at sunrise."

He moaned. "I just *hate* when that happens."

They both laughed at their silliness as they cleared the table. The ringing of her cell brought them back to reality.

Who could be calling this late? "Hello."

"Hi, Janet. It's me."

She stiffened then sat down. It took a second for the voice to register. "Matt?"

Pat came to attention and paced around her chair and mouthed, "Is something wrong?" Janet shrugged.

"Yeah, it's me. Do you know where my dad is?"

"Yes. I think I can get in touch with him." She touched Pat on the hand to stop his pacing. "Is anything wrong? Do you need to talk to him?"

"No. I need him to pick me up. I'm at the airport."

"What airport?"

"Your airport."

"St. Louis?" She whispered to Pat, "He's here!"

"That IS where you live, isn't it." Matt chuckled.

"Yes, but I don't understand."

Pat was making choking motions with his hands muttering, "What has that kid done now?"

Janet put her finger to her lips to shush him. "Are you alone?"

"Yes. Vernon loaned me the money for the ticket. He and I discussed the educational advantages, as well as the social advantages, of travel and we thought—"

"Matt, I think maybe you'd better think up something a little more believable before your dad gets there."

Pat was shaking his hands in the air and still threatening death and destruction.

"Well I really wanted to see you again, Janet." Matt's voice dripped with sweet honey. "But Vernon really *did* say travel was educational and Josh is taking care of Carlyle."

"Wanting to see me is the best reason I can think of." She wrinkled her nose at Pat. "I'll try to explain it to your dad...kind of cushion the blow. However, I know he'll be delighted to see you. He's been missing you."

"Thanks. I knew I could count on you."

"Your dad and I will be there shortly."

She hung up and smiled at Pat. "That was your son."

"I *know* who it was. What's he doing here?!"

"He wanted to see me again."

"Oh, for crying out loud."

"Well thanks a lot!"

"No...I didn't mean it like that."

"I know. I could have told him you were here but you were too irate. I didn't want you to say something that would upset him. I myself can't wait to see him." She laughed. "Vernon loaned him the money for the ticket. He said something about the educational advantage of travel."

"I swear the world is not safe with him *or* you on the loose."

She chuckled and playfully pulled him to her and kissed him until she convinced him to let Matt live. "We need to get going. We have a small, lonely child stranded at the airport."

"Maybe if we ignore him long enough, he'll take the next flight out."

She nipped him on the nose.

"Ow!" He rubbed where she bit him as they went out the door. "Have you had your rabies shot?"

*****

After picking up Matt and a barrage of hugging and kissing, they formulated their plans. Pat decided it would be best for him to use the company suite alone and Matt could stay at Janet's apartment with her. That way no one would see him and Matt together.

"It will only be for a couple of nights." Pat looked stern. "I mean it, Matt. Two days and then it's home...no whining...home in two days at the most!"

"Oh, I meant to tell you." Matt cleared his throat and went on as if his dad hadn't said a word. "Roger told me to tell you he would make arrangements for you to take next week as an extended vacation and Josh is taking care of Carlyle."

"That's great!" Janet didn't even try to keep her excitement in check. "That will give us time to do everything you've always wanted, Matt."

"Hold it!" Pat let his breath out in a huff. "Who in the heck died and left you two in charge of my life?"

Janet sighed tolerantly. "It's a dirty job, but someone's got to do it. Besides you're out-numbered. There's Matt and now Roger and Vernon."

"Don't forget Doyne, Josh and Carlyle." Matt smiled

sweetly.

"I give up. I'm too tired to argue with the two of you. It's late. Let's get going. Just drop me off at the hotel. I'll go to the office in the morning. No one will be there. I can go over the last quarter's figures to make sure I didn't miss anything. You two can start your sightseeing without me. I've seen St. Louis."

Janet and Matt smiled at each other.

"Here take this." Pat handed Janet a wad of bills. "You'll need it. The kid doesn't come cheap. If you run out, let me know."

"Do you want to meet for breakfast?"

"No, you guys get started on your outings. I'll see you for dinner."

CHAPTER TWENTY FIVE

After cereal and juice the next morning, Janet asked Matt if he'd like to go to the zoo.

"Righteous!"

"I take that as a yes. Afterwards, do you think you would be okay staying in the apartment alone for a little while? I need to go to the hospital to see your Grandpa."

"Let me go with you."

"Matt don't be absurd."

"Please, please, pretty please."

"Don't even think it. I made your dad a promise...so did you!"

"But I have a plan. We only promised to keep it a secret that I'm his grandson. I have a plan and he won't even know who I am."

"No!"

"It'll work. Just listen to the way I have it worked out."

"Matt...I smell trouble."

"Does the hospital have a place that patients can go to visit people? You know in their wheelchair or something?"

Janet thought for a moment. "Yes, there is a sunroom where families meet to visit...no! I'll not be a party to this."

"Pleeease! I won't even talk to him. I only want to see what he looks like."

"It would have to be in the afternoon when it's warmer.... No." She shook her head. "I can't believe I'm even entertaining the thought, let alone planning the strategy. Absolutely not."

Matt settled back in his chair. "We'll talk about it after we see the zoo. Fate tells me he is going to feel good enough to go to the sunroom."

She glanced at him and watched him cross his arms in front of his chest and breathe a contented sigh. He never gives up, reminding her of herself. When something is worthwhile, you just can't give up. Maybe it would work. Christopher wouldn't even have to see Matt. Matt could just observe from afar. It might be the boy's only chance to get a glimpse of his grandpa. She tried to convince herself it was the right thing to do.

*****

Right after leaving the zoo, she received a call from Pat.

"How are you two doing? Is Matt begging for everything in the world?"

"He's being an angel." That was stretching it a bit.

"Hope you don't mind. Cal wants to have dinner with me and tonight is the only time he has."

"That's great. I'll order in a pizza for Matt and me."

"See you tomorrow then. Thanks for babysitting."

"Ha. Babysitting! Hardly a baby."

They both laughed and she was relieved she wouldn't have to face Pat tonight if she went through with Matt's plan. She knew she would have to tell him but tonight she welcomed the private time to find the right words to explain it all to him.

After parking the car at the hospital, Janet turned to Matt. "You know we're going to be in deep trouble with your dad just doing what we're doing so please don't make it worse by revealing yourself." She breathed a shuddering breath. "I'm still not totally convinced this is right."

"Don't worry. Just show me where you're going to bring him and I'll find an appropriate vantage point."

She arched her brow. "An appropriate vantage point?" She laughed. "Sometimes I think you're a college professor in an eleven year old body."

He smiled and showed that irresistible dimple. "It's a gift."

She took him by the hand and led him to the sunroom. "Well, take your *gift* and hide it behind that potted evergreen in the corner." She arranged one of the chairs behind it for him to sit on. "Stay there and don't make a sound."

She stood back to see if he was hidden, then nervously pushed the plant a little nearer his chair to hide him better. She could still see him a little. "Matt, it just isn't going to work."

"Will you stop worrying? Even if he does see me, he won't know who I am."

She waved her hands in the air and hurried to Christopher's room. Maybe the doctor won't allow it. That would solve all problems.

One look at Christopher sitting in his wheelchair told her he was feeling a lot better.

"Thought you might take me for a stroll up the hall. I'd like to see something other than this room."

Matts 'fate' is working overtime.

Her delight in seeing him looking so much better pushed aside any trepidation she had as she wheeled him to the sun deck.

"This is nice in here." He leaned back against the pillow in his chair and breathed in the fresh air coming from the open window. "One forgets the beauty of nature until it's almost snatched away."

"Well, you're going to be seeing a lot of nature. You

are going to be up and out of here in no time. God's not through with you yet."

He turned his head, reached up and patted her hand. "You are such a dear child." Before he turned back he squinted to get better focus at something. "I wish I'd brought my glasses." He craned his neck toward the plant. "Who's that lurking behind that tree?"

Janet turned his chair sideways away from Matt. "I don't see anything."

"Really, Janet! Turn me around."

She reluctantly turned him back. "It's a boy. You there. Come out of that corner."

Janet felt faint, her heart jumped up and down in her throat.

Matt peeked around the plant, his big brown eyes round as silver dollars. "You called me, sir?"

"What are you doing hiding in the corner like that? Don't you know you could scare someone?"

"Well, it certainly scared me." Janet turned his chair toward the hall. "Shall we go back to your room now?"

The old man raised his hand to stop her, then turned back to the boy. "Speak up. Cat got your tongue?"

"I'm sorry, sir. I didn't mean to scare anyone. I was just waiting to see Grandpa." He smiled the same smile that captivated Janet the first time she saw him. As the corners of his mouth turned up, the dazzling dimple dented right on cue. She wanted to take that dimple and hit him with it. She was numb, unable to do or say anything except cross her fingers, stare anxiously at Matt and pray for lightning to strike.

"Well, your grandpa must be very proud to have a handsome grandson like you." Christopher seemed to take on unexpected strength.

"Thank you, sir."

"What perfect manners." Christopher smiled. "What's your name?"

Matt's eyes darted to Janet who was still frozen in place unable to speak. "Matthew."

"Matthew. That's a fine name. Tell me, Matthew, do you go to school around here?"

"School's out."

Christopher chuckled at the boy's cocky response. "Puts me in the mind of someone." He directed his statement toward Janet. "Does he you?"

Janet managed a choking, "I think he looks like a boy on T.V."

"I'm sure if your grandpa knew you were here, he'd want to come right away. Should we get the nurse to see what's taking him so long?"

"No, that's okay. I'll just sort of hang around. I don't mind."

"Well, tell me what you like to do now that school's out."

"I went to the zoo this morning."

"The zoo. That's nice. What else you like?"

Janet became more nervous by the minute as Matt and Christopher chatted incessantly about everything under the sun. Matt suddenly became blind to her frantic hand signals behind Christopher's back to get him to go to the car and wait. She knew he was pretending not to understand what she wanted so she pointed to him and then put her hands around her neck in a choke hold. He got the message.

"Guess *Grandpa* is not feeling well enough today. I'll see him later. You get well. Oh, and I think you have a very pretty daughter there." Janet glared a hole through him. He smiled sweetly. "She'll make some boy a perfect mother someday."

Janet rolled her eyes and mouthed "Wait 'til I get you home!"

"Couldn't you stay just a little longer? I've really enjoyed our visit. I don't get to talk to young people much these days."

Janet patted Christopher on the shoulder. "I don't want you to get too tired. We need to get you back to your room."

"Nonsense. I feel fine."

"Do you play cards?" Matt paid Janet no mind at her frantic hand signals.

She wilted when she saw Matt pull a deck of cards from his back pocket. *What eleven year old carries a deck of cards with him? Help me, Lord?*

Christopher's laughter was music to her ears and she prayed this would all go well.

"I used to play a lot of cards. What's your pleasure?"

"Stud poker." Matt pulled a small table over to Christopher's chair and took the cards out of their holder. He tore a page from an old magazine in the rack and tore it into small squares for betting. "I'm not allowed to play with real money. I usually play with wooden matches but this will do. Jokers, deuces and one-eyed jacks are wild. Four of clubs is missing."

Christopher laughed so loud he didn't hear the rest of Matt's crazy rules but after a couple of hands, made up some crazier rules of his own.

Janet found herself laughing along with them. For Christopher's and Matt's sake at least the sham has been a success, but for her personally, the sacrifice was going to be devastating.

Suddenly the laughter came to an abrupt halt and Janet looked up to see what the problem was. Her eyes met Patrick's blazing back at her. Matt frantically gathered up the cards and Christopher turned the wheel of his chair to see who Matt was staring at. The old man's mouth dropped open and a gasping, "Son?" escaped his lips.

"How I prayed my suspicions were wrong. Cal had to cancel dinner and when I couldn't reach you or Matt on your cells, I remembered you turn them off while you're at the hospital." Pat's voice was flat as he looked coolly toward his father, then back to Janet. "It was all for him, wasn't it? It was all just a vicious trick! All for him no matter who you hurt!" His voice raised in pitch. "Nothing matters as long as Christopher gets what he wants!" He ranted, not giving Janet a chance to say anything. "You used every womanly trick in the book to get me to come back to St. Louis. Nothing's too low for you is it? Not when it's for the good of the company...or dear old dad!" He raked his fingers through his hair roughly then made a fist and beat it into the palm of his other hand. "Damn! I feel like a drowning man. My whole life is flashing before my eyes. It's just like twelve years ago all over again!"

"Son, what's wrong?" Christopher stretched his arm toward Pat.

Matt came from behind the table. "Dad...wait. It's not her fault."

"You!" Pat pointed at him. "Not another word. Wait in the reception area. I'll deal with you later."

"But—"

"Go!"

Matt hung his head and trudged down the hall.

"Matthew is your son?" Christopher was clearly shaken. "My grandson?" His brow knitted. "Now I know who he looks like...it's Sylvia!"

Pat gave his father a scathing look. "Don't try to hoodwink me any further. You and your *pet* here have done enough already."

"He *didn't* know, Patrick." Janet tried to convince him his father had nothing to do with this. "Please listen to me. I was going to tell you everything. It all got so out of hand..."

"When!? During our next *pillow talk*?" The contempt in his voice made Janet shudder. His features were hard and angry and the force of his seething eyes riveted her to her chair. "Give me a break, Miss Raye. Save the theatrics for the music troupe!" His voice was sarcastic and belligerent as he spun on his heel and walked away.

CHAPTER TWENTY SIX

$\mathcal{J}$anet stiffened indignantly and bolted from her chair, taking three steps to his one to keep up with him.

"You're right! We *do* live in two different worlds. You're stubborn and opinionated. No one's right but you, but worst of all, you're vindictive! You not only deny yourself the joy of having a father, but you're destroying something very precious to Matt. You're too self-centered to put aside your bitterness long enough to see the good things you're throwing away." Her voice softened and tears sprang to her eyes. "I'm not saying what I did was right, but was it all that wrong? I guess down deep I had always had a ray of hope for us...that maybe we could share something special. I know that's gone now. I know you think I betrayed you. If you would just let me explain."

"It's too late." He did not look at her. His eyes stared straight ahead cold and impersonal.

"I know it's too late for us." She took hold of his sleeve to slow him. "Patrick, please, PLEASE don't do this to your father. Not now. Don't you see what the shock of all this could do?" She tugged at his jacket. "Don't do this to Matt. I beg you Patrick." He jerked away from her hold. "Think what you will of me, but don't take away the love Christopher and Matt could have for each other. God doesn't want us to hate. Pray about this, Patrick. Let Him guide you."

She slowed her pace and watched him disappear into the waiting area. Turning with a deep shuddering sigh, she walked back to the sunroom, her heart heavy. She hated to think what damage she had done by all this to Christopher...for that matter, to everyone, including herself. *God, forgive me for failing you. I know what I did was wrong even if I did it for the right reasons. I ask for Your forgiveness but will have a hard time forgiving myself. I am so unworthy of Your love but I ask for guidance to find the right words to make amends with Patrick.*

Christopher sat slumped in his chair, his head in his hands. Janet knelt to the floor and leaned against his legs. "I'm so sorry, Christopher. I've been such a fool."

"No, my dear. The fool was me years ago."

"But if Patrick wasn't so stubborn."

"No, he's not being stubborn."

"What?"

"He has every right to feel as he does. In fact, he's probably been exceptionally kind in his rendition of the story. He probably wants to save your feelings for me. I can't blame him for keeping Matthew from me."

"I don't understand."

"Don't get me wrong. I love my son. I always have. I just had a difficult time showing it. I never once told him I loved him."

Janet gasped. "That is so sad. We shouldn't keep those feelings inside."

"I loved him, but I was also jealous of him. His mother loved him much more than she loved me. Oh, she didn't hate me, but we never...well, there wasn't that closeness that husbands and wives usually share. I had her committed when the drinking got out of hand instead of trying to help her myself. It hurt Patrick but her feelings, his feelings meant nothing to me then. I had enough money to have any woman I wanted and I had several. Mostly young ones. I had no scruples."

"Don't. You don't have to tell me all this."

"Oh, but I do. I don't want you to place all the blame on Pat. It's taken me a long time of soul searching and praying to God to admit all this even to myself."

"But you must have cared a great deal for him. You wanted him to be a part of the company to be successful."

"I wanted him to be a part of the company so I could show him what a great success I had become. I secretly wanted him to fail."

"No."

"Yes! Even when I bought the plastics company and made him President it was to show him just how hard it would be to stay at the top." He took a breath. "Then Sylvia came along. Beautiful Sylvia."

"This is tiring you. Let me take you back to your room."

He went on, dismissing her suggestion. "I didn't like her at first. I judged her just like I would a piece of machinery. It either worked for me or it didn't. She didn't. Pat was determined to marry her, so I fine-tuned her, making her fit the mold I had cast. Somewhere along the way, I fell in love with her." He laughed. "Ironic, isn't it? There's no fool like an old fool. I was flattered by all the attention she gave me and felt very smug that I could have a woman who belonged to my son. An old man like me winning a prize like Sylvia from right under my son's nose. Oh, it was a high I had never experienced. Then, as with all highs, there was the crash. She didn't want me. She wanted my money. I didn't care what happened to my son in the process. All I could think of was getting even with her. In the end, I gave her what she wanted...money. I never heard from her again."

"She died right after Matt was born." The sordid pieces fell into place. No wonder Pat was so skeptical about her relationship with Christopher. Now she understood what it looked like to him when he found her and Matt today.

"I didn't know she was dead. When Pat left town that day, I was busy wallowing in self-pity. Pat made it very explicit that I consider him dead. For the next year I pretended not to care. I never tried to find him. Seeing him would only remind me of Sylvia."

"But you've always been so wonderful to me...so much like a father."

"Cal helped pull me back to life. He sat me down and told me just what a fool I had been. The women, the carousing, buying my way into anything and out of anything. Strange, I never got mad at Cal. I guess he didn't tell me anything I wasn't beginning to realize myself." He cleared his throat. "I woke up one morning and I was all alone. I mean really alone. Cal called Pat and tried to patch things up between us, but it didn't work. That's when I found God. I decided the best way to show my love for my son was to leave him alone and give him complete freedom from me."

Janet patted his hand. "That must have been a sad time for you."

He nodded. "That was just about the time you came to work for us. The same time I was experiencing a major turning point in my life. You've heard of people *seeing the light*?"

"Yes."

"I saw the light. I decided to live my life as a better human being. I never interfered with Pat's life again." His eyes misted. "Sometimes you have to love someone enough to let them go. Do you understand that?"

How well she understood that. Her face grew sad and the old man drew his shaky hand across her hair.

"I've discovered the hard way that the things I thought I cared for...money, prestige...meant nothing without family. Through my own doing, I lost my wife, I lost my son and now my grandson. You've been my family these past ten years. In a way, I've used you."

"Used me? How?"

"I've used you to pour out all the fatherly love I kept bottled up inside for so long. I did to you what I should have done to Pat. I gave you guidance, but not interference. I helped you but not to the point of hindering your growth."

"You *did* do all that and I love you for it. A real daughter couldn't love you more."

"You *are* a real daughter to me. Promise you'll always be my daughter for as long as I live."

She patted his hand. "Of course I promise." She rose slowly and hugged his shoulders, vowing to herself never to forsake him, though her heart would always belong to a certain cowboy in Montana.

Back in Christopher's room while he slept, Janet prayed again to God for guidance as well as forgiveness. There was no need to go home. Pat had a key to her apartment and could get Matt's things. She wouldn't subject him to her presence again...not today. Perhaps later she would write him a letter explaining her reasons for bringing Matt to the hospital and that she did not *use* him, she loved him. *Loved? Not past tense.* But did she love him enough to let him go? Those were Christopher's words, *sometimes you have to love someone enough to let them go.* It was a hard test to pass, but she knew in her heart she loved him and she would have to let him go to live the life he wanted.

She didn't realize when she dozed off, but she woke when a young girl brought in the evening food tray. Christopher offered to share the meal with her but she declined. She wasn't at all hungry, she was only heartbroken. She started to turn on the T.V. knowing he always liked to watch the news while he ate. He asked her not to. He would rather just talk.

"I hate to see you so upset."

Now it was Christopher who was fussing over her. There was really nothing that could be said to ease the pain. "Oh, Christopher. I did such a foolish thing bringing Matt here. It wasn't supposed to turn out like it did. I pray it did not upset you and cause you anymore distress with your heart."

"My dear, don't you worry about me. I know Matthew's visit was not as planned, but you don't know how marvelous it is to know I have a grandson like him. He's a delight." He smiled broadly. "What a lad! Sure, I hate I may never see him again, but I'll always have him in my heart and the joy we shared playing cards and laughing. I can't remember when I laughed so much."

"It *was* nice watching the two of you getting along so well."

"I don't want you to be so hard on yourself over this. As for me, you did me a favor. I'll never forget this afternoon with Matthew."

*****

Later in the evening, just before she was preparing to leave, she heard footsteps approaching the room. Janet's heart quickened as she detected the familiar stride...another thing she had memorized. Momentarily Pat appeared in the doorway.

"May I come in?" His eyes darted quickly toward Janet, then back to his father.

"Have a seat, son."

"No thanks. I just came to say what I have to say and then leave. It won't take long enough for me to sit down. Matt's waiting in the lobby. I wanted this private time to tell you what's on my mind."

He stepped into the room and Janet rose to leave.

"Stay, Janet. I have things to say to you, too."

"I think we've said all there is to say."

"You said all there was for *you* to say. Now it's my turn."

She wilted back down in her chair.

Pat looked toward his father. "Dad, we'll probably never understand each other, but as has been pointed out quite often lately..., he glanced at Janet, you're still my father and I'm still your son. A long time ago that meant a great deal to both of us. It's a memory I'll always cherish. I think it's important you know that."

"Me too, son. You'll never know how sorry I am for shattering those memories."

Pat cleared his throat. "It probably never will be the same between us." He hesitated, his eyes again turning to Janet, scanning her face but not really seeing her. "But for *my* son's sake I want to try to put a few of the pieces back together. At least some line of communication between us."

"I'd love that. I've prayed many years for just that."

"I've been also praying about it lately and God's been working on me." He let out a soft chuckle and pointed to Janet. "Along with her help. She actually seemed to work harder than God. She tells it like it is and she never lets up."

Christopher chuckled also. "She's a God-send, that's for sure. Just ask anyone who knows her."

"Well, I'm still working on my feelings about the past and I'm not saying everything will be fine and dandy right away, but maybe someday..." His voice trailed to a whisper and Janet somehow managed to look him in the eye, hers brimming with tears. "Matt told me what happened. I know how persuasive he can be. He's used that tactic on me many times. I owe you an apology, Janet, for saying some things—"

"No. I'm the adult. I should have never listened to Matt's scheme. I am so very sorry."

"It doesn't change things, however. We still live in two different worlds. I see how much you are needed here.

Your life is in St. Louis and mine is in Montana."

"I know." Janet knew he was right and there were no words that could be said to alter the circumstances.

Pat turned his attention back to his father. "We're leaving on the next flight, but I promised Matt if you got well enough he could come back for a week. That is if you want him."

"Oh, son." The old man's voice cracked and tears spilled down his cheeks. "That's the best tonic anyone could give me."

"It's just for a short visit. No way will I allow him to stay more than a week and believe me he WILL try to convince you to let him stay, but you have to stay firm."

"I understand. That's all I ask. I'll never undermine your wishes ever again, son."

"Well...then this is goodbye." He looked back at Janet, his eyes red and vaguely distant. He was looking at her but his remarks were addressed to his father. "It must be a great thing to be loved so loyally by someone."

Janet raised her hand to him, but when she looked, he was gone.

CHAPTER TWENTY SEVEN

June was one of the blackest months of Janet's life. Even though Christopher was making a remarkable recovery looking forward to Matt's visit soon, Janet's spirits could not be lifted. She just went through the motions at work.

Christopher was able to come into the office a few hours a week, making the stockholders very happy. The company was flourishing, yet Janet found this all very secondary. Nothing mattered anymore. Her birthday was only a few days away and her usual excitement over hearing her sister Jeanie sing Happy Birthday over the phone could not lift her spirits this year. She had lost weight, she couldn't sleep and it had gotten to the point that others were commenting on her ill health.

Janet looked up from her desk and was pleased to see Christopher standing before her looking extremely well and happy. "What a pleasant surprise. You look on top of the world."

"I am. I heard from Matthew. He'll be here for the Fourth of July. We're planning to view all the fireworks displays we can together." He chuckled with delight. "He's a fine boy. Pat's done well raising him."

Janet nearly broke into tears and bit down hard on her lip to keep them back. "Yes, yes, he has."

Christopher took a seat and studied Janet's face for a moment. "I have something especially nice this year for your birthday. Something I think will erase those dark circles under your pretty eyes."

She smiled lovingly at him. "I'm afraid there's no such thing, Christopher...though I wish there were." She quickly added, "Seeing you well and happy is the best present you could give me."

"Oh, I think I know something a little better than that." There was a lilt in his voice.

She raised her brows. "What's that?"

"This." He handed her an envelope. "I know it's not quite your birthday yet, but I thought you might need a couple of days to make plans."

"If you're giving me airfare to so see my sister, I just don't want to leave right now."

"It's not that. Open it. I think in the long run, you'll be happy."

She opened the envelope while he talked. When she pulled out the pink dismissal slip she became puzzled. "You're firing me? I don't understand. Have I done something..."

He was almost laughing out loud. "My dear, I may be old, but I know love sickness when I see it and if Matt is any judge of character...well we suspect Pat's feeling the same way. Go to him."

"But I promised to never leave you."

"You're not *really* leaving me. I couldn't be happier. I can find another assistant, but I couldn't find another daughter-in-law that I would rather have. Besides I don't plan to spend so much time with business anymore. I'm going to enjoy my family...something I should have done a long time ago."

She was joyous, her voice bubbly. "Do you think Pat will forgive me?"

"I think he already did when he apologized to you at

the hospital. He's no fool. By the way, the rest of your gift is waiting for you at the airport...a one-way ticket to Montana."

He was still talking but in one quick movement she flung her arms around his neck and kissed him loudly on the cheek, then bolted out of the office, calling goodbyes to everyone she passed and promising to write.

*****

She wasted no time in packing most of her personal belongings and making a definite decision to stay several days this time...maybe forever.

I'm the happiest girl in the world. I gotta call Jeanie!!

"Sis?"

"Hey you. What's up?"

"I've found the man of my dreams. Are you ready to be a bride's maid?"

"Congratulations! When?"

"I'll have to get back to you on that. He hasn't asked me yet."

"Janet." She breathed out noisily. "What's going on?"

"I'm on my way to Montana. It's Christopher's son. I'm in love."

"Christopher's estranged son?"

"They're not so estranged anymore. He also has an eleven year old son whom I adore. Oh, Jeanie, I want you and your family to come to Montana for the wedding and meet everyone."

"Hold it. You said he hasn't asked you yet."

"He will or I'll ask him. Believe me, there *will* be a wedding and soon if I have my way."

"And you usually do have your way."

Both women laughed and exchanged news about Jeanie's husband getting a promotion and the kids growing like weeds.

"Love you, sis."

"Love you too. Have a safe flight and keep me in the loop so I can make travel plans."

"I'll pay for everything. Christopher gave me a very lucrative severance."

She took a cab to the airport, leaving her car in the apartment garage. She didn't know exactly how long she would be in Montana but she certainly knew she would be staying until she convinced a stubborn cowboy that his life would be miserable without her.

After landing at the small airport in Montana, she nearly fell over when she saw Patrick in the terminal. Christopher must have called him, she thought at first, but then the surprise written on Pat's face made her think otherwise.

"You didn't know I was coming?"

He looked bewildered and shook his head. "No.

"Then what are you doing here?"

He held up a ticket. "I couldn't stand it any longer. I was coming to get you...kidnap you if necessary since we've had some experience with kidnapping recently. You know, blindfolds, putting you in the trunk..."

"No need. I'd have come willingly."

"But..." He was still puzzled. "What are *you* doing here?"

She smiled broadly. "You know, I think Matt's *fate* must be working overtime to bring us here at the same time."

"Funny, Matt was very specific as to what flight I took. I think *fate* had a little help. Matt and Dad have been having a lot of hush, hush phone conversations lately as well as that skype stuff you're so proud of. I think the two of them are in cahoots."

"Whatever...I'm not going to question it."

"Me either. This has been the most miserable damn month I've ever spent."

"If you would stop cussing long enough, I'd love to kiss you."

"If that's all it takes, I'll never say another swear word again."

She showered his face with a thousand kisses.

"Hey, leave some of my hide. It might not be much, but it's all I got."

"By the way. I'm unemployed. Your dad fired me."

Pat smiled. "Good for him. Are you looking for another profession out here?"

"What do you have in mind?"

"Oh, maybe a wife and mother to a conniving twerp of a kid."

"I thought you'd never ask." She kissed him again. "I don't want to ever stop kissing you."

"You have an enormous appetite for this, don't you?"

"You stir up my hunger pangs. I love you so much!"

"And I love you too...mmmmm." He kissed her long and hard and pulled her to him with a hold that possessed her very soul. "Matt is so right about one thing. We DO need *a woman's touch* around here."

"I'll give you all the *woman's touch* you can stand."

"I plan on it."

"That *was* a marriage proposal you gave me a few seconds ago wasn't it?"

"Yes."

"Okay, here's how I see it. My birthday would be a good time for a wedding. That gives us one week to plan it."

"One week!?"

"Is that too long to wait. I could plan it in a day if I had to."

"No, no. A week will do. I'll get right on it finding a preacher, best man..."

"Jeanie will be here with her family. We'll make reservations for them at the motel."

"They can stay in Vernon's guest house."

"Righteous! That's what Matt would say. I hope you won't mind if I ask Christopher to give me away?"

"Not at all. He needs to be here. Matt would throw a colossal fit if he weren't."

"You have made me so very happy."

Pat laughed. "God knows why you'd want an old worn out cowboy like me, but I want you under any conditions...just as long as it's forever."

"You're not so worn out. After all you danced with me all night when I was here. I thought you did exceptionally well for a guy who wears pointed toed boots."

He smiled seductively, his voice husky. "I've got moves you haven't seen before."

"Well, what are you saving them for, cowboy?"

"I was waiting for a cute little cowgirl to come along."

She stood back and struck a silly pose. "Will I do, stranger? I've been told I look good in western wear."

"Do you ever!" He pulled her back in his arms and kissed her tenderly on the lips.

"So you think this will make up for all your stubbornness?"

"Yes."

"Pretty cocky, aren't you?"

"No, not cocky...scared. I'm scared to death. I'm afraid this is a dream and I'll wake up and you'll be gone."

Her compassionate nature took over and she smoothed a finger across his knitted brow. "Don't be scared, darling. It's going to be the most wonderful life we could ever imagine."

He kissed her again. "I need to see if I can get my money back on this ticket."

As he left her to go to the counter, she called out to him. "One more thing."

He turned slowly. "There always is. What?"

"I want babies. Lots of babies."

A Woman's Touch

He looked a little pale but then gained his composure. "Looks like I'd better get started soon on the house I planned to build out on the ranch."

EPILOGUE

FOUR YEARS LATER

"Bradley! Watch out for your little sisters! Don't pull them so fast in the wagon. They'll fall out." Janet never tired of watching her three-year-old son play with the eighteen-month-old twins. Lynn and Lori had been a surprise, but such a blessing.

Pat put his arm around her and they rocked back and forth in the glider on the back veranda. "Don't be such a worry wart, Mom."

"Cute, aren't they?"

"They take after their mother."

"Bradley looks just like you. I sure hope he's not as stubborn."

"Ha! Stubborn? Didn't I build you this big house on the piece of land Vernon gave us? And didn't I quit the Rangers so I could be home more and just do the cowboy stuff so I could help with all these babies you brought into the world?" He laughed.

"You love it! I told you I was going to produce our own little farm hands."

"You're right. Life couldn't be better."

"They worship their big brother. Matt is so good with

them."

"Where is Matt?"

"He's riding his horse practicing for the rodeo this weekend. Christopher is flying in to see him."

"And spoil the little kids to pieces."

She laughed. "That's what grandparents do. We'll be there one day."

Pat's expression grew serious. "I know how you *hate* to say I told you so, so I'll say it...you told me so."

"What?"

"What my dad and I have now is priceless. You were right. When I let the bitterness go and turned my hurt around, God took over and gave me a blessed life."

Janet patted him on the cheek. "I know. We are *all* blessed." She brought his hand to her lips and kissed it. "One more thing."

"You and your *one more thing*. What is it now?"

"I'm pregnant."

He stopped the glider and looked into her beaming face. "When are you due?"

"A few months. Long enough for you to add a couple of bedrooms on the house."

He stared at her, his brows raised.

She smiled brightly as she produced a picture of the sonogram from her pocket. "Meet your twin boys, Bobby and Robby."

"Yikes! You wouldn't have a cigarette on you, would you?"

"Shut up."

"Make me."

"My pleasure."

Their lips met and said it all. Their life was full of love and happiness.

*****

In a world of uncertainty, two people found each other. Different, yet alike. Their love was all they needed to grow together in harmony. Everything was right in God's grace and they were exceedingly grateful for all their blessings.

ABOUT THE AUTHOR

Norma Eaton is author of full-length romance novels, magazine articles and short stories. She was a long time member of Ozarks Romance Authors as well as other writing groups. She and her husband sing gospel in and around Branson, MO. and reside in Springfield, MO. She thanks God for giving her the joy of writing.